"Brace yourself. I'm going to kiss you."

He was going to kiss *her?* Libby's heart pounded. "I don't—"

Cooper put his finger to her lips. "Don't think. Experience. Isn't that the real reason you went searching beyond the borders of Sentinel Pass to find someone to father your child? You wanted to feel something new, something fresh and exciting?"

"But I never planned to..."

To what? Get emotionally involved with her baby's father? Was that even possible? Once someone entered your life, you were involved. But how much that affected you was your decision.

Wasn't it?

Dear Reader,

I fell in love with the Black Hills of South Dakota while visiting my older sister who lived in Rapid City. She'd take me to explore magical places such as Rockerville, Keystone, Hill City and Deadwood. To a "flatlander" like me, the Black Hills was another world entirely.

Sentinel Pass is where I'd live if I called the Black Hills home. It's an amalgamation of the unique hamlets I visited. I "found" Sentinel Pass with the help of my cousins, Janie and Stan Petrik, who acted as my tour guides last fall. Stan scoured National Forest Service maps for the best trails for my characters to hike, and he accompanied me to the top of Harney Peak in twenty-degree weather for a breathtaking view—if you had any breath left. Janie introduced me to her lovely family and friends, who answered all my questions and reminded me of what I love most about the Hills—the people. Although Sentinel Pass exists only in my imagination, it came into sharper view thanks to these two kind and generous souls. But you can absorb only so much in a week, so any mistakes are mine and mine alone.

I'd also like to thank postmaster Glenda Miller for helping me to understand what it's like to be the person everyone calls when they need to know what's happening in their small town. What would Cathey's Valley do without you?

I hope you come to love Sentinel Pass as much as I do.

Debra Salonen

BABY BY CONTRACT
Debra Salonen

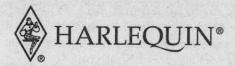

TORONTO • NEW YORK • LONDON
AMSTERDAM • PARIS • SYDNEY • HAMBURG
STOCKHOLM • ATHENS • TOKYO • MILAN • MADRID
PRAGUE • WARSAW • BUDAPEST • AUCKLAND

ISBN-13: 978-0-373-71492-6
ISBN-10:   0-373-71492-0

BABY BY CONTRACT

ABOUT THE AUTHOR

Debra Salonen's stage career was limited to a high school production of *JB*. She played a prostitute, and her only line was "I'd rather be home in bed with a good boy." This caused quite an uproar, and the following night her line was changed to "I'd rather be home in bed with a good *book*." Irony notwithstanding, the pressure was simply too much for her and she never acted again...although members of her family might claim otherwise.

Books by Debra Salonen

*Texas Hold 'Em

This first book in the Sentinel Pass series
is dedicated to Stan and Janie Petrik.
Not just for being such kind and generous hosts,
but for living the kind of life I wish for all my
characters: rich in terms of friends and family,
accomplished in terms of careers and service to
country and community, and filled with a love so
real and enduring they are still best friends
after forty-plus years of marriage.

CHAPTER ONE

Malibu, CA

PAY UP OR DIE.

Cooper Lindstrom stared at the memo line of the e-mail and fought the urge to put his fist through the screen of the desktop computer.

One, he couldn't afford a broken hand. Two, he couldn't afford a new computer. And three… He didn't know what three was.

He deleted the message without reading it. There would be others. So far he'd received half a dozen, each one escalating the level of violence that would befall him if he didn't make good on his mother's online gambling debt.

"I wonder what comes after death?" he muttered. "This moron isn't a deep thinker. He should have hung on to loss of life until he'd exhausted the removal of all body parts."

He sighed and shook his head. He hated the way his brain worked. When he was supposed to be concentrating on the weighty matters of his life—of which there were many at the moment—his "butterfly brain," as his mother often referred to his mind, would flit off to another, more interesting flower.

His mother.

Lena Lindstrom. Powerhouse backstage mom who had watched after her only child and his career with a devotion most people found…unusual, if not faintly disturbing.

But not Cooper. He'd loved her—even when she'd hovered. He'd loved her enough to overlook her faults. Until she suddenly collapsed in a casino in Vegas, then died the following morning, hanging on just long enough for him to reach her, touch her hand and say her name. But not long enough for anything else he'd wanted—needed—to get off his chest.

That had been eight weeks earlier. Eight life-altering, eye-opening, icon-shattering weeks. He could no longer say he loved his mother.

He looked at the four-inch stack of bills that had accumulated on his desk. The ten-thousand-dollar piece of acrylic topped by a fake surfboard was designed to look as if it were bouncing on the waves just beyond his floor-to-ceiling Malibu window. Prior to Lena's death, he'd only sat there twice—for photo shoots.

Sighing, he pushed away from the screen and rocked back, plopping his bare feet on a footstool that looked like an elephant foot. He hoped to God it hadn't once belonged to a real elephant, but this is what happened when you gave a set designer full reign and an open checkbook to decorate your home.

At the time he bought this house, his prime-time, mid-season fill-in reality show called *Are You Ready for Your Close-Up?* had just moved into the top slot in the ratings. Viewers couldn't seem to get enough of watching semi-talented aspiring actors go head-to-head—or "chest-to-boobs," as one critic called it—competing for a studio contract and a chance to appear in an established network show. As its host, he'd been raking in the dough. Life had been good.

But that had been two seasons ago. Even with the carefully hinted-at scandal that made headlines at the beginning of the viewing year, the show now routinely scored in the bottom half of the numbers. The same celebrity gossip magazine that had teased readers with hints about Coop's supposed affair with one of the contestants was now predicting this would be the last year for *Close-Up*.

Which was fine with him. He was tired of arbitrating the nasty infighting between the celebrity judges, two of whom were actually having an affair. And he'd had it up to here dealing with the inflated egos of the young actors who were put through a grueling pace to learn lines and perform scenes that the judges critiqued and the viewing public voted on.

He closed his eyes to the pacifying view beyond the window. The waves, which usually grounded him, now felt as though they might swamp him. He could almost picture a giant tsunami that retreated for a couple of miles, then nailed his three-million-dollar beach bungalow, leaving every other celebrity's house intact.

"God, what a drama king," he muttered, shaking his head and forcing his eyes open. Wide open.

These bills wouldn't pay themselves, as his mother would have said if she'd been there.

Mom. He hated how the word made his throat tighten and tears start to well in his eyes. He blinked a couple of times and pushed away the thought that she would never be paying his bills again.

"Grow up, Cooper," a familiar voice snapped. So clear he almost looked over his shoulder to see if she'd returned from the dead to scold him.

He knew what she would have thought of his despondency. Lena Lindstrom had had no time for sentimental *ennui*. A word he'd picked up from his mother and had used frequently until one of the studio tutors pointed out—in front of the other students—that the word was pronounced "on-we" not "en-new-ee."

He was reaching for the top envelope—an angry yellow color, when the phone rang.

He looked at the display before picking it up. Good timing. He needed a diversion—even a predatory one. "Hello, Tiffany. I wondered if you'd ever get around to calling to express your condolences."

"The old gasbag would roll over in her grave if she thought I'd fake any kind of grief over her death."

Tiffany Fane, his first ex-wife, had spent more of their eighteen-month marriage fighting with his mother than she had interacting with him.

"So why the call?"

"Your check bounced."

"Which check is that?"

"The one that is issued to me monthly in agreement with our divorce settlement. It's called spousal support, and your mother set up the draw as an auto-deduction from your account so she didn't have to see my name in writing."

That sounded like something his mother would do. She'd called Tiffany and, to a lesser degree, Morgana—his second mistake—predatory she-bitches. Both women felt the same about Lena.

"Well, I don't know what to tell you. Mom handled the money, and I've been a little too busy handling her affairs to even look at mine. And, honestly, I'm not sure where to begin."

She made a petulant sound that he'd once thought cute and childlike. "Don't play the poor, pitiful son card with me, Coop. We had an agreement and I expect you to honor it." She took a breath. "Or else."

"Else what?"

"I had a tabloid reporter snooping around the other day, asking about you…and your mother's reputed gambling problem." She spoke slowly and succinctly, as if he needed time to digest the threat. "I knew you before *Close-Up*, Cooper. I know where the bodies are buried, so to speak."

"Tiffany, I hate to point out the obvious because it might

take the edge off your smugness, but if I had money, it would be in the account and the check would have cleared."

"Surely the old hag had insurance."

Not so far as he could see. "I'm worth quite a bit dead. But Mom...not so much."

"Or alive," she muttered. "Well, don't just sit there on your oft-photographed tush, Cooper. I'm not waiting forever. Do something. Try selling your Emmy on eBay. You're still hot, even if *Are You Ready for Your Close-Up?* is slipping in the ratings."

Oft-photographed? Who says things like that? He wondered if she was trying out for some kind of summer-stock production of Shakespeare.

"Are you listening to me, Cooper? I said, sell your Emmy. Better than letting the world see what a twisted freak your mother was, right?"

Cooper looked across the room to the glass bookshelf where the statue he'd embraced as joyfully as a newborn not so long ago now sat collecting dust. His mother had been his date that evening. She'd wept on camera. Then had slipped out of the party at the Governer's Ball to play in an online poker tournament because she'd been certain her son's "luck" had rubbed off on her. Not exactly a tribute to his skill or talent.

When Tiffany—or T-fancy, as he used to call her, a nickname that later changed to Infancy—hung up, he turned back to his computer. It took a few minutes to figure out how to prompt a search engine, but eventually he made his way to that giant online auction house: eBay. Not to sell his pride and joy. No way. But if... He glanced at the pile of bills again. Just in case it came to that, he could see what such things were going for.

Since his statue looked like gold, he entered that word alone in the box where his cursor was blinking. "Go."

His screen filled with possibilities. Gold coins. Gold doubloons. Gold mine.

A gold mine? Really?

He scanned a little further but found himself backtracking. He wasn't sure why. Maybe because one of his first big-screen roles had been the son of a Gold Rush-era miner whose wife died on the Overland Trail. The actor who'd played his father was a belligerent drunk off camera, but he'd been surprisingly convincing as a man torn between following his dream of getting rich and settling down to make a life for his child.

"Actually, I could use a gold mine," he muttered, tapping the mouse. "To hide out in from my mother's psycho bookie, if nothing else."

He double-clicked on the item and read: *Will trade: quarter share in working gold mine for viable sperm resulting in pregnancy. Restrictions apply.*

"Sperm I got. It's gold I need," he said with a laugh. To his trained ear, the sound was edged in bitterness not in keeping with his happy-go-lucky, blond-to-the-roots public persona.

He tapped another blue-highlighted link that promised details. A woman's MySpace page came up. A woman named Libby McGannon.

He hunched forward and started to read, slowly, memorizing each word as his mother had taught him when he first began trying out for speaking parts at age six.

Directors don't have time for flubs, Cooper. You only get one chance to make a bad impression. He'd been in his twenties before he'd learned what a malapropism was.

Libby McGannon was offering to trade half of her half interest in the Little Poke mine, a family enterprise in the Black Hills of South Dakota. "The Little Poke," he murmured, letting out a low chuckle. The name alone was priceless irony.

He didn't know much about the Internet, but he'd heard plenty of stories of people faking things to pull suckers into some kind of scam. But the more he read, the more he decided this woman was for real. She included the kind of facts most people couldn't—or wouldn't bother to—make up. But more importantly, there was something straightforward and sincere in her manner. Something very human.

One of his acting teachers once told him that "desperate circumstance, irony and farce are the building blocks of comedy." Cooper hadn't understood that at the time, but he did now.

This would make a good sitcom.

A millisecond later a tingle coursed through him. It was not unlike the electrical shock he'd received when a malfunctioning toaster on the lot had brought the paramedics running and given the late-night talk show hosts their opening gag.

"Bingo," he cried.

He thought a moment, then jumped to his feet and pumped his fist in the air, changing his call to, "Eureka."

See, Mom? I listened in a couple of history classes.

His mother's expensive ergonomic chair shot like a bullet across the bamboo floor and collided with a curio cabinet containing the many Lladró figurines he'd given her over the years. The delicate porcelains never went with the decor in his office, but since Mom had been the only person to use the room, he'd let her include as many personal items as she'd wished once the photo shoots had been over. She'd loved the figures that he found slightly anemic-looking and too melty for his taste.

He stared at the cabinet a moment, then smiled. "Thanks, Mom."

He knew what he'd sell on eBay. The collection had cost him a fortune over the years. He could get even more for the pieces if he sold them under his real name, but that wasn't possible. He didn't want anyone to know how hard up he was for money. If they did, they'd ask why.

He'd do just about anything to avoid answering that question. Even if it meant using the money from the figurines' sale to finance a trip to the Black Hills of South Dakota to see a woman about a gold mine. Not the one she was selling on eBay but a gold mine of a different kind. The only thing that would pull him out of this financial crevasse of his mother's making was a new hit television show.

He returned to his chair and sat. With elbows on the desktop, he steepled his fingers and rested his chin on his hands. He stared at the computer screen, studying Libby McGannon's photo. What kind of woman would sell a share in her family business in exchange for sperm?

A desperate one, of course. And that was something he could relate to all too well.

With a long sigh, he cracked his knuckles and started typing.

"ELIZABETH JANE MCGANNON, that's the dumbest thing I've ever heard. Tell me you're joking."

Mac's face had turned an unhealthy shade of red—the color he and Libby had referred to as "maroon gloom" when their father had been ranting about something. Their father was gone now. Killed in a cave-in in the Little Poke mine. Where her brother was following in their father's footsteps.

"I've not only made up my mind," Libby said calmly, aware of the three spectators to this unplanned sibling debate, "the deed is done. I posted the information on my MySpace page and I'm already up to twelve-hundred hits."

His groan made her wince. "Nuts. Completely crazy." He snatched his Denver Broncos ball cap off the chair and stalked to the door. He paused to look at the three women who had arrived at Libby's house half an hour earlier expecting to drink wine and discuss their monthly book club selection, not be drawn into the middle of a family argument. "Maybe you can talk some sense into her. Who in their right mind would place an online ad offering to trade a share of a mine in return for sperm?"

He spat out the last word as though it were poison.

Her friends—Jenna, Kat and Charlene—exchanged looks that Libby had no trouble interpreting. Libby had suspected her idea—which had come to her in the middle of the night when she was rocking her niece to sleep after the child awoke from a nightmare—might cause a bit of a stir. That was one reason she'd held off telling her best friends until they were all together. She knew she was going to need them on her side when the news got out.

After all, she was postmaster of a small town in the Black Hills. Sentinel Pass had only gotten high-speed Internet a few months earlier. Most home computers, including Libby's, were now able to access the world. But that didn't mean its citizens were ready to embrace the changes that came with that two-way street.

She locked the front door to deter a return visit, then walked to the rocking chair where she'd been sitting enjoying her dinner before Mac stormed in. He'd entered the house through the kitchen and circled through the dining room where she'd placed a chafing dish and a salad bowl along with a copy of their book club selection and three little flags. Her guests had oohed and aahed over the table as they'd filled their plates, then carried them to TV trays in the living room. Libby had planned to break her news to her friends in a cozier, less formal setting.

"I was going to tell you about this. *After* we finished talking about the book." Tonight the four mainstays of the Wine, Women and Words book club were discussing *Eat, Pray, Love* by Elizabeth Gilbert and drinking Chianti to complement the spinach-and-cheese-stuffed ravioli that Libby had prepared. Dessert would be gelato.

She took a long pull from her wineglass, then said, "For the past two weeks I've been involved with an online chat group made up of people like me. Women who are pushing forty to the ever-steady beat of the biological clock. They helped me figure out how I wanted to do this."

"Wait a minute," Jenna Murphy, closet poet and substitute postmaster, demanded. She wiped a trace of pasta sauce from her Angelina Jolie-shaped lips. "You took your problem to strangers?"

"How could you?" Kat Petroski cried, sitting forward from her spot in the middle of the sofa. "We're your best friends."

The tremor in the petite blonde's voice was more hurt than outrage.

"Of course you are. But none of you have walked in my shoes, so to speak. Kat, you're so fertile you could conceive after an evening of talking dirty. Tag and Jordie prove it." Her sons by two different husbands were eight and six.

"Jenna doesn't want kids," Libby went on, moving her finger to the woman on Kat's left. "And Char…" She looked at the woman with short spiky hair that she dyed anything from orange to purple, depending on her mood. At the moment she resembled a rock star—black with pink highlights. "Char has always been surprisingly mum on the subject."

All started talking at once. Libby moved the TV tray to one side and picked up the venerable five-foot-long yew branch that was a part of every meeting. "Stop. Everyone. I have the talking stick. That means I speak and you listen. Without jumping to conclusions or rushing to judgment. Remember?"

When they'd started the group two years earlier, Char had suggested they borrow the idea from a Lakota friend who ran a free clinic on the Pine Ridge reservation. The talking stick was empowering to the speaker and symbolically reminded listeners they could get whacked over the head if they didn't shut up and pay attention.

"Kat, you know I've been thinking about this for a long time. Even before Misty died." Mac's wife had been killed in a car accident the previous fall.

"What does your slutty sister-in-law have to do with your decision to get pregnant?"

Libby shook the stick at Jenna, who even on the best of nights was rushed for time and tended to cut off every long-winded discussion topic to keep things moving. This attitude partly stemmed from the fact she was a downtrodden caregiver whose only night off from caring for her difficult, hypochondriac mother was spent counseling her friends, whose lives seemed to be shrinking to one solitary point of focus—men.

Or, rather, the lack of them.

"Misty—for all her faults—was only twenty-eight when she died. Twenty-eight. In a few months I'll be thirty-five. That's two decades of menses wasted every month instead of nurturing a new life. I've read that some women are starting to enter perimenopause in their early forties because of stress and the environment. I need to do this. Now. And I'm willing to pay for it."

"But—"

She shook the stick. "But the only thing of value I own—outside of this house—is half interest in a gold mine. We all know it's never going to be the next Homestake, but what man wouldn't want to brag that he owns a share in a gold mine?"

"What about your mom's settlement money?" Jenna asked, ignoring the stick.

"You all know how I feel about that. Dad called it 'blood money' and refused to touch it. After he died, Gran set up trusts for Mac and me, but we both decided the money should go to our children. Of course, that was before Misty got hold of it." What happened to a good-size chunk of the money was still a sore subject that Mac refused to talk about. "Megan will inherit what's left of Mac's share, but I…I don't even have a cat to leave it to at this point."

She lowered the stick, indicating that the others were free to ask questions.

"Why now?"

"Why online? There are all kinds of kooks and weirdos out there."

"Why didn't you ask Clive? He's been in love with you since grade school."

Libby finished her wine in one gulp, then turned to Jenna, her closest and oldest friend, who knew better than to suggest such a thing. Clive Brumley was a nice guy. One of Libby's most reliable rural carriers. But he'd never be anything more to her than a friend. "He kissed me when we were in the third grade. I remember because it was so traumatizing. I ran home to Gran and told her his lips were soft and slimy and his breath smelled like fish sticks. To this day a part of me thinks of him as Fish Lips."

Char's slightly upturned nose wrinkled.

"Exactly."

A moment later Kat said, "Libby, I think you're one of the smartest women I've ever met. You're capable and strong and a born leader, but being a single parent is the toughest thing I've ever done—and I started out with a partner. Both times."

Libby smiled at the compliments. Wouldn't her friends laugh if they knew how terrified she felt? She'd agonized over this decision for weeks and still, at times, was certain she was a self-serving fool. But, ultimately, her rationale would come back to Kat. "Kat, you're partly the reason I decided to do this."

"Me? I work two jobs and have two kids from two ex-husbands who make me jump through hoops to get my sons' monthly child support. What part of this madness I call a life do you find attractive?"

"You're a single mom getting her teaching certificate while juggling part-time work and child care. Jordie and Tag are great kids who adore you and don't seem to resent the fact you're not married to their fathers. That was my biggest concern. Would my child hate me for not giving him or her a standard, two-parent upbringing?"

Char leaned in. "Of course he or she will hate you—at some point. No matter what you do."

Char could always be counted on to salt the pot of controversy with a dash of negativity.

"On the off chance that's true, I've decided I need to meet the father face-to-face. No anonymous donor list for me. I don't have time to court some guy and fall in love—and we all know the pitfalls that come with love. But if I handle this as a business transaction, there won't be all the angsty emotions that could turn us into enemies." *The way Mac and Misty were at the end.* "We'll stay in touch. By e-mail. From a safe distance."

Nobody said anything, so she added, "And he'll be available in case anything happens to me. My child will never be an orphan." Her voice faltered on the last word, as it always did. She looked at her lap, hoping her friends wouldn't notice. She didn't want their sympathy, only their support.

"So you're not planning on having sex with this guy?"

A telling question, Libby noted. Not surprising coming from someone with Jenna's history.

"No. Absolutely not." *Even though I feel like a dried-up shell and am afraid my soul is too barren at this point to host a fertilized egg.* "After I've narrowed down my search, I'm going to require the applicant I choose to come here for a week. I haven't worked out all the details, but I figure he can stay in Gran's cabin out back. If we both agree that we can work together on this project, he'll deposit his sperm at the clinic in Rapid City and leave. My doctor gave me a bunch of information about hormone shots and whatnot. Once she says it's time, I'll go in and we'll let nature take over."

There was a bit more muttering and shaking of heads, but Libby carefully laid out her baby-by-contract strategy. These were her friends. They knew and loved her. If she couldn't convince them this was a good idea, then her plan was doomed where the rest of the town was concerned.

And did the town's opinion matter to her? Of course it did.

She'd known most of the residents of Sentinel Pass all her life. But was she willing to give up becoming a mother just because her postal customers didn't approve?

She'd wrestled with the question on more than one sleepless night, and the answer, she'd finally decided, was no. This was her life, and there came a point when even a people-pleasing good girl had to put herself first.

I can do this. I will *do this.* Provided she could find the right sperm donor. Someone who was more interested in claiming an interest in a gold mine than actually getting rich from it. If such a man didn't exist, she would fall back to plan B and pay him a portion of her trust fund for his contribution to her private sperm bank. But ideally he'd want that money to go to their child. In a perfect world.

CHAPTER TWO

"I HAVE A PLAN," COOPER announced, breaking the uncomfortable silence that had grown to elephant-size in the few short minutes it had taken his friend and colleague Shane Reynard to read the e-mail threats Coop had decided to show him.

Shane's dark head appeared to one side of the computer monitor. "Does it include leaving the state before some psychotic loan shark rearranges the bones in your trademark face?"

Coop glanced at the now-empty display case where his mother's collection of figurines had once rested. "Yes, actually, it does. I'm going to the Black Hills of South Dakota. Your old stompin' grounds."

Shane stood up and walked to the window to stare at the view. Coop wondered which of the sights the reticent and very private man was taking in. The bikini-clad coeds playing volleyball on the sand? The slightly past-her-prime actress strolling hand in hand with her latest boy toy? Or was he checking for paparazzi?

"Not exactly," Shane said, his back to Coop. "I grew up in Minnesota and went to college in Brookings. That's on the eastern edge of the state."

Coop walked to the window, too, his flip-flops *shush-shushing* on the smooth floor. "Close enough. You know where South Dakota is, anyway."

Shane looked at him. "I do," he answered drily. "Although I have to say I'm a little surprised you do. Didn't you once tell me you're geographically challenged?"

"I can never keep Ohio and Iowa straight."

"Ah. Four letters each. Three of which are o's. Could happen to anyone." His narrow lips lifted slightly at the corners. A Shane Reynard excuse for a smile. "So what exactly is the big draw to the Black Hills?"

"Gold. I'm trading sperm for a quarter share in a gold mine." He rushed to get out the spiel he'd been practicing in the mirror before Shane could recover from his obvious shock. "It's a win-win situation. It's not like I'm using that sperm at the moment. In fact, most of it just goes down the drain of the shower."

Shane made a sound of disgust and backed up a step.

"This is a joke, right?"

"Nope. My little swimmers are going to buy me part ownership of a mine."

"What does your lawyer say about this?"

"He doesn't know." Arthur Brannigan was his mother's age and conservative to the extreme. He and Lena had had a love-hate relationship that at times had bordered on obsessive, yet Lena had insisted Arthur was the only man she'd trust with her son's finances.

Too bad Arthur had put a similar trust in Lena.

"If he did, he'd tell you you're insane."

"If Arthur were privy to the specifics of this situation—like the death threats I showed you but nobody else—he'd say, 'Go for it.' Because think about it, man, this is all good." He paused a moment. "Actually, it's more like win-win-win, because you're going to benefit, too."

"Your sperm and I have something in common? Lord. Do I even want to know?"

Coop walked to the printer beside the filing cabinet where he'd stashed the towering stack of unpaid bills and picked up the copy he'd made of Libby McGannon's home page. "As you're reading, think about the story behind this woman's situation. The pathos. The humanity. The universality of her goal."

Shane's left eyebrow went up at the three-dollar word Coop had pulled from his research.

He waited for some kind of remark. When none came, he added, "Think of the demographics we'd reach with a television show centered around that goal. Every single gal over thirty is going to tune in every Thursday night to see what becomes of this woman on her quest toward motherhood, love, happiness…you get the picture."

Shane glanced up. "You've already picked the night? Don't you think the networks are going to have some say in the matter?"

"Not when they hear our pitch."

The piece of paper lowered. "*Our* pitch? How did I get involved?"

"I'm the idea guy. You're the producer. You take my ideas and make them workable. And I dare you to tell me this isn't a great idea. Think *The Bachelor* meets *Northern Exposure*."

Shane's poker face didn't give away much. He finished reading Libby's bio, then said, "Where exactly do you come in? You're not serious about donating sperm to father this woman's baby, are you?"

Coop smiled, feeling both relieved and validated. Questions meant Shane was intrigued. "I am. That's part of what makes the story work. Popular actor and TV personality with an irate bookie on his back decides to answer this woman's call for help and at the same time hide out in the Black Hills until he, a, gets enough gold to pay off the loan shark or b… Things get a little fuzzy here. Maybe the bad guy shows up and the locals protect the hero."

"Why would they do that?"

"I don't know. I'm tossing out ideas here. Maybe the postmaster lady dies in childbirth and the hero moves in to raise the kid. You've got that whole fish-out-of-water thing."

"But you lose the single-mother vote. And any chance at

a love interest. And what about the bloodthirsty loan shark? Is this a comedy or a *Sopranos* spin-off?"

Cooper flipped him off. "Quit jerking me around, man. I'm serious. I know you. You've taken smaller ideas than this and turned them into hits."

Shane was quiet a good minute. "Okay. The initial concept has a certain ring to it. But we could work on this idea without you handing over your sperm. For God's sake, Coop, think about the consequences. A kid means some major bite-you-in-the-butt opportunities for the next eighteen years. Or more."

Coop hated to be told to think. His mother had used that expression all the time—particularly when she didn't want him to use his head. And Coop *had* been thinking. He'd done nothing but ponder his fate and future ever since he'd discovered his nearly depleted bank balance. He refused to tell Shane he was broke. That was too humiliating. How dumb did you have to be to put your complete trust in a woman with a gambling problem?

"The kid's mom will be in charge of that. Unless something happens to her, I'm just a name on a birth certificate. Fifth-string stand-in."

"You're crazy. You know that, right?"

Crazy. And desperate. But nobody was going to know just how desperate. Not even Shane.

"Are you going to sleep with her? What if she's a dog? Hell, she must be a dog if she has to buy sperm over the Internet."

Cooper walked to the computer and pulled up the Web site he had bookmarked. "Here's her photo. She's no beauty queen, but she's not ugly. In fact, she looks nice. Responsible. She has a government job with great benefits. The kid will have a trust set up, but she's got this thing about not leaving her kid an orphan." *Like me.*

He pushed the thought away and quickly added, "And, to answer your question, no. I won't be sleeping with her. I'm staying in her guesthouse for a week so we can get to know each other and decide if this is what we both want. Then it's me and a *Hustler* magazine in some clinic in Rapid City. Her doctor takes it from there. Simple."

"Right. Like anything in your life has ever been that easy."

Shane's cavalier tone made Coop's pent-up anger snap. "Hey, some of us aren't born with a golden touch. Isn't that what the reviewer for *People* said about you, Mr. Wonderkid?"

"*Kind*. Wunder*kind*."

Coop made a snarling sound and gripped the edge of the desk. "Yeah, we all know you're a brainiac. But are you smart enough to see the potential in this story? I don't have all the answers. I don't even have a plot. But something tells me I'll find what I'm looking for—storywise—once I get to Sentinel Pass."

Shane sighed and crossed his arms. He studied Coop in a way that made Coop antsy, so he quickly sat at the desk and moved the mouse around.

"Maybe it would be a good idea to leave town for a week or two. But all joking aside, what if this bookie tracks you to South Dakota? You'll be out of your element, Coop. Anything could happen. At least take your assistant along."

And pay her how?

He clicked on his e-mail icon. "The postmaster wants me to come alone. I'll have my cell phone. It's not like I'm going to Fiji or something."

Shane walked to the pointed end of the surfboard desk and rested one hip against it. "Still…did you ever see the Hitchcock movie *North by Northwest*? Cary Grant and Eva Marie Saint? They filmed part of it at Mount Rushmore. It didn't end well, as I recall. And, knowing you, if something can go wrong, it will. Wanna bet?"

Coop scrolled down his list of new messages. The latest one from his mother's bookie was accompanied by a fierce red exclamation point. "Sorry, pal. You have me confused with my mother. I don't gamble."

LIBBY DROPPED HER purse to the floor beside her chair. The long day was finally over. She'd been waiting all day to rush home and check her e-mail. Would his answer be here? Would today be the day she decided? Or would his answers to her questions be enough to make her wake up and admit what a farce this had become?

She clicked on the little envelope icon and waited. It made no sense to keep corresponding with someone like him. A guy so far out of her league they weren't even breathing the same atmosphere. But, if she were being honest, she had to admit that his fame and high-profile lifestyle were faintly titillating, if nothing else. How often did a postmaster in South Dakota get to communicate one-on-one with a TV star? She really couldn't believe it was him and not some goof-off in Outer Mongolia using his name.

But they'd finally worked past her suspicions and doubts. She was convinced—well, ninety-eight percent sure, at least—the man calling himself Cooper Lindstrom really was the actor and TV personality Cooper Lindstrom.

She hoped.

She scanned the page on her screen and quickly spotted his e-mail name. She ignored the other three hundred and fifty e-mails to click on his.

Good morning, fair mayden. I'm looking at the first hint of dawn on the ocean. More gray than pink. Another day in paridise.

She couldn't help but smile at his typos. They made him more human. Which was good. Because if she went by his photos and all the information on his Web site—interviews, press releases and hype—she'd have thought he was perfect. She was too much of a realist to put her faith in perfection.

But he couldn't spell worth a darn. And neither could she. At least they had that in common, she told herself.

I'm wondering if this will be the day your going to agree to let me come to the beautiful Black Hills to meet you in person. I've been doing some homework, and everything I've read about your area sounds like a place I want to visit. Dinosaurs? You have dinosaur bones in your town? For reel?

Only one. His name was Seymour. Or See-More, if you wanted to be crass, Libby thought.

The mortuary people delivered my mom's ashes yesterday. C.O.D.

He'd included a sad face made up of a colon, a dash and an out-facing parenthesis. Her mind flashed to the cold, gray morning they'd lowered her sister-in-law's casket into the ground.

She didn't leave any instructions about what to do with her remains. I don't think she planned on ever dying Or maybe she thought I'd keep her on a shelf with my Emmy.

Emmy? He has an Emmy? Was he trying to impress her? Maybe, but she didn't think so. He wouldn't bother if he knew how rarely she watched television. She wasn't too impressed with anything she'd seen recently—even his program.

I'm rambling. Sorry. I'm not usually up this early, but I've started a new workout routine so I can hold up my part of the bargain where the mine is concerned. Is your brother starting to come around?

She'd told him how unhappy Mac was about the idea of bringing a stranger into the mine. She'd even had her lawyer draw up a separate agreement stating the person she chose wouldn't sue them if he got hurt on the job.

Well, time to lift weights. I'm hoping to hear back from you. Tell me when to book my flight. Coop.

Coop.

She closed her eyes and rocked back in her chair. Honesty was a trait she valued above all others. And if she were being honest now, she had to admit that this man sparked her interest in a way none of the other applicants had. She wasn't sure why. There was something very human about him. And she liked it that they had things in common. Not outwardly but deep down.

They were both alone—although she had a brother and a niece. Both orphans. Both had careers not of their choosing. She'd completely related to his story of his mother pressuring him to try out for roles. Her brother had been the one twisting Libby's arm to apply for Gran's job. "It has great benefits, Lib. And you're a shoo-in."

A shoo-in who'd had to compete with ten other applicants and suffer through three interviews. But she didn't regret her choice. She loved her job. Most of the time.

She looked at the calendar. She could drag this process out forever. Or she could go with her gut.

Smiling, she hit the Wine, Women and Words group e-mail and typed: Emergency meeting tonight. My house. Kids okay, Kat.

An hour and a half later, as she poured iced tea into four glasses for the women sitting around her kitchen table, she said, "I think I found the guy. We've been e-mailing. He interests me more than any of the other responses." Looking up, she added, "Why didn't any of you warn me about spam?"

Nobody answered. They knew she was stalling.

"Yesterday was Mother's Day. I know because I personally processed a couple thousand card-size envelopes last week. It might be why I decided to act now rather than drag out this process. I've picked a candidate."

A candidate whose first e-mail had seemed to jump off the screen and into her lap.

I'm an orphan, too. My mother just died and I never knew my father.

Her heart had done a flip-flop that hadn't occurred when she'd read any other inquiry—not even the one from a surgeon in Boston.

"So tell us about him," Jenna said, wiping a hint of sweat from her upper lip. It was only the middle of May, but the Hills had been experiencing an unusually warm spring, and the six-block stretch between their homes was straight uphill.

"You may have heard of him. His name is Cooper Lindstrom. He's an actor. I think." Did hosting a talent competition on TV qualify as acting?

Her friends looked at each other for a heartbeat or two, then all started talking at once.

"The guy from that *Close-Up* show?" Jenna blurted out.

"He's handsome. And famous," Kat said.

"Never heard of him."

The last was from Char. She often bragged that she didn't own a television, but Libby knew she kept abreast of popular culture because every week Libby placed a *People* magazine in the woman's mailbox.

Libby finished her task, then passed out the glasses and sat. "Apparently the show just concluded. I missed it. I've checked every night for a week, but there's only been basketball on that channel. Anyway, I don't care about that, but when I did an Internet search, I found the official Cooper Lindstrom Web site. And several fan clubs."

"Why would a famous guy do something like this? A publicity stunt?" Kat asked. She took a quick sip, then rose from the table and walked to the picture window to check on her sons, who were playing soccer in front of the house.

"The thought crossed my mind," Libby confessed. "In fact, I figured this was some kind of joke and I deleted his first message. But he kept e-mailing me. Not really trying to get me to change my mind exactly, but…" She hesitated because what she was about to say sounded silly and presumptuous given the fact he was a celebrity and she was a nobody. "He sounded lonely. And a little lost."

Jenna made a *pff*ing sound that sounded just like her mother—a woman who tried everyone's patience at times. "He's a star. He has people for that."

"His mom just passed away."

Char snapped her fingers. "*That* Cooper Lindstrom. I read something about his mother. Came from a small town in North Dakota. Got hired by a studio but was seduced by some mogul on a casting couch. He was married, of course. Ruined her career, but she took the high road and wouldn't tell anyone who her son's father was. The implication was she used blackmail to get her son a few breaks along the way."

Libby stared at her friend so intently Char blushed and threw up her hands. "What? I might have saved the article, if you want it."

Kat tapped on the window, gave a thumbs-up to someone outside, then rejoined the group. "So are you saying you feel sorry for him?"

"Of course, not. He's rich and famous. But I know how that kind of loss can make you reevaluate your life."

"And you think that's why he's doing this?"

Kat always asked the tough questions.

"Why else?" Libby held up her hand and, starting with her pinkie, named the objections she'd raised with him via e-mail. "I asked him if this was a publicity stunt. He said he'd come here with no press, no entourage. The only person he plans to tell is his best friend."

Ring finger. "When I asked what part the mine played in his decision, he said, 'A big one.' His mother's death really rocked him. The tabloids have been hounding him, and he sees the mine as a way to duck out of sight—literally."

Jenna's jaw fell open. "You mean he actually plans to get dirty? Libby, my mother loves that stupid show, so I am forced to watch it every week. Believe me, this guy doesn't look as though he's ever broken a sweat in his life. He's too pretty."

Libby had managed to catch a few clips on another site devoted, it seemed, to poking fun at televised talent shows. In all honesty, she'd thought the same thing, but it felt faintly disloyal to say so.

"Why risk life and limb on a hazardous job like mining when he's rich? He is rich, right?"

Libby studied the beads of moisture on her glass. "I don't know. When I asked him how important the money was, he was kinda evasive. He said his mother had been in charge of financial matters and he was still trying to sort out everything." She looked at Jenna. "Didn't you tell me you felt the same way when your dad passed away?"

Jenna nodded. "Dad was a control freak who never let Mom or me even peek at the checkbook. Fortunately, he was also very conservative, so once we put together all the pieces, we could breathe a little easier." She frowned. "Although if the Mystery Spot doesn't open on time, we might be in trouble."

Libby didn't know the nature of the latest crisis at the Murphys' summer business, but she knew better than to ask. "Then you know how he feels. Maybe his mother was good with money, too. But I got the impression that wasn't the case."

"So money is a factor," Kat stated. "But it's not like the mine is making money hand over fist. You and Mac wouldn't be working second jobs if that were the case. Did you tell him that?"

"Not exactly." Libby dropped her hand to her lap and sighed. "When I wrote the ad I thought I made it clear that this wasn't a get-rich-quick scheme. I figured the words *gold mine* would attract a lot of attention, but anyone reading deeper would see that my offer was more about bragging rights than actual profit. I'm not sure Cooper took it that way."

When no one said anything, she groaned and plopped her cheek on her hand. "I'm a liar and a fraud, aren't I? And now I've convinced a television personality to move in and father my child."

Kat reached out and squeezed her shoulder. "Lib, you're the most honest person I know. I went to your Web site. I think your disclaimer is very frank and forthright. Only a person who couldn't read would think he was going to get rich from this. Obviously this Cooper person can read, so it's probably safe to assume he's not doing this for the money."

Libby sat up a little straighter. "He does seem like a really nice guy deep down. Maybe a little shallow on the surface, but that could be from growing up in L.A. I mean, he was making commercials at an age when you and I were collecting pollywogs in Sentinel Creek," she told Jenna. "He didn't exactly have a normal upbringing."

Jenna seemed to consider the argument.

"Well, I've been giving some thought to the reason behind your decision to have a baby," Kat said. "And despite how my life has turned out—the two divorces and everything—I can't imagine not having my boys. They're the best part of me. So no matter how you go about this, my friend, I'm behind you."

Libby sat up a little straighter, surprised by how good those words felt. "Really? You don't think I'm crazy?"

Jenna laughed. "She didn't say that. But I'm in your corner, too, pal. You know that, right?"

"Me three," Char chimed in. "And if you think Cooper Lindstrom is the right one, then go for it. I bet only half a dozen people around here would even recognize him if they passed him on the street. And it's not like he's bringing Hollyweird with him."

Libby smiled, but a shiver of uneasiness passed through her. When she'd first imagined this happening, she'd pictured the sperm donor as a sort of shadowy figure who hung around the cabin making sure the woman who would be mother to his child was qualified for the job. She had no reason to believe Cooper Lindstrom had another agenda, but somehow she couldn't picture him hiding out quietly in a tiny log cabin. He seemed too colorful and vital for that.

But maybe that was a good thing. He didn't seem the type to want to stay in Sentinel Pass for long—or even return for a visit. His home was in Malibu. The ocean, the glamour, the proximity to Hollywood all seemed to fit the persona he projected on his Web site.

And that was fine with her. She liked her rustic little village just the way it was. Sentinel Pass had been a great place to grow up. Safe. Carefree. There were aspects of it that might seem a little confining to her at times, but as a single mom with a child to worry about, she wasn't in any hurry to see it change.

CHAPTER THREE

"HOW 'BOUT WHOSE SPERM IS IT?"

Shane's eyes narrowed intently. "Let me make one point perfectly clear, Coop. I will never allow my name to be attached to *any* show that has the word *sperm* in the title."

Shane was driving Cooper to LAX because Coop had insisted it would give them time to brainstorm about the Sentinel Pass project. He hadn't mentioned the gesture also would save him the cost of a limo.

"I had no idea you were so sensitive. Do you like *Honey, I'm Pregnant?*"

"No. I thought you wanted this to last more than one season? A pregnancy is nine months. Once the kid is born, the title no longer applies."

"Good point. How 'bout—"

"Wait." Shane held up his hand as he checked the rearview mirror, then stepped on the gas to shoot into the on-ramp. "Before you toss out another gem, let's try to pin down the high concept behind the story line. Because, frankly, Coop, I'm having trouble seeing it. If it's just about some woman trying to get pregnant, then count me out. I really don't want to get sued."

Cooper ignored the last comment. "Think of it as a fish-out-of-water story, only this fish brings his water with him."

"Huh?"

"The gold-for-sperm thing is a fabulous hook, but the real

story is what happens *after* the hero and heroine meet. And I've been thinking about who we could get to play the postmistress. Ashley Judd."

The black Hummer hesitated for a fraction of a second before weaving seamlessly into the traffic flow on the 405. "I could be wrong," Shane said, focusing on his driving, "but I think I remember hearing that the word *postmistress* is archaic. Like a *stewardess* is now a *flight attendant*. A woman who is the head of a post office is called a postmaster."

"Really? Um...okay. If you say so. So would Ashley Judd make a good postmaster?"

"I've seen your postmaster's photo, Coop. She's nice-looking but hardly beautiful. Ashley is gorgeous."

"True, but she can do plain. Remember when she played a woman who went to jail for killing her husband, and Tommy Lee Jones followed her—"

"*Double Jeopardy*. But she's an A-list star. Give me a television actress."

Cooper frowned. He'd been pondering that very subject earlier in the day when his second ex had called—also unhappy because her pin money was late in coming. Thankfully, Morgana had her trust fund to fall back on. Not that that had kept her from going for blood in the divorce, but her established wealth had kept her from taking him to the proverbial cleaners.

"I hate to say it, but one person who might be perfect is my ex."

"Which one?"

"Tiffany."

"She's gorgeous, too."

"Yeah, but you haven't seen her in the morning. She does ordinary very easily."

"I'll take your word for it."

Shane drove more conservatively than Cooper liked, but

for once Cooper wasn't running behind schedule. Usually when he flew, unhappy airline personnel were holding the plane door for him as he raced down the concourse. Shane, who didn't like to be rushed, had insisted on picking him up an hour early.

"You like drama? Call a cab," he'd said when Coop had complained that if he arrived too early, he'd be at the mercy of fans in the airport.

More important, although he hadn't mentioned it, was the fact that an early departure meant leaving a couple of undone things. Like giving Rollie—the old guy who lived next door— everything edible left in his refrigerator. The man was eighty and at one time owned a couple of miles of prime Malibu real estate. But his trusting nature had made him a candidate for victimization. Coop watched over him as much as he could. Lena had called Coop a sap. Not for helping the old man but for not letting his publicist use the fact in press releases.

He'd called Daria, his twenty-four-year-old assistant, and asked her to check on Rollie when she came to collect the mail and feed his fish.

"Not a chance," she'd said, her voice thick with sleep. Or drugs. Or both. She was a partier like her role models, Paris and Lindsey. "Old people give me the creeps."

Maybe she considered Coop old. Maybe that was why she'd stopped flirting with him.

Or maybe she'd stopped flirting with him because he'd made it clear he had no desire to sleep with her.

Why don't I want to sleep with her? He didn't know the answer. And didn't want to think about it.

"So who plays you?" Shane asked, drawing Coop's attention back to the present.

"Me, of course. At least in the pilot. This is my idea, remember?"

"Actually, the idea came from the postmaster. It's her life.

You don't think she's going to be just a little bit upset when she figures out you're only using her for the sake of a television show?"

"The Internet is public domain, man. I had lunch with Arthur yesterday and tried to pick his brain about the legality of this without really telling him anything. You know what a gossip he is." He rolled his eyes and muttered, "Client privilege, my butt."

"Arthur said you could do this with impunity?"

Cooper didn't know the word, so he ignored the question. "We talked in hypotheticals. Hypothetically, if I spotted an interesting idea or concept that someone applied to their life and they made that idea public via the Internet, I—or anybody who was so inclined—could take it and run. You can't copyright ideas."

"I know that, but you're not the only person who knows about this. I'm assuming hundreds, if not thousands, of men have replied to her ad. That means that no matter how much we change this plot, the basic element—a woman trades a gold mine for sperm—is going to point to her."

"So?"

"We're talking about creating a comedy around a woman's decision to have a child, Coop. A lot of people aren't going to find that funny. In fact, if she goes public or tries to sue, your reputation could be toast."

The thought had crossed his mind, but he hadn't let it linger. "I hear you, but remember your high concept. This is *my* story now. What happens when a popular actor on the run from a nefarious loan shark answers a woman's ad so he can hide out in the Black Hills of South Dakota?"

"So there isn't a baby now?"

Questions. Coop hated winging answers. He was always terrified of saying something so completely wrong everyone would know he wasn't too bright.

"There might be." His need for some quick cash hadn't changed. It would be weeks before he and Shane saw any money from this project—if they could interest backers. It would be months before they saw network money...*if* there was a pilot. "I don't know yet," he admitted. "But, if the show turns out to be as hot as I think it will and it makes boatloads of money, the *postmaster*," he said pointedly, "will be able to send her kid to Harvard. What mother wouldn't endure a little public ridicule for that?"

Shane didn't say anything right away, so Cooper added, "Besides, if we use this part in the script, that will be my sperm in the Petri dish. Doesn't that make *me* just as open to humiliation?"

Shane nudged his Ray-Bans lower on his nose and looked at Cooper. "Sometimes you surprise me."

"Because I'm not as self-serving as everyone thinks?"

"No. It's still all about Coop. But you're deeper than anyone would guess. I assume you keep that a secret for a reason, though, so I promise not to mention it to either of your ex-wives if we end up auditioning them."

The observation pleased Coop but made him uncomfortable, too. Shane saw too much. "Good. Mom called them piranhas for a reason. Any hint of weakness and—" He put a hand out to brace himself when Shane stomped on the brakes.

Taillights flashed red across all lanes, and Shane cursed under his breath. He looked in both oversize side mirrors, then began jockeying for position with a Jaguar. The owner of the smaller car laid on the horn but gave way to superior size and wheelbase.

A few miles later they took the exit leading toward a grouping of giant pillars. The unusual outdoor sculpture would be glowing like multicolored Jedi swords that evening. "I know what a blow your mom's death was, Coop. I can't help wondering if the reason you're so gung-ho about this project is that it's a way to avoid thinking about all the things you don't want to think about."

Coop shifted uncomfortably in the soft leather seat. "I didn't realize you had a degree in psychology."

He hadn't meant his tone to come off quite so sharp, but he knew it had when Shane sighed. "I'm not saying the idea doesn't have merit, but if you're not up front with this woman from the very beginning, the whole thing could blow up in your face."

Cooper was sick of thinking about the negatives. His bank balance. His last review. His exes. And the unrelenting death threats—you don't get much more negative than that. He needed to make something positive happen in his life, and what could be more positive than helping a woman fulfill her dream of having a child?

"I can be honest," he said, scanning the overhead gate signs for his airline.

"You're an actor, Coop. Are you sure about that?"

He turned to look at his friend. "Hey, I'm not the bad guy here. I'm not the one who gambled away money that didn't belong to me. And let's not forget about the bookie who wants my heart on a plate. I plan to do whatever it takes to make this happen, but I promise you, I'll take…um—" he had to think a moment "—Libby McGannon's situation into consideration. As far as we know, she's going to love the idea of turning her ad into a hit show. And why wouldn't she? It's win-win. She gets a kid. Her Podunk town benefits from the publicity. I make enough money to get my mother's evil monkey off my back. Everybody's happy. End of story."

Shane heaved a sigh as the monster SUV came to a stop in a no-stopping area. He put a hand on Cooper's shoulder and squeezed. "I know you, Coop. You're more a brother to me than my own twin. But I'm worried about you, man. You've been acting weird since your mom died. Have you made the club scene even once in the past month? No. You're busy hiding out at your house…alone. No parties. No dozen or so *assistants* hanging around. I don't know what's going on, but I don't want to see you jump into something for the wrong reason and wind up getting hurt."

Hurt? The only woman with the power to hurt him was dead. "Thanks, Shane. I appreciate that, man, but I'll be fine." He opened the door and got out, then retrieved his carry-on from the backseat. This was the first time in his adult life he'd traveled anywhere without a minimum of four suitcases.

Shane leaned across the seat to shake his hand. "What if she meets you and decides you're not the right man for the job?"

Coop's heart lurched uncomfortably. "Are you crazy? Why would she do that? I'm Cooper Lindstrom."

He slammed the door and stepped up onto the curb. He couldn't be sure, but he thought his best friend's last words were, "My point exactly."

THE RAPID CITY AIRPORT had taken strides to modernize, but Libby imagined to someone as worldly and well-traveled as Cooper Lindstrom it would look small and ordinary. She'd been to New York once. With Jenna and her mother when the two girls graduated from high school. Libby had saved for three years to afford it. She'd loved the adventure—the Broadway shows and interesting food—but she'd felt a profound relief to return home. She'd found it depersonalizing to walk for blocks and blocks without seeing someone you knew—or even making eye contact. Here, she was someone. People recognized her, respected her; and feeling that she was a vital, tangible part of a whole mattered to her.

She'd been to a few postal conferences in places like Minneapolis, Houston and Phoenix since then, but Libby always returned home knowing she would never live anywhere else.

She took the escalator to the second floor since nobody was

standing around the baggage area. Cooper's plane from Denver was twenty minutes late. Wind sheers at the Denver airport, she overheard someone say.

"Are you waiting for family?" a voice asked.

Libby looked at the elderly woman standing a few steps away. Probably ten years younger than her grandmother. Spry. The way Gran had been most of Libby's life. "A friend," she answered. "You?"

"My sister. She and her second husband moved to Tucson so they wouldn't have to shovel their driveway."

"We were pretty lucky last winter. Not much snow to shovel."

"That's what I told 'em. Then he had heatstroke and had to have his knee replaced from too much golf. Poor Ruby has been nursing him for months. Finally she came back here to pay their property taxes and get a break." She shook her head. "Makes me glad I'm single. I'm Bea, by the way."

"Libby. Nice to meet you."

"You married?"

"Nope."

"Smart woman."

Libby smiled. During the truly awful period when her brother's marriage was coming apart at the seams, she'd been glad to have avoided the marriage trap. Lately, not so much. She would have liked to be loved by someone, even once. Then she wouldn't have had to go to such extremes to conceive a child. But since that wasn't going to happen...

She started to ask the woman where she lived when Bea suddenly let out a squeal that could have come from a thirteen-year-old girl. She grabbed Libby's arm and pointed. "Look. Look there. That's Cooper Lindstrom. Live. In person. I can't believe it. Here. Right here. Not twenty feet from my sister. And she doesn't even see him, the twit."

Libby assumed she meant her sister was a twit, not Cooper. Her heart sped up as she watched the man who obviously rocked Bea's world stride into hers. He was taller than she'd pictured. Fabulous posture. Chin high—to avoid making eye contact, she guessed. Dark glasses that also helped in that effort. Trademark blond hair looking perfectly tousled.

His black pants were made of some lightweight material with just enough pockets to appear both trendy and functional. His unbuttoned long-sleeve white cotton shirt worn over a black T-shirt apparently took the place of a coat, although she'd warned him that spring in the Hills could include showers and a cold spell. His black lace-up, low-rise boots were a combination of leather and mesh fabric. They looked pretty ordinary but probably cost more than she made in a week.

He moved with purpose, like a person who knew his place in the world and was comfortable with that. Libby was envious. Until she reminded herself that he was an actor. He was probably trained to evoke a certain persona even when he wasn't on stage.

She cautiously stepped away from the woman who'd moved her hand to her chest as if she might swoon. "Excuse me. My friend's arrived. Nice talking with you."

She didn't like the way her knees suddenly turned wobbly, but she forced herself to intersect the stream of pedestrians headed toward the stairs and the first-floor luggage carousel where they'd agreed to meet. "Ahem," she said, joining him in stride. "I'm Libby."

He stopped as though he'd put both feet in glue. His chin turned. Was that hint of a cleft real, she wondered or the result of surgeon's scalpel?

"You are?" he asked, removing his shades. "Your photo doesn't do you justice."

She felt her cheeks heat up under his scrutiny. She knew she couldn't hold a candle to some of the young starlets he'd dated—if the tabloids could be trusted. But she had applied a tiny bit of foundation, blush and mascara that morning.

"How was your flight?"

His grin provoked a collective inhale from the people around her. "Windy. We circled Denver for nearly an hour before we could land. Then it was hold-on-to-your-hats, boys, we're going in."

She liked his voice. It sounded chipper and bright. "Wind sheers are dangerous. I'm glad you didn't crash."

"Me, too." He quickly glanced around. "Um…maybe we should keep walking. Makes me less of a target for autograph seekers."

Libby looked around. Nobody seemed that interested in him, although she spotted a few people looking their way. "Luggage?"

He lifted the shoulder with a black leather strap over it. "I'm traveling light."

There was something in his tone that made her think the common phrase meant something more. She pointed toward the main entrance. "My truck is in the short-term lot."

"Short-term lot," he repeated, his head cocked to one side as if hearing the expression for the first time.

"They don't have hourly parking in L.A.?"

He blinked. "What? Oh, no, of course they do. I was thinking about something else." He replaced his sunglasses.

Libby shook her head and dug out her own pair. Six dollars at Target. She was pretty sure Cooper Lindstrom couldn't say the same about his.

They were three feet from the door when she heard a high-pitched voice call "Woo-hoo, Libby. Wait a minute, please."

Libby paused and looked over her shoulder. Bea—the woman she'd been making small talk with—was approaching at warp speed, a giant pink suitcase in tow and another woman following behind looking frantic and confused.

Libby let out a low groan and leaned toward Cooper. "She's a fan of yours. Recognized you before I did."

He looked at her a moment, then turned around, smiling

as if he was just about to meet his best friend in the world. "Hello, there. Lovely to meet you two, but we're in a bit of a hurry. I hope you can forgive us."

"Oh, please. Just one photo," Bea pleaded. To her sister, who was breathing hard enough to worry Libby, she snapped, "Tell me you have your camera."

Flustered, the silver-haired woman started digging in her purse. Seconds later she triumphantly held up a disposable that she nearly dropped when she tried to pass it to her sister.

Libby could see where this was going, and curious onlookers were starting to back up behind them, so she herded the two older women to one side and motioned for Cooper to follow. "I'll take the photo. Let's move over by this wall so there won't be so much glare. Here we go…"

She positioned the women where she wanted them, then looked at Cooper archly. "Well…"

He responded to his cue adroitly, hopping into place between the sisters. He looped his nicely muscled arms carefully about each woman's shoulders.

"Smile."

She couldn't prevent the slight intake of breath when she met his gaze through the viewfinder. My God, he was handsome. Alive and vital. Perfect. Her stomach turned over and whatever was left of her breakfast nearly came back up. She swallowed harshly and snapped the shot.

Oh, Lord, what have I done?

THE DRIVE FROM THE airport circumvented, for the most part, the sprawling town of Rapid City that Coop had observed from the air. He made a mental note to visit it at some point then gave his attention to the scenery as they headed into the mountains. Despite one traffic stop for road construction and an amazing number of motor homes on the highway, the pace was so noticeably different from what he'd left that morning he felt the muscles in his neck and shoulders begin to relax.

Although Libby, he observed, was gripping the steering wheel so tightly her knuckles were white. Poor girl probably would have suffered a meltdown if she'd been on the 405 that morning.

He didn't feel right about openly taking notes—that would raise questions he wasn't prepared to answer—but he tried to pay attention to their route and the general lay of the land, since he'd promised to provide Shane with some idea of what kind of logistics the production crew would be facing once they started filming.

"We don't have time to stop anywhere today, but I'll try to point out some sights on the way home," she told him. "That big dome is part of Reptile Gardens. It's a popular tourist attraction. We're going to pass by the Stratosphere Bowl, although the road is blocked off now and you have to walk in a mile or so to see it."

"What's that?"

She rattled off something about meteorological records that he didn't quite get.

"It was made by a meteor?"

She looked at him several seconds before replying, "No. The bowl is a natural depression. I'm not sure how it was formed. My friend Jenna's dad could have told you. He was a geologist. But it's famous because someone launched a weather balloon into the atmosphere from there and it made some kind of record. I haven't been there in years."

"Oh," he said, feeling dumb.

A few minutes later she pointed to a road sign that said Rockerville. "Was a mining boomtown. Then it became a tourist boomtown. Then the new highway went in and that was the end of Rockerville's popularity," she said.

He leaned forward to look around her as they zoomed past. Although it was difficult to see clearly through the trees, he spotted what could have been a movie set of an Old West ghost town, deserted and falling into disrepair.

They passed by the charred evidence of a forest fire that had obviously jumped both lanes of the highway. Her voice changed as she filled him in on the details. "Mac's a volunteer firefighter. He was on the line for three days with this one. He says the ones that are started on purpose are the hardest to swallow."

"What are the winters like here?" he asked, changing the subject.

"Some people call this the banana belt." She looked at him, her lips pulling to one side of her face wryly. "All things being relative, of course. We still get our share of below-zero temps and snow. But nothing like it used to be in my grandmother's day."

The four-wheel-drive SUV provided a marvelous vantage point—except in those spots where the land fell away into cavernous voids protected by rather flimsy-looking guardrails. He didn't think he was afraid of heights—he'd skied in Vail, for heaven's sake—but he subtly leaned his elbow on the center console and turned his attention on her.

She glanced at him, then returned her gaze straight ahead, giving him a clear view of her profile. Firm, straight jawline ending in a femininely rounded chin. Her nose was small, almost delicate in relation to her other features. He really liked her lips, generous and creased in the corners just enough to tell him she smiled a lot. But she could stand to have her eyebrows waxed, he decided.

She put on the blinker and stepped on the brake.

"Are we almost there?" he asked, wishing he'd paid more attention to the directional signs. "Do we go past Mount Rushmore? I've never been there. Can you believe that?"

"No. No. And…yes."

Definite humor in her tone.

"Are you making fun of me?"

She looked appalled. "Of course not. I was making light of the fact that you haven't been to the Black Hills before. Despite the number of motor homes we just passed, South Dakota isn't the premier destination for most vacationers."

"Okay. I was just making sure you don't have a blond bias."

"Not at all. One of my best friends is blond. And she's very smart. In fact, she's working on her teaching credential."

Cooper wasn't really worried about what she thought of him—not yet, anyway. He generally didn't have any trouble getting women of all ages to like him. But he was curious about her. She seemed surprisingly aloof for someone who wanted his sperm.

Neither spoke for several minutes. Cooper was content to mentally catalog the mountain beauty that was neither Tahoe nor Rocky Mountain National Park. The more he saw, the more he unwound. He almost felt as though he were coming home.

Which made no sense at all.

The road followed the shore of a dazzling blue lake. Libby told him the name as they passed by a historical marker, but he missed it. His brain was preoccupied with figuring out a way to work the location into his story. He really hadn't expected to be impressed by the land's beauty.

A few miles farther, she slowed again, this time putting on the opposite blinker. She had to stop to wait for oncoming traffic to pass.

Cooper looked around. The road made a T, and on the inside corner, to the right of where they were turning, sat a huge white tepee flanked by two log cabins. Four or five cars and a camper trailer were parked in the gravel lot near a billboard inviting shoppers to buy Native American crafts—pottery, carvings, leather moccasins… The list went on, but Libby turned sharply, cutting off his view.

"I'd like to come back and look around sometime. Interesting place. Is the owner Native American?"

"In a past life, maybe," she said with a little laugh. "My friend Char owns it. She's as white as me, but she claims to feel a spiritual affinity for the American Indian and has been ritually adopted by at least one Lakota tribe."

The narrow two-lane strand of pavement wound through tall, silvery-green pines that seemed to crowd the road. The early-afternoon sun felt warm through the windshield, but when he cracked the window a few inches, he felt cool, pine-scented air rush in.

"How much farther?"

"Sentinel Pass is ten miles off the main road," she answered, adding under her breath, "Ten miles and twenty-five years."

He wondered what she meant, but instead of asking said, "There aren't really three dinosaurs in your town, are there?"

"Not anymore. There were three skeletons discovered a few miles from here years and years ago. They were moved to the School of Mines for research purposes. To make up for stealing our dinosaurs, the state paid to have a replica of one erected at the visitor center. His name is Seymour."

"How did they know his name?"

She smiled as if actually amused by his question, but she didn't take her eyes off the road. "People tended to be more casual with Paleolithic discoveries in the past. Remember the Tyrannosaurus named Sue? The others might have names, too. Seymour is the only one I know personally because he gets about a hundred letters every year from schoolchildren who have visited here on field trips."

"Does he write back?"

He didn't expect an answer to his quip, but she turned and looked at him. "Yes, actually, he does. Through me."

"You speak dinosaur?"

Her smile made his heart stop for a second. Something he could honestly say had never happened before in his life. It didn't hurt exactly, but it freaked him out enough that he missed the first part of her reply.

"…expect you to be that interested in our town. You'll have to meet my grandmother. Even on her bad days she still knows more about Sentinel Pass than anybody else does on their good days."

An elderly character, he thought. *Excellent idea.* "I'd love to meet her. And your brother, too. Is he still not thrilled with your decision?"

She turned to face the road and stepped on the gas. "He's a man. He has a daughter. He doesn't get it."

If Cooper were honest, he'd admit that he didn't understand her motivation completely either. Why choose such an extreme—and public—process to get pregnant? He'd probably never know, but since his former acting coach used to tell him motivation was key to getting into a character, he asked, "Is it your desire to have a child that he doesn't get or the way you've chosen to go about this?"

"Both."

He frowned. Short, succinct answers weren't going to cut it. He'd never met a woman who didn't go on and on about herself, the reasons behind her choices and her future expectations when given half a chance. "Do you think you've made the right choice?"

"Time will tell, as my grandmother always said." She made a gesture with her right hand. "This is it. Sentinel Pass. Try not to blink, you might miss it."

Another rather biting comment about a place that on first glance looked far more real and charming than the tourist town they'd passed earlier. No stereotypical false fronts. Well, maybe a couple, but mostly the main thoroughfare seemed quaint, rustic and…perfect for what he had in mind.

"I like it," he said honestly.

She slowed to let a woman dragging an upright metal cart of some kind cross the street. The woman waved at Libby and gave Cooper a curious squint but scurried faster so they could pass.

Cooper followed her with his gaze. She'd make a fabulous extra. The Sentinel Pass version of a bag lady.

"I'll bring you back into town after you get settled," Libby told him. "Right now I need to get home and call the post office to check on Jenna. Is that okay with you?"

He pulled his attention from the two-story hotel made out of some rough brownish-colored stone he'd never seen before. "Huh? Oh, yeah, sure. Whatever works for you. We're on Libby time."

She blinked at that but kept driving.

They passed a bar midblock with swinging doors and a funky old sign that looked like something out of bad film noir. He could totally picture a film crew using the exterior as a location shot. The interior could be anything Shane wanted it to be.

A few doors down, on the corner, sat a café with honest-to-goodness blue-and-white gingham curtains in the window.

"Quaint," he murmured, suddenly craving a cup of coffee and a piece of pie. "Tell me they serve homemade pie. Apple à la mode."

"Pardon?"

He swallowed the surfeit of saliva in his mouth. "Oh, nothing, just mumbling to myself."

He mentally noted two antique stores, a barbershop, a coin-activated laundry and a tiny one-pump gas station that appeared to be operational. "From your description, I pictured it more…desolate."

"Really? I don't remember what I said that gave you that idea. I suppose I kind of take the town for granted. I grew up here. Not much has changed in thirty-odd years. The hardware store got a face-lift a while back." She shrugged.

Then, abruptly, the buildings turned to houses. Mostly old. Some squeezed together as if land had been at a premium; others were set back from the street with spindly trees and a minimum of landscaping inside the twisted wire fences.

The road climbed steeply, causing the car's transmission to downshift to make the grade. Two curves later she flicked on her turn signal. "Here we are."

She pulled into a gravel driveway that led to a narrow, two-story house the color of L.A. fog. Three or four outbuildings were scattered behind it. The nearest neighbor he could see was a mere hint of color through the branches of trees not quite fully leafed out.

He studied the house as she drove past it to park in front of a detached two-stall garage. The most prominent feature was an enclosed porch that stuck out like a woman's stiffly starched skirt. Inside the glass windows he glimpsed a table, several chairs and a large sofa. He didn't see any screens and wondered how much the area got used.

"Okay. This is it. Home, sweet home."

She turned off the engine but didn't get out right away. Coop looked around. Five old cars succumbing to varying degrees of rust and degeneration were clustered beneath a tall stand of pines like a strange lawn sculpture.

Great set decoration. He had to remember to write that down when he had the chance.

He got out. Except for the broken-down cars, the place was meticulous. Lawns mowed. Sidewalk between the house and garage edged. Even the five-foot-tall stack of wood was perfectly even.

"Nice place."

She made a skeptical sound, as if doubting his sincerity. But he meant it. Maybe because the house fit the town and the town fit some ideal image he had of the kind of place he would have liked to grow up in. "Really. It's not some cookie-cutter tract home. It has personality."

"All that's missing is the ocean," she said drily.

Well, he couldn't argue with that. This wasn't Malibu, but he actually felt more relaxed here than he had in months. He took a deep breath and let it out. "No smog. L.A. can't say that."

She joined him. He couldn't help noticing she left the keys in the ignition. Something only a fool would do in L.A. That impressed him, too, but he kept his comment to himself. Maybe she was acting slightly self-deprecating about Sentinel Pass because she didn't want him to become too comfortable here. He didn't blame her, considering what they were planning.

"Come on. I'll show you the house. It's nearly a hundred years old. The root cellar goes back to the mining days. My great-grandfather built the log cabin first, then, when he could afford it, put up the big house. It survived two fires. You can still see the charred beams in the attic."

His mind was racing, trying to catalog impressions. Finally he gave up. He was going to be here a week. He could take his time sifting through what he wanted to use for the show. "Whose cars are those?" he asked, getting his Louis Vuitton bag from the backseat. He slipped the strap over his shoulder and soundly closed the door.

It felt bulkier than when he'd first packed it because he'd remembered at the last minute to add his Dsquared cropped jacket in case the weather turned cool.

"A couple are Gran's. The rest belong to my brother. I keep telling myself this is the year they go, but somehow I never get around to getting them towed off to the scrap yard. I don't think I'm a sentimental fool, but...who knows. There they sit."

Interesting attachment, he thought.

"Let's go in. I thought maybe you'd like a little time to yourself to, um, unpack?" She looked at his bag a moment, then shrugged. "As I said, I need to check on my rural routes and make sure the drop box is picked up, but I'll show you around first."

She started off, obviously expecting him to follow. A narrow, uneven sidewalk separated two stretches of thick yellowish-green lawn. "The guesthouse is out back," she told him, pointing off to the left. "It used to be Gran's place."

Cooper jogged to catch up.

"There's running water, of course, but the bathroom is kinda small and sometimes the toilet backs up." She frowned. "I should probably put in a new septic, but it doesn't get used much and there are so many other places to use the money."

"How come you don't have a sewer hookup?"

"There's one in town, but we're too far out. When Gran was a girl, they used the outhouse." She pointed toward a slope-roofed building with a crescent-moon cutout in the door.

"No shit."

She groaned.

"Sorry. Terrible pun, but I couldn't resist."

Her smile seemed indulgent. Motherly. That was a good thing, right? Since she wanted to be a mother. But it wasn't the reaction he was used to getting from women, and that bothered him.

"Feel free to use it if you have any problems in the middle of the night." She paused before adding, "Or you're welcome to use the facilities inside the main house."

"Your house."

She nodded, looking at the building in question. "Yes. It was my parents'. Gran moved in to take care of Mac and me after Dad died. She deeded it to me when she retired from the post office. Mac's house is on the lot just behind this. His place used to belong to Gran's second husband. When he passed away, she gave it to Mac and his wife."

"How many times has your grandmother been married?"

"Just twice. Widowed both times. Now she's living in sin with a younger man." She paused, her lips puckered in a smirk. "Calvin. He's eighty-four."

"Oh, my. I don't think I want to try to picture that. Nope. Definitely not."

She shrugged. "They're very sweet together. Cal likes to say that Gran's mind is going and his body is shot, so together they almost make a whole person."

Delicious. His fingers tingled with the need to get yet another gem on paper.

"This way," she said, heading off again.

He followed, happy to use the time to study her. Long limbs but graceful. Her shoes were black, functional, zippered leather. Nothing delicate or sexy about them. He knew neither of his exes would be caught dead in shoes like that. On Libby they just seemed to work.

Her jeans were well broken in and faded in places that drew his eye. He knew without asking that the faded places weren't factory-issue. Her maroon V-neck sweater topped a white shirt. The tiniest hint of a postal emblem or name tag showed above her chest.

He was a little surprised she hadn't dressed up more to meet him.

"Does the cabin have DSL? I'd like to check my e-mail."

She stopped and turned around. Her eyes—an unusual shade of golden brown that could have sold a fortune in contact lenses if it could be duplicated—opened wide a moment before she burst into laughter. "Sorry. I guess I should have sent you a picture of the place before you came. My dad ran power to it when Gran was living with us, but there's no phone. Or TV. We don't get cable. Some people in town have satellite, but it's never been high on my list of priorities." She looked a little worried. "Are you going to be able to handle that?"

He shifted the strap that was biting into his flesh on his

shoulder. "Of course. I just assumed that since you reached me via the Internet, I'd be able to do the same."

"Oh, you can. In the house. I have a desktop computer. In my bedroom," she added softly. "I...um...I'll see about moving it to a more central place—the dining room would probably work—so you can use it, too."

She's a prude. Suddenly, he felt an overwhelming need to test his theory. That's what his character would do, he was sure of it. So he slipped the strap from his shoulder, letting the heavy leather bag drop to the ground, and cleared the distance between them.

She stared at him questioningly, mouth slightly agape.

"You can leave it where it is," he said, removing his sunglasses so they were looking straight into each other's eyes. "After all, we're going to be sharing genetic material. That should entitle me to at least *see* the inside of your bedroom, shouldn't it?"

Her bottom lip moved up and down, but no words came out. For the pure hell of it, he leaned in and kissed her. Neither of them closed their eyes, so he could read her instant shock. But she didn't pull back or react in any other outward response.

That lack of reaction never happened when he kissed a woman. He'd been kissing women long enough and often enough in front of other people to know that he was damn good at it. She should be swooning. Unless he'd lost his touch.

Determined to trigger a reaction, he pulled her against him and tilted his head. This time he did close his eyes. He felt the thudding of her heartbeat that was outpacing his.

His brief moment of satisfaction was lost, though, when she let out a tiny moan, followed quickly by a sharp, "What the hell are you doing?"

She pushed on his shoulders with a strength that surprised him. He stepped back—and promptly tripped over his carry-on bag. He went down gracelessly and hard.

A pain shot down his leg and straight up his spine. "I think I've broken my coccyx."

"Good. Then it will save me kicking it."

He looked up, startled by her tone. "What? We're going to make a baby together. Shouldn't I kiss you?"

She put her hands on her hips. "Shouldn't you wait until I've made up my mind whether or not you're the one I pick? Shouldn't we get to know each other a little bit first? Good grief, don't they teach you any manners on the West Coast?"

He shifted to one side and gingerly touched his butt. The pain wasn't as bad as he'd first thought. Reaching under him, he discovered he'd actually landed on the handle of his bag. But he could have been hurt, and her lack of sympathy made him wonder if she was going to be equally hard-line about his plan.

"I thought you midwesterners were big on hospitality. What if I'd needed to go to the hospital?"

She rolled her eyes. "Oh, good grief. Nobody has ever died from a broken butt bone." She held out her hand. "I can bring you some ice if it's starting to swell."

Like your big head, he imagined her adding.

Pride made him resist her offer of help. As he was brushing reddish dust and grass clippings from his Emporio Armani Techno pants, she picked up his bag and hefted it over one shoulder like an empty mail sack. She marched toward the one-story log cabin with a green metal roof and shabby gingerbread ambience, mumbling something about giving him "time to settle in."

He got the impression she couldn't wait to get away from him. He followed, frowning. Women—except for the two he'd married—generally liked him. He hadn't known Libby McGannon long enough for his charm to wear off, so he had to attribute her standoffishness to her situation. Alone. Desperate for a baby yet unmarried. But also fiercely proud.

The way Mom was when she found out she was pregnant with me? The unwelcome thought sent a shiver down his spine.

"The woodstove actually runs on propane and can be turned on by remote control, if you're cold," his hostess said, apparently noticing his reaction. "The place gets real cozy. Megan, my niece, and I sometimes camp out here when we need some girl time." Her smile seemed to be peace-offering and Coop felt his tension leave him.

No. Libby was nothing like his mother. She was real and honest and didn't hold a grudge. She would make an excellent female lead—even if he still wasn't quite clear on the plot. But he was more determined than ever to write the pilot and get the show on the air.

Everything he'd seen so far—even Libby's reaction to his kiss, which, although personally humbling, would look great on camera—confirmed what his gut had told him. There was a gold mine here storywise. He just needed to start digging.

CHAPTER FOUR

LIBBY DIDN'T OWN A cell phone. Service was so spotty in this part of the Hills it wasn't worth the monthly fee, she figured. So once she dumped Cooper Lindstrom's suitcase—a leather bag the color of the pipe tobacco her father used to smoke and so soft she'd had to fight the urge to rub her cheek against it— on Gran's antique spindle bed, she made a dash to the main house to call Jenna.

"Sentinel Pass Post Office." Jenna's crisp voice resonated with the authority worthy of Libby's PMR—an acronym for Postmaster Relief. The postal service loved acronyms, and Libby had to fight the tendency to abbreviate things in her real life.

"Not so loud," Libby shushed, closing the storm door behind her. "He might still be wandering around outside."

"Libby? Is that you? I can't hear you. Why are you whispering? Oh, my God, he's with you, isn't he?"

"Not yet. I put his bag in the cabin and suggested he unpack, but he said he needs to go online to check his Nelsons or something, so he—"

"Nelsons? Do you mean Nielsens? How can someone so smart be so socially unsavvy?"

Libby walked to the window at the kitchen sink so she could keep an eye on her new guest's activities. Plus, there was a chance she might throw up. Nerves, of course. She'd experienced the same feeling twice before. Both times had involved death, not birth. The end of hope, not hope embodied.

She squeezed the phone between her shoulder and ear and turned on the tap. Taking a glass from the cabinet she'd refinished last winter, she filled it to the brim and made herself take a slow, long drink. "Better," she said, smacking her lips.

"Isn't it a little early to be hitting the wine bottle? What's wrong? Were you mobbed by adoring fans and the paparazzi at the airport? Is that why you're upset?"

"No. Just two old ladies who bowled me over to get his autograph. I got the impression he was a little surprised and maybe even slightly piqued that there wasn't more hoopla, but he was nice to his two fans. Nicer than I expected. I got to play photographer." Invisible. As ever. "That's not why I called. He's just as pretty as his pictures and seems very pleasant, but…I think I made a mistake. A big one. Huge." She swallowed against the bile rising in her throat. "Jen, why didn't you stop me? He's not the right guy for this. Remember the book we read? *Men Are from Mars, Women Are from Venus*? His planet is actually spinning in a galaxy far, far away."

She held her breath, waiting for her smart, practical, conservative friend to agree with her. "Oh, quit it, Libby. You always do this. You meet a guy and immediately dissect his every flaw so you can dump him. Or, if he doesn't have any obvious flaws, you dredge up your own—real or imagined—to you prove why you're not good enough for him. Not this time, Lib."

I do that? "Why not this time?"

"Because there's a potential child involved. You have to think of the bigger picture. If you were a kid, would you rather have a father—even one who wasn't on-site—who is handsome, rich and famous or smart, boring and anonymous?"

Libby set down her glass and started pacing. She was used to thinking on her feet. From the breakfast nook window she could see that the front door of the cabin was still open. Because he was waiting for someone to close it? She pushed aside the snarky question. True, she'd gotten the impression Cooper was privileged, but he'd also been kind to the elderly fans and he'd asked intelligent questions the entire drive. A lot of them, actually. "I don't know," she answered honestly.

"Well, think about it. Not from your protectionist point of view. From a kid's point of view. Seriously. For once in your life act, don't react."

The words rang a bell in her head. They sounded like something her grandmother would have said. *Gran.* A sudden sense of calm, like a large, warm hand on her shoulder, made her heart rate slow down a notch. She'd take Coop to meet Gran. If Gran approved, then Libby would stick with her initial decision. Even if he did scare her spitless. Witless. And about every other *less* you could name.

In the background of the phone, Libby heard the overhead doorbell ding-dong. Seconds later a loud voice boomed. Marva Ploughman—or "the Mouth," as some people called her. Gossipmonger extraordinaire.

"Hang up. Hang up now," she said. "Gran used to say the woman was psychic where gossip is concerned. I don't even want her to know you're talking to me. She'll hear about this soon enough and won't stop talking till she's six feet under. I'll be in later to lock up. Bye."

As she replaced the cordless unit on the receiver, a flash of movement from outside caught her eye. Her new guest had left the cabin to stand in the middle of the yard. Hands on hips, he looked around like a conquering hero surveying his domain. The midafternoon sunlight made his golden-blond hair glisten as if he were filming a shampoo commercial.

She tried to tell herself he looked silly and out of place, but the sad truth was he probably couldn't look silly and out of place if he tried. In fact, he looked confident, capable and curious. It was the last that made her push her fears aside and decide to do what her best friend suggested. She'd act, not react.

Her late sister-in-law had once called Libby narrow-minded and judgmental. Misty had been drunk at the time and had apologized profusely the next day, but the criticism had stuck in Libby's mind. Maybe she did jump to conclusions about people without giving them a chance. She didn't know this guy from Adam and she'd invited him to travel halfway across the country to "interview" for the position she'd offered. Surely she could let down her guard long enough to get to know him before she decided he was too much trouble.

She polished off her water and put the glass in the dish strainer in the sink, then started toward the door. She'd only gotten two steps when the phone rang. "Hello."

"Libby girl, is that you? I called the P.O. and that redheaded girl told me you were at home. You're not sick, are you? You're like me—never sick a day. Do you know I've never had a headache in my life?"

Libby had probably heard that boast nine hundred times—in the last year alone. "Hi, Gran. No, I'm fine. Just had some errands to do. Had to pick up a friend at the airport. I told you he was coming, remember?"

"Of course I do. I'm not old, you know. Just sometimes the days get away from me. When are you bringing him over for me to see him? I can't recall his name at the moment. Mason?"

"No, Gran, that was Grandpa's name. My friend is Cooper."

"Is he a barrel maker?"

Libby's eyes went wide. Her grandmother's mind was becoming a convoluted maze with bridges to plateaus of lucidity that constantly surprised her. "No, Gran. He works on TV."

Her grandmother made a groaning sound. "Too bad. With a good barrel you can catch enough runoff to wash your hair for a week. Nothin' like rainwater to keep your hair smooth and shiny."

Libby had a vague memory of her grandmother rinsing her hair with water from a large barrel that used to sit at the corner of the house. She wondered whatever happened to it. Now there was a metal gutter and a downspout that channeled rain to the lilac bush.

She glanced out the window to check on her guest, and her heart rate jumped. Mac was midway between their two homes, headed straight for Cooper. And from her brother's body language it was easy to tell the simmering pot was about to spew its lid.

"I'll call you back, Gran. I have to go stop Mac from committing homicide." The word made her shiver. There'd been talk after Misty died… No, she had enough to worry about without thinking back to that terrible time. Mac was a good man. A good father. He couldn't help it he wasn't any good at marriage. She doubted she'd be any better, but now at least, if things did work out with Cooper Lindstrom, she wouldn't have to worry about that.

Unless her brother scared him away.

COOP STUDIED THE small screen of his cell phone. No service? How was that possible? he wondered, walking into the middle of the yard to escape the shadow of the tall pines in case they were blocking the cellular waves.

Not that he had a clear concept of how a cellular phone worked, but the attractive young woman who'd sold him this particular phone had promised that he could get service on Mars.

"Apparently the red planet's more accessible than this part of South Dakota," he muttered, folding the phone with a snap.

Either that or he'd been too distracted by the young woman's boobs to read the fine print in his contract. Breasts had long been his downfall.

And wouldn't you know the postmaster had a fine pair.

He looked toward the main house, wondering if he'd given her enough time to regroup or call for reinforcements or whatever women in this part of the country did when they were having second thoughts about a decision they'd made.

A noise made him turn to look over his shoulder. A man with a square, powerful-looking upper torso was bearing down on him with a fierce scowl on his face. "Call for reinforcements," he murmured, fighting the urge to flee like the cowardly dandy he'd been called once or twice.

But on the off chance Libby was watching, he held his ground and waited to find out if this was who he figured it was: Mac McGannon. Libby's brother.

As he got closer, Cooper could see a certain resemblance through the jaw and cheekbones, although Libby's eyebrows were fairer and her hands were completely different. Feminine. This man's hands, which he balled into fists and released half a dozen times, were the size of the plastic discs Coop and his friends tossed around the beach.

Cooper searched his memory for a movie character who matched this guy. A man's man. Honest. Forthright. No bull. An Ernest Borgnine kind of guy, only better looking.

"Mac, I assume," he called, facing the guy head-on. He took a step toward him, one hand out in greeting. "I'm Cooper Lindstrom. My gut says I'm probably your worst nightmare."

The man stopped, looked at Cooper's hand, then took another step closer. He didn't make any attempt to shake. Instead he shoved his fists in the pockets of his hunting jacket—the kind with pockets that probably held all sorts of ammunition. "Yep, you could say that," he answered, his voice a raspy growl.

His Denver Broncos cap made it impossible to tell much about his hair color or style, but he was clean shaven, and a scent of Old Spice told Cooper Mac had cleaned up prior to coming to meet him.

"You live nearby?"

He nodded in the general direction over his shoulder. "Our properties adjoin."

"Convenient."

"What's that supposed to mean?"

"Nothing. I just…you have a daughter, right? It's probably nice that she can run back and forth between your houses. That's all."

"Oh."

Coop looked toward the house, hoping his salvation might arrive soon. "Um…do you hunt?"

The question seemed to take Mac by surprise. "I used to. No time now. Why? Do you?"

"No. Went deep-sea fishing once. Didn't catch anything, but the rest of the people on the boat did very well." Probably because Coop had been so seasick he'd "chummed" the waters the entire morning they'd been out. "I saw a jacket like that in one of the *Outfitter* magazines in a doctor's office."

A distinct smirk made Coop guess that her brother associated California doctors with plastic surgery. In fact, he'd been there with this mother. Finally talking her into having a complete physical. Not that it had done any good. Instead of following the doctor's urging to have bypass surgery, she'd headed to Vegas.

"So you're a movie star, huh?"

"No. I'm an actor. At the moment I host a television show." *Or did*. Past tense. He was pretty sure *Close-Up* wasn't getting picked up again next season. Which was why he was here.

"Same thing, isn't it?"

He could have gone on at length about the differences between his present line of work and what "real" actors did, but he decided to save his breath. "Pretty much. I work in the entertainment industry."

Mac took a step closer. "Well, I don't find what you're thinking of doing with my sister all that entertaining."

Since making a baby normally involved sex, an image of making love to Libby appeared in Coop's head. Quite vividly, to his surprise. Complete with the beautiful naked breasts he'd been speculating about earlier.

He shook his head and forced his attention back to the man in front of him. Besides, that kind of intimacy wasn't going to happen—which might be the only reason this man hadn't beaten the crap out of him.

"You don't approve of me. I can appre—"

"I don't give a shit what you appreciate or don't appreciate. I don't care how big a star you think you are. I know what a star is. It's a ball of burning gas. Stars glow for a while, then burn themselves out. I don't want my baby sister getting singed in the process."

"In case she didn't tell you, the physical part of this trade will take place in a doctor's office. We'll be half a continent apart when it happens. No singeing going on, I promise. Or are you more worried about Libby trading part of her share of your mine for a baby? Even if that baby would be your daughter's cousin?"

The guy was a father. Surely mentioning the B-word would soften him up.

If anything, Mac's scowl intensified.

"Listen, Mac, I started this as a way to get away from all the crap I had to deal with after my mother died, but now that I'm here, I think I can learn a lot from this experience. And maybe leave a positive mark on the place when I go."

"The sooner you go, the better."

Damn, even the dead-mother card didn't work with this guy.

"I didn't put that ad on the Internet," Coop reminded him.

"No, but you answered it. What I want to know is why."

Good question. Not one he was ready to answer truthfully. "Escape."

"Huh?"

"Aren't there some days when you just don't want to be Mac McGannon? And you'd give anything to be anyplace but where you are?"

Mac didn't answer, but Cooper could tell he finally had established some kind of connection.

"My life may look glamorous from the outside, but when I read your sister's MySpace page I realized I know nothing about this part of the country. I've never even flown over it, as far as I know. The only image I had was from watching *Dances With Wolves*, and that open-space thing appealed to me. Very few people and lots of trees. Just what I need right now."

Mac studied him intently a few moments, then his upper lip curled back. "Bullshit. Guys like you don't do *alone*. You don't know the meaning of the word."

"Well, maybe you can teach me."

Before he could reply, the sound of a screen door slamming made them both turn and look toward the house. Libby cleared the steps in two light leaps and hurried toward them. "Mac, you promised to stay away until Cooper had a chance to get acclimated."

"Acclimated. Hell, Lib, it's not like we're in the Rockies. Besides, I figured I could save you both a lot of grief if I cleared the air right off the bat."

"Go away."

"Are you going to tell him the truth or do you want me to?"

"Shut up and go away."

"I don't know what *really* made you answer Lib's ad, but you need to know one thing. You aren't going to get rich working the Little Poke. I don't care what Libby implied. You just won't. Doesn't matter if you dig all day and all night for the next twenty years."

"There's no gold?" Coop tried to keep his shock from registering in his voice.

"There's gold, but by the time you pay to get it out of the rock and the government gets it share of your taxes, you're probably looking at enough profit to put the same amount of gold back in your left molar."

Cooper looked at Libby, whose face had turned a bright shade of crimson. Her eyes were narrowed in the same glare her brother had worn a few moments earlier—only it was directed at Mac, not Cooper.

That's when Coop knew her brother was telling the truth.

"So what he's saying is a quarter share of nothing equals nothing."

Libby gave her brother one last look that easily bespoke an excruciating torture at some later date, then turned to face Cooper. "The deed will bear your name. The value of the land is going up. And if Mac ever decides to give up working the mine, we've talked about turning the place into some kind of dude ranch or bed-and-breakfast. You actually could see a large return on your investment—if this were about money. But you said the gold wasn't your main reason for doing this."

He did say that. He hadn't wanted his financial debacle spread all over the Internet. But money was a factor. Especially when he had an irate bookie breathing down his neck. Even if Shane sold the network on the new project, it would be months before he saw a big fat check. He could be dead by then…or missing body parts.

Before he could get a reply together, she said, "I have a trust fund. I'd planned to save it for the baby, but if you'd rather not get involved with the mine, then I can pay you the going rate for donated sperm."

Cooper didn't want to ask how much in front of her brother. He was afraid it would make him look too greedy. Or needy. "Hmm, well, I think I'd like to see the mine before I make a decision. Is that possible?"

"Today?" Libby looked at Mac, who shook his head. "It's getting kinda late. Mac has to pick up Megan at the sitter's, and I need to stop by the post office to make sure everything gets closed up. How 'bout tomorrow? I could take the afternoon off. Would Barb keep Megan a little longer?" she asked her brother.

"Maybe. I'm hauling rock in the morning." He looked at Cooper and added, "I spread gravel in the summer and plow roads in winter. Those are my real jobs. The ones that pay the bills."

With that, he turned and walked away.

Coop waited until he would be out of earshot then said, "Cheerful fellow."

"He used to be."

The cryptic response wasn't followed up with any more information, so he looked at her. Her expression was almost as intense as her brother's had been. He waited for a cue.

"I'm sorry. I should have been more up front about the mine. Like I said, I'll write you a check for the same amount I would have paid a sperm—"

He didn't want to hear her say the words, so he cut her off. "You were right about me needing time to get acclimated. How 'bout we hold off on negotiations till later? I haven't seen where you work. Or met Seymour."

Her smile started out small, undecided, but once she committed to it, humor radiated outward like a small sun. He basked in the brief moment of joy and goodwill and suddenly realized he had no desire to be anyplace else. He didn't know what that meant exactly, but for the first time in a long time he was content.

CHAPTER FIVE

ALTHOUGH LIBBY HAD offered to drive him back down the hill to town, she'd also made it sound like something a sissy would do, so he'd insisted on walking. A form of exercise he very rarely did unless he was trying to impress a cute chick on a nearby machine at the club. Occasionally he and Rollie would take a stroll on the beach, but since Rollie was eighty, Coop rarely worked up a sweat.

"How's your, um, behind?"

Coop didn't think he'd ever met a woman who couldn't bring herself to say the word *butt*. He had to work to keep from grinning. "Better. Still a little sore but nothing compared to what it would have been if your brother had given me the swift kick he was contemplating."

"He told you that?"

"No. I read it in his body language. It's something they teach you when you're studying theater. Body language is almost as important as voice projection on stage."

"Oh. Did you act in plays?" She was a few steps ahead of him, navigating around a sunken grate designed to catch runoff. "I glanced at your bio online, but I can't remember if I read that or not."

He made a wide detour. "Summer stints at Knott's Berry Farm when I was a kid. I played all kinds of roles, including—but not limited to—a singing bear."

"Oh. Not exactly Macbeth, but I bet it was more fun."

"Maybe. I can't remember."

She stopped walking. "You can't remember if you had fun as a kid?"

He tried to picture the kinds of things she'd call fun: playing with friends, camping, swimming in a lake, skateboarding…. "My mother didn't do recreation. My career took center stage from the time I could talk. Before, actually. I made my first commercial at six months."

"For what?"

"For the money."

"What were you selling?"

"Oh. Vacuum cleaners. The woman was vacuuming with a baby in her arms. Me."

They continued walking without further comment. Since there wasn't a sidewalk, Coop was limited in how much he could look around. He'd already fallen once in her presence and didn't want to look like any more of a klutz.

The air temperature was as pleasant as a winter day in southern California, but the pine scent definitely told him he wasn't in L.A. anymore. That and the quiet. He could actually hear bug sounds in the trees. That was a first.

"How many people live in Sentinel Pass?"

"The sign outside of town says nine hundred and seventy-two, but I think at the last census we were over a thousand. We add a couple of new mail addresses every year, but some of those are somebody's kid moving home or someone splitting off a lot for an aging grandparent or something."

"So you must know a lot about everyone's business."

She looked at him. "I try not to pay too much attention beyond what I need to know to make sure the mail gets to them. Why do you ask?"

"Just curious. Until you mentioned it, I hadn't really given your job much thought. Do most people get their mail delivered to their homes or do they have postal boxes?"

"Half and half. Some do both. Some have businesses and home delivery. A few have a box in Rapid City so they can have more privacy. I figure if they need that much privacy, I don't want to handle their mail in the first place."

She sounded okay with that, but he had a feeling she was offended that anyone of her townsfolk wouldn't trust her. He guessed that she took her job very seriously and wouldn't appreciate anyone who violated her trust. That made him a little uncomfortable.

She continued. "There might have been a time when the postmaster could ascertain certain facts from mail that passed through his or her hands. Nowadays there's too much volume to even think about individual pieces of mail. I barely have time to read my own, let alone worry about someone else's."

He frowned. There went one of the ideas he'd been toying with for a story line. He hated it when reality messed with his version of life.

"Do you know everybody who lives here?"

"Pretty much. I'm usually the first to meet someone new. And, of course, I've lived here my whole life, so I know all the family connections." She made an offhand gesture. "Which comes in handy when I get a letter addressed to Uncle Joe and no other information. If there's a return address, I can usually figure out whose box to put it in."

"Wow. That's a skill."

She shrugged. "I don't always get it right, but my grandmother was uncanny. She can still remember people who have been dead for forty years. Where they lived. What they did for a living and how many kids they had."

"She's your town historian."

"Was." She took a deep breath and let it out. "Her mind is still sharp…at times. But more and more often there are days when she doesn't remember even the people closest to her."

"Bummer."

"I know."

"Could I meet her?"

"Sure. I'll take you there after I check in."

He could hardly wait. Every good sitcom—hell, every good story—needed a wise old person. *Andy Griffith* had Aunt Bea. *Cheers* had Coach. And his would have Granny… somebody.

His speculation was interrupted when Libby stopped abruptly. "This is a good view of downtown. Four blocks, pretty much, although there's Smiley's Garage and a couple of other businesses on the edge of town. My building is one of the oldest. The bank, the original jail and the hotel were built first, but the hotel burned down twice."

She continued to talk about the town's history as they walked. Although her voice was well modulated and her delivery devoid of any hype, he read a certain amount of pride. This was home to her, and even if she knew it was an apple to Malibu's orange, she liked it here.

He regretted leaving his camera in his bag. He hadn't wanted to look too much like a tourist. Besides, Shane would send someone to take stills when they were farther along in the process.

"Is there a coffee shop or restaurant? They don't feed you on the plane anymore."

"Even in first class?"

He mumbled something about not liking the entrée because he didn't want to admit that he'd only been able to afford economy class.

"Hmm…sure. The Tidbiscuit is open at six every morning. The Icee Hut—that brown shack-looking place with the watering trough in front—is set to open next week. Phyllis and John, the owners, are snowbirds. They spend the winter in Arizona. They make frozen mochas and things like that. If you want a Starbucks, you have to go into Rapid."

"Regular coffee and a sandwich will do. I'm not a foodie." Because Mom wouldn't allow it. *You'll eat what I give you or you'll go hungry*.

She gave him a speculative look. "Do you cook?"

He shook his head. "I've been told I'm a danger to myself and others when I try to whip up something in the kitchen."

They'd reached the sidewalk that fronted the stores on each side of the street. Progress was slow because they had to pause at intervals to let other pedestrians cross in and out of shops. Libby greeted everyone with a friendly singsong hello. Most appeared to notice him, but not one showed any sign of recognition.

He wasn't sure how he felt about that. He was used to being recognized. He couldn't walk anywhere in L.A. without having to stop and sign an autograph. Here, he was just a stranger walking with Libby. People might be curious, but not a single one exclaimed over him. For possibly the first time in his life he knew what it was like to be a regular person. Normal.

"Out of the way. Out of the way. Big package coming through," a booming voice warned.

Cooper automatically reached out and pulled Libby to one side to let the person behind them pass. The contact set off alarm bells that distracted him so much he didn't manage to get his own body positioned safely. A solid object collided with his right kidney area.

"Umph," he grunted as his body propelled into hers.

"I warned ya," the grouchy person grumbled in lieu of an apology.

"Rufus Miller," Libby said sharply, shifting away from Coop. "What's your hurry? The lobby window doesn't close for another ten minutes."

The man, Rufus, who resembled a woolly mammoth from the back, made an abrupt turn into an open door without answering. Overhead, swinging from two hooks, was a sign bearing the red-white-and-blue U.S. postal logo.

Libby motioned for Coop to follow. They stepped into the building that cried time warp. Pine wainscot gleamed with a soft patina from years of touch-up varnish. Posters—honest-to-goodness Wanted posters—were scattered among informational notices and advertisements for stamps. The ornate overhead light fixture looked right out of the Long Branch Saloon.

The giant bear of a man dumped his armload of mismatched boxes on a chest-high table across from the open window, which was so quaint and old-fashioned Coop almost smiled. Except his new ache was still throbbing. *Where's my stunt double when I need one?*

"Sorry, Miss Elizabeth," the man mumbled through his thick beard and mustache. "Didn't know it was you. Whatcha doin' on this side of the cage?"

Cage? Coop looked again. Sure enough, wrought-iron bars protected a double-hung window of frosted glass bearing the emblem U.S. Mail in gold-and-black lettering. He assumed it could be lowered when the office was closed.

"This place is perfect," he said. "Quaint. Charming. Historic. I love it."

Libby gave him a look that made him regret his exuberant outburst.

"I mean…you must love working here."

She gave a skeptical snort. "Oh, I do, except for the fact it was built in the late eighteen-hundreds before anybody ever heard of junk mail. Today, our volume is about a zillion times what it was back then, but our space is still the same. Come Christmas, it's a real zoo around here, isn't it, Rufus?"

The man's broad shoulders, clothed in a faded plaid shirt that seemed too warm for the weather and gave off a distinct odor of old sweat and cigarettes, rose and fell impressively. "You always get the job done, Miss E."

The average person might have heard the name as "missy," but Cooper knew the man was still paying his respect to a woman younger than himself that he regarded as a person of authority. Intrigued, he turned to watch Libby interact with the man, who could have been anywhere from forty to sixty-five.

"Thank you, Rufus. Now, what have you got for us today? Nothing alive, I trust."

Alive? He looked at her questioningly.

She shook her head and mouthed, "Later."

A small thrill he couldn't account for zinged through his chest and landed somewhere below his belt. *Later* held all sorts of connotations, and he was certain she didn't mean the one his mind instantly jumped to, but still…they were to have a *later*. He liked that.

"No, ma'am," the giant replied. "Learned my lesson on that one. Snakes don't do well in the belly of an airplane. These here are some rustic crafts I decided to sell on that there eBay place. You heard of it? Miss Kat, over at the adult learnin' center, showed me how to put 'em up for sale, and darned if three didn't go like hotcakes."

Libby put her hand on the man's shoulder, causing a red flush to color the small areas of skin visible between the brow of his hat and the start of his beard. Cooper felt another odd twinge. One that didn't like or approve of her touching a man who was so visibly affected by her touch.

"That's wonderful, Rufus. I'm glad for you. And I'll be sure to tell Kat what a great job she's doing at the center. Keep up the good work. And if you give me your URL, I'll check out your art."

The man's woolly caterpillar eyebrows met above his nose. "Huh?"

"The Web address of your listing. Never mind. I'll get it

from Kat. We'll get out of your way now so you can make today's cutoff. Bye."

She motioned for Cooper to follow, then used a key she'd withdrawn from the pocket of her jeans to open a door that blended so well with the paneling he hadn't even noticed it. She held it for him to enter first.

Two people scurried about the small, crowded square room that featured a high ceiling of pressed metal. The tall windows on two sides of the place also featured prisonlike bars. An open door at the rear of the building led to another room.

"Jenna, Clive, this is Cooper Lindstrom. He's renting Gran's cabin from me for a couple of weeks."

Renting? Interesting. "Cooper, Jenna Murphy—my PMR, as I told you earlier. And back there is Clive Brumley. He's our—"

"HCR," Clive hollered before Libby could complete her sentence. "That stands for Highway Contract Route."

Cooper gave him a mock salute, since the man's tone sounded military.

"I take it Sandy's gone for the day?" She looked at Cooper and explained, "Sandy is called a rural carrier, but she delivers to the homes and businesses around town. Clive handles everyone else."

The pretty redhead pushed her glasses up on the bridge of her nose to get a better look at him. With the right makeup and wardrobe she could be a knockout, he thought. Did he have a place for a redhead in his cast? Geekish best friend, maybe?

She took a step closer. Instead of shaking his hand, as he expected, she gave him a squinty look. "Lib's my best friend. I've got her back. Just wanted you to know that in case you're planning anything funny."

Coop held up both hands in surrender. "I promise I won't even make her smile, let alone laugh. If that's the way you want it."

Libby rolled her eyes and shook her head. "Knock it off,

Cujo. We're just passing through to see if you need any help closing. It's been a while since I took any time off."

Her friend shook her head but continued to watch Coop intently until a customer—Rufus, the artist backwoodsman—shoved one of his boxes through the gap below the bar. "Gonna have to unlock the door for the rest of these, Jenna Mae."

The redhead let out a grumbling sound and walked to the door. "I told you not to call me that, Rufus. Just because you played Snidely Whiplash to my mother's Poor Penelope Plaingood does not give you the right to use my ridiculously outdated middle name."

Coop pulled his attention away from the exchange at the window to Libby, who had moved farther into the enclave. Two beehive-looking cubicles with wide metal desks below sat across from each other. A man about Libby's age sat at one of the desks, hunched forward on a high stool. He didn't look happy.

"Clive, what are you still doing here? Did your route run late today?"

Blondish hair at the beginning stage of a comb-over. Baggy jeans that exposed a gap of flesh between his blue-gray polo shirt and his belt. Tightie whities, Coop noted. Underwear of choice of most men in this town, he'd bet.

"Nope. I was waiting to talk to you. I think I finally figured it out. I knew something was up. You've been all secretive lately, rushing home to your computer every day after work. But, holy heck, Libby! Online dating?" He looked at Cooper, his expression turning from concern to antipathy. "Do you know how dangerous that can be? Any kind of kook or weirdo could show up at your door."

Coop looked at Libby. Her emotions weren't as clearly broadcast, but her sigh told him she didn't want to deal with this roadblock. He stepped around her. "Listen…Clive, is it? I'm sure everybody is going to have an opinion about what Libby should and shouldn't do with her life, but when it comes down to crunch time, she's the only one who can make that decision. She's a smart lady, wouldn't you agree?"

Clive's lips puckered as if he'd eaten a sour grape. "Of course, but—"

"And as her friend and colleague, you want to see her happy, don't you?"

"Yes, more than anything. But you don't know her. You shouldn't even be here. She didn't need to go looking outside for someone to love her. I—we…all do."

Very telling slip, Coop noted. A shy, unrequited lover in the picture. *Perfect.* Audiences loved that kind of character, one part of his brain noted. Another part—the one trained by his mother—knew it was time to start his spiel. He put a reassuring hand on the man's rounded shoulder. "That's good to know, Clive. Because if things don't work out between me and Libby, she's going to need that kind of support. I feel better knowing Libby can rely on you and her other friends."

He looked at Libby. Her raised eyebrow told him he'd laid it on a little thick, but Clive heaved a big sigh and nodded. "You know I'm here for you, Lib. Don'tcha?"

She smiled her real smile. "Of course, Clive. And I appreciate your concern. Really, I do. And even though Cooper is here, we haven't…um…we're still getting to know each other. So I'd really appreciate it if you'd keep this to yourself."

Clive gave Cooper another once-over. His expression didn't hold much hope that that was going to happen. This man would gleefully begin a smear campaign if he thought it would keep Libby from making a huge mistake. Coop realized this wasn't a slam-dunk. He was going to have to sell himself if he wanted Libby's consent and cooperation where his project was concerned.

"Now, if you guys are okay, I'm going to introduce Cooper

to Seymour and Gran." Her smile turned to a grin. "It'll be interesting to see which impresses him more."

Coop already knew the answer to that question. Granny McGannon, of course. He had an image of her in his head—and an actor in mind to play her.

"*THIS* IS SEYMOUR?"

The disappointment in his voice made her smile. She couldn't help herself. Even though she'd been expecting it.

"To scale," she said, studying the miniature replica of the gigantic dinosaur which had once roamed this region. The size of a pony, Seymour was a surreal shade of green with a white underbelly and blunt concrete ridges along his back. These had been worn smooth by countless schoolchildren who had climbed up on him for a class photo. "I might have forgotten to mention that. Happens a lot around here."

He fingered a spot where the concrete was showing through—Seymour was due for a touch-up—then looked at her and burst out laughing. "I love it."

"You do?"

"Absolutely. He's perfect."

"For what?"

He sobered. "I mean…he seems to fit the town perfectly."

She agreed, but she wasn't sure she liked a stranger jumping to the same conclusion after only a couple of hours in her beloved hometown. "He's an important educational tool and a lot less maintenance than the full-size models on Dinosaur Hill in Rapid."

He didn't argue or ask for more information, so she continued talking, telling him the same spiel she usually gave to tour groups that called ahead asking for a docent. She was a bit surprised by the level of interest he seemed to take in Sentinel Pass. His blue eyes were as wide as those of some of the children who visited Seymour for the first time.

She gave herself a mental tsk. She should be happy that he appeared intelligent and curious. Those were great traits to pass along to a child.

They left the History Center—which also served as the chamber of commerce office and the civic meeting hall—by way of the back door. The building butted up to the three-stall Volunteer Fire Department and, in the shared patio area, the Sentinel Pass VFD Auxiliary held its annual chili cook-off fund raiser. "I thought we were going to your grandmother's?" he asked.

"We are. This is a shortcut. Are you okay? We can go back for the car if you're tired."

He straightened indignantly. "Not at all. This is great." He took two quick steps to catch up to her.

She didn't buy his enthusiasm. Despite the well-sculpted body mass she could not only see but also had felt on two occasions since his arrival, she had a sense that he didn't work out regularly. Or maybe he did but wasn't used to the altitude. "This isn't Denver, but you do live at sea level. The altitude can do a number on a person until your body gets acclimated. Maybe we should get the car."

"No, really, Libby. I'm fine. The weather is gorgeous. Is it always this mild?"

She snickered softly. "Weather is the main topic of people coming to the post office. I don't give it much thought since I can't do anything to change it."

His laugh was a rich rumble that came from deep in his chest. Maybe that formal training for stage again, she thought. He was an actor, she had to remind herself. Even though there were times when he seemed genuine.

They walked in silence, Libby leading the way along a narrow trail that wove between several residences. A couple of dogs came toward them barking, but once they saw it was her—a regular on this path—they wagged and returned home.

"Are there wolves in these mountains?"

"I don't think so. Naturalists reintroduced them in Yellowstone, but that's pretty far to the west. I haven't heard of any. There are a couple of people in town who have wolf-mix dogs. Or so they claim."

"Nice stream," he commented a minute or two later. "Does it have a name?"

The tiny waterway in question was seasonal, giving the town a quiet joy and a lush abundance of wildflowers for a few months each spring.

"Not really. It runs into Rapid Creek, which feeds Pactola Reservoir—that big lake I pointed out on the way here. Gran might know if it ever had a name."

"How old is she?"

"Eighty-seven."

"Wow."

"Yeah. She's pretty amazing. She was driving up till last winter. Something happened. We don't know what, but one day she hung up the keys and said, 'I believe it's time I had a chauffeur.' Fortunately, Calvin still has a license."

She glanced over her shoulder. His smile was accompanied by a nod, as if she'd just confirmed something. Baffled, she overlooked a fallen limb and tripped. She went down on one knee. The damp pine needles and layers of decomposing deciduous leaves provided a soft cushion, but the denim fabric turned dark blue from the moisture.

He took her elbow and helped her up. His manner was a great deal more concerned than hers had been a couple of hours earlier when their positions had been reversed. She felt herself blush.

"Are you bleeding?"

"No. I'm fine."

"I could give you a piggyback ride."

She couldn't prevent the laugh that erupted from her throat.

"I could. I work out."

She fought back the grin that wouldn't stay suppressed. "I'm sure you do. Really. You've got muscles. I felt them. But I'm fine."

"You're sure?"

"A hundred percent."

He nodded, then stepped back so she could proceed.

"I think I owe you an apology," she said, walking more slowly now that they'd reached Hayden's Meadow, where as young girls she and Jenna used to collect wildflowers and harass bees on lazy summer afternoons.

He drew up beside her. "You do?"

"Uh-huh. I had a certain image of you. Probably from your press photos and some of the things I read on other sites. I figured you'd be soft and used to having people do everything for you. And when you fell at my house, I wasn't very nice."

"You were brutal," he said, but the gleam in his eyes belied the criticism. "Actually, not as tough as most of my critics. Some have drawn blood."

"Well, people in the public eye set themselves up for criticism. Even someone like me, who is a public persona in a very limited sense, has to be prepared to take the heat for what I'm doing. There will be people in Sentinel Pass who won't approve of my decision. Others will think I'm crazy. And some will stop talking to me…for a while."

"Critics all, my mother used to say. She believed that you could never please everybody all of the time, so you had to listen to your own heart."

"A wise woman. In case I didn't say so in my e-mails, I'm sorry for your loss. I know how difficult it is to lose your parents."

He lifted his chin and swallowed. "You did. Online, I mean. You were nice. That's one of the reasons I wanted to do this."

One. "Can you explain the others? I'm still a little unclear about why you'd come all this way for…well, the gold, of course, but…"

He looked away, a frown marring his perfect looks. "It probably sounds cowardly, but I really needed to get away. Escape, if you will. Too many memories everywhere I turned."

She understood. And sympathized. Even if she wasn't sure his explanation was the whole truth. But she let the subject drop because her grandmother's house was just around the bend. One part of her wanted to warn him about Calvin's unusual home, another wanted to see his unrestrained reaction.

"Holy shit," he exclaimed a minute later. "A real live Hobbit house."

The tiny one-story rammed-earth home was an engineering masterpiece with rolled eaves, one-of-a-kind chimneys on either end of the building and a quirky fence made from antique metal bed frames. The landscaping was an overgrown jungle of green punctuated with flowers. Behind the house, if given an opportunity, Calvin would proudly show off his vegetable gardens, which he lovingly cultivated with heirloom plants.

"Cal was a very successful pharmacist in Sturgis. He sold his former place for over a million and decided to have fun with this one. All the doors and bathrooms are wheelchair-accessible. Perfect for an elderly couple—although Gran would skin me alive if she heard me use that word. She still tells people she doesn't know what she wants to be when she grows up."

"I like her already."

They walked to the front door, which Gran had painted flamethrower-red—"Just to get people excited."

"Nice color."

"She likes it. Or did," Libby added under her breath. Lately her grandmother's mind seemed to slip out of the present and into a reality that didn't seem to have a time and place.

She turned the knob and walked in. "Knock-knock. Gran? It's me, Libby. I brought someone for you to meet."

An excited high-pitched yipping obscured her grand-mother's answer, if there was one. "Onida," she whispered. "Gran's toy poodle mix. Brace yourself. She doesn't have enough teeth to hurt, but she does bite people's shoes and the occasional ankle."

She shook off her postal uniform windbreaker and tossed it on the couch, which was littered with crocheted throw pillows. Springing quickly, she managed to catch the small apricot-colored dog before it could attack Cooper. "Quiet there, Oni. Good girl. Be still. You'll have plenty of time to devour Cooper after he meets Gran."

The woman in question pushed a streamlined black walker that Libby had never seen before into the room at a brisk pace. She stopped about a foot from them and looked from Cooper to Libby and back. "'Bout time you got here," she said with a nod of her pure-white head.

An odd shiver slid down Libby's back. She was certain Gran meant that statement as a criticism for not coming to visit her for a few days, but she'd been looking at Coop when she said it.

"Gran, I brought someone for you to meet. His name is Cooper Lindstrom."

"I knew the Landstroms back before their jewelry became so popular. And expensive. There was a time you could only buy it in the Black Hills. Now you find it at Wal-Mart." She gave a snort that made it clear how she felt about that.

"No relation," Coop said, stepping forward while making sure to stay out of reach of the dog that still shivered with bared teeth in Libby's arms. "It's a pleasure to meet you, Mrs….um…McGannon?"

He looked at Libby for confirmation.

She shook her head, but before she could correct him, Gran answered. "I was that once upon a time. Then I was a Tyler. I liked that name pretty well. Now I don't know what I am."

Libby set down the dog with a warning not to cause trouble and went to her grandmother, putting an arm around her thin, stooped shoulders. "You're still a Tyler, Gran. Mary McGannon Tyler. That's your full name. Remember?"

Supplying the missing information seemed to put her at ease. She smiled and nodded. "Well, there you go. The facts as we all know them. My granddaughter likes facts, don't you, Libby?"

"That I do."

"The truth and nothing but the truth, so help me Goliath."

Libby laughed and hugged her as tightly as she dared. To Cooper she explained, "Goliath was our St. Bernard. When I was a little girl and I did something wrong, I used to blame Goliath. Gran would make me swear to tell the truth or she'd punish Goliath."

Gran looked at him and added, "One thing you should know about my granddaughter—she's got a tender heart. She could never stand by and let a poor, dumb dog take the blame for something she did. That's how she learned that the truth hurts for a minute, a lie for a long, long time."

"Very profound," Cooper said, his tone oddly stiff. "What happened to Goliath?"

"Perforated bowel. Ate something sharp. Poor little Libby cried for a month."

She hadn't thought about Goliath in years, but suddenly the memory was very fresh. She'd blamed herself for his death because she'd left her Barbie dolls outside and the dog had dismembered one to the point where they never found an entire leg. A few weeks later, when the vet suggested the damage to the dog's intestine might have been caused by a sharp object—possibly something plastic—she'd picture the leg poking clean through his belly. She'd had nightmares until her father assured her Goliath's death wasn't her fault. But Gran hadn't been that generous.

We'll never know for sure, but your conscience is going to believe one thing no matter what your pa says. Next time someone tells you to put your dolls away, you'll do it, won't you?

How funny, she thought, that Gran would bring up Goliath at a time when Libby's conscience was working overtime. There was a reason Libby hadn't mentioned her baby-making plan to her grandmother. Even now, Gran would have cut through Libby's weak rationalizations like a surgeon with a laser.

CHAPTER SIX

COOP DIDN'T HAVE A chance to call Shane with an update until the next morning. Libby went to work well before the sun had crested the tops of the trees behind his little house. She'd left him a note on the tiny table beside the kitchenette.

Coffee in the fridge. Cream and sugar, too. (Ants.) He assumed that was meant to explain why the sugar was refrigerated, not that he was welcome to add ants to his coffee if he was so inclined. *Lunch at the P.O.?*

He glanced at his watch. It was only ten. He had two hours to kill, and the morning was too pleasant to spend at a computer in her house. He'd made an effort to help her move it out of her bedroom to a more central location the night before, but they'd encountered a stumbling block. The old house didn't have a lot of phone jacks, and there wasn't one in the dining room.

She'd assured him he was welcome to use it where it sat, but he was oddly reluctant to enter her bedroom. He didn't want to examine the reasoning behind that disquiet. So, in the meantime, he could use his cell phone…if he could find a spot with a clear signal and enough bars.

He held it out in front of him like a divining rod. Finally, on a slight rise near the path leading to Mac's house, he got four bars. He punched in Shane's number.

"Reynard here."

"Her grandmother looks like Yoda."

"And good morning to you, too, Cooper. By the way, just a suggestion, but if I were you, I'd refrain from making that comparison when you're talking to Libby."

"Well, duh. I'm not that dumb. This is just between you and me. When you're casting the role, think Yoda-esque."

"Got it. Does she speak in the same singsong backward thing?"

"Not, I think, so much. But if I were Luke Skywalker, I'd be a lot happier."

"Why is that?"

"Because somehow she tricked me into going hiking with Libby. If I were Luke, I could use my Jedi powers to get out of it."

"Can't you simply say you don't like to hike?"

Cooper cleared his throat. "She implied that I wasn't fit enough to keep up."

"Of course, he might not be able to handle Daugherty Gulch," the old woman had said. "His flatlander feet might do better on something nice and flat like that trail they made on the old railroad line."

Shane hooted. "She threw down a gauntlet you were powerless to refuse. Brilliant. I wonder how she knew you couldn't resist a challenge—even one you were sure to fail."

"When have I failed?"

"I can name two triathlons."

Coop felt his cheeks heat up. "I had bad bike juju. You were with me in Hawaii. Come on, man. Two cracked rims? What are the chances? And the time before that my entire wheel assembly fell off. I'm jinxed."

Shane's laugh grew louder. "Uh-huh. So when are you going?"

"Depends on the weather. Maybe Saturday. Libby wants me to get better acclimated. She drew me a map outlining a couple of short hikes in the area. Nearby, where I can't get lost. Did I tell you she didn't take off work? My God, she's supposed to be deciding if I'm going to be the father of her child and she doesn't take any time off to hang out with me. What's that about?"

"Maybe she needs the money and would prefer to spend any vacation time taking care of her new baby."

"Oh. Good point. I hadn't thought of that."

Because you never think of other people first, Cooper, he could almost hear his mother say. *I think of you first, but do you think of me when you're making your big plans? Of course not. You never think, son.*

He'd heard that complaint often enough.

"Anyway, I'm going to check out the Mystery Spot. Don't you love the image that provokes? Libby says it's a local tourist trap that her best friend's father built forty years ago. Apparently he was some eccentric genius physicist who spent the summers running the place. It's about a mile outside of town."

He'd really enjoyed sitting beside her at the lunch counter of the small café on Main Street while she'd been drawing her map. Her pride in Sentinel Pass came through even though she tried to downplay what a special place it was. He thought he understood why she didn't go on and on about it: she didn't want him to get any ideas about moving there.

Not that that would happen. As much as he liked what he'd seen so far, he was only interested in how it served his purpose.

At least that's what he kept telling himself.

"Are you taking pictures?" Shane asked.

"When I can. I'm trying not to be too overt. I don't want anyone to ask why someone who is leaving right away wants photos of the place. Did I mention that Libby's grandmother said I have flatlander feet?"

"You know I hate it when you jump from topic to topic without warning. But it makes sense. You live at sea level… literally."

"Still. That was blunt. Even Yoda wouldn't have said that. But I think it's something we can use."

Shane was silent for so long Coop thought he'd lost the connection, which was sketchy even if you stood in one place. The night before, he'd tried to reach Daria, his assistant. He got through once, but not for long enough to find out how Rollie was doing.

Maybe I could talk Shane into swinging by and checking on him.

"Coop," Shane said, his voice low and serious, "I've been thinking we should try to find another way to dig you out of this mess. Have you seen the gold mine?"

"Not yet. But from what Libby's brother says, it's not going to produce the kind of return I need to get Mom's monkey off my back anytime soon. There's gold there, but the cost of getting it out makes it almost not worth the effort." Libby had left him at the cabin shortly after they gave up their aborted attempt to move the computer, then marched through the trees to the house she'd pointed out as her brother's.

"I was afraid of that."

"Which is why I really need this show to come through, Shane. And the way things are falling into place here, I swear this was meant to be. Sentinel Pass is funky as hell, but it'll make a perfect setting for our story. Are you working on a script?"

Shane sighed. "I have other projects, Coop. Previous contracted obligations."

"Yeah, yeah, I know. You're a busy guy. But I need a favor. Could you run out to my house and check on my neighbor? He's an old geezer who will talk your leg off if you let him. He hasn't got any family in the area…well, none that's worth a plug nickel, as Mom would say. Just make sure he's got something to eat in his fridge, okay? And find out if my house has been raided by the police because of the wild parties my assistant has been throwing."

"Can't hear you. Losing the connection."

Coop wasn't sure he believed him. "Okay. Later then."

He closed the phone and dropped it into a pocket of his Calvin Klein cargo pants. He rubbed his hands together, looked at his feet cushioned in four-hundred-dollar running shoes he'd bought when he'd had iron-man aspirations. They didn't fit quite right, but he was determined to show Libby and her grandmother that he was made of stronger stuff. Nordic stuff. His ancestors sailed the icy waters of the North Atlantic, pillaging and plundering. He'd keep up with Libby even if it killed him.

"Flatlander feet," he muttered, setting off on the trail he'd memorized from Libby's sketch. "Ha."

He was out of breath long before he felt he should be. Of course, her drawing hadn't looked uphill. Hearing the roar of an engine coming up the road behind him, he stepped into the grassy border and paused to catch his breath.

As the sound got louder, he turned to watch a jacked-up truck of mixed body parts slow to a stop beside him. The beast was too tall for him to see into until the passenger door flew open.

"Hey."

Coop stepped back in surprise. Mac. "Hi."

"Want a lift?"

"I'm supposed to be acclimating. Your sister is taking me hiking on Saturday."

"In those shoes?" Mac shook his head. "Get in. I'll show you the mine, since you're gonna be part owner."

A silent voice warned that this was not a good idea. Mines had dark holes where a body might go undiscovered for years. On the other hand, he needed to know about the mine for the show. And while Mac hadn't been exactly friendly, he hadn't lied about the mine's productivity, either.

"Okay. But I'm supposed to meet Libby for lunch." He climbed into the four-wheel-drive truck and closed the door. "Will we be back in time?"

Mac put the floor shift in gear and let out the clutch with a long, grinding squeal. "Maybe. Maybe not."

"I CAN'T TALK FOR LONG. Cooper's supposed to join me for lunch." Libby nodded toward the insulated cooler sitting on the picnic table situated under the cottonwood tree behind the post office. She'd hired Mac to create the small, square patio a couple of years back. The wood-and-metal table was slightly warped from exposure to the elements, but it was functional.

"Just give us a quick update."

"What's your gut telling you?"

Kat and Jenna had popped into the office a few minutes earlier to invite Libby to lunch.

"Well…I introduced him to Gran and Mac. And Calvin. Gran called him a flatlander, but other than that she was pretty cordial. Calvin didn't recognize him, which was good. You know how he can carry on when he wants to impress somebody."

Both women nodded. Everybody adored Calvin…except when he started to describe his past accomplishments.

"How'd Mac behave?"

Jenna asked about Mac quite often, Libby had noticed. Probably more than was necessary. Libby hoped her friend wasn't considering him as a romantic interest. Mac was a great guy, but Misty's death had left him an emotional basket case. "They spoke. I wasn't privy to the entire conversation, but Coop was still in one piece when I got there."

Kat pretended to wipe a bead of sweat from her forehead. "Whew. Close call. Did Mac tell him about the mine?"

"Yes. But I don't think Coop believed him. Actually, I don't know what Coop thinks. Or why he's here." She gave in to her growing sense of disquiet. "I know he's an actor, but he seems to really like it here. I can almost see him taking mental notes about the place, the people. It's weird. Do you think all actors are like that—everything in their lives is fodder for some future role or something?"

Jenna answered, "Mother used to talk about acting all the time. Her life in the *theater*," she said, putting air quotes around the word. "And she said life is the palette that colors every role. Or something like that. So it's possible."

"Well, I don't know what his motivation is, but I plan to lay out what I want to see in our contract today. Or maybe Saturday. I'm taking him hiking."

"Why?" Kat sputtered. "To see if he's physically fit? You know it doesn't take that much effort to deposit sperm in a cup. I'd be willing to bet he can handle it."

Libby groaned at the obtuse pun. "Gran insists him I show him the real Black Hills, not just the tourist spots. She suggested we hike the Daugherty Gulch trail. Apparently she used to walk that way to the Slate Creek School when she was a girl. I don't know if I believe that, but I've been out there hunting with Mac and the view from the top of the ridge is pretty nice."

"You can cover more ground if you bike the Mickelson," Jenna said.

"I actually suggested that, and he went into a long story about his previous triathalon experience. He's quite funny, you know." She hadn't expected him to be so personable and self-deprecating. She had to keep reminding herself that he was an actor, and that meant he knew how to manipulate an audience.

"That's the other side of Tigerville, right? I could drop you off near the McVey place and pick you up afterward. I know right where that trail comes out on Mystic Road because Mom and I got lost out there trying to find the slate quarry."

Libby looked at Kat, wondering what had changed to make Jenna suddenly so helpful where Cooper was concerned. "I thought Saturdays were reserved for your mother's weekly shopping trip."

Jenna made a face. "She twisted her ankle. No swelling but enough pain that she doesn't want to risk reinjuring it. I'd planned to wash windows at the Mystery Spot, but I could do that while you're hiking."

"Thanks for offering. I'll run the plan past Cooper, then let you know, okay?" Libby checked her watch. "He should have been here by now. I'm going to have to eat. Do you guys want some? I have plenty."

She opened the red-and-white plastic cooler and grabbed a tuna salad sandwich. Both friends shook their heads. "We're going to iron out Kat's day-care schedule for the boys this summer. I'm hoping Tag can work for me a couple of mornings a week once the Mystery Spot opens up."

"What will Jordie do while Tag's working?" Libby asked after chewing a bite of her sandwich. Finely minced red onion was her secret ingredient, and she'd been looking forward to seeing if Cooper liked it.

"That's what we need to discuss," Kat said. "The boys are inseparable but partly out of my need. I think it would be good for them both to have some time apart, and Tag is old enough to handle a few hours at a job. But Jordie will be jealous when his brother has spending money and he doesn't. We'll see."

Libby wondered if parenting one child would be half as complicated. Probably not.

Jenna snatched a couple of chips from the open bag Libby offered, then turned to leave. "Sorry to abandon you, but we want to get a table at the Tid before it fills up. Call me later."

Since Libby's mouth was full, she nodded, but before the two were out of sight she remembered something she wanted to ask. "Hey, Kat, what's Rufus Miller making that you liked enough to suggest he sells it on the Internet?"

Kat murmured to Jenna and they both laughed. To Libby she called, "I'll tell you later. You might want to buy one."

The pair continued on their way, but their laughter lingered in the quiet of the alley. Libby might have been annoyed if she weren't so worried about what had happened to Cooper. Was he lost? Impossible if he'd followed her directions.

"Flatlanders," she muttered, remembering something her grandmother said at the onset of every summer. "More trouble than they're worth."

Trouble, maybe. But that didn't mean she wanted anything to happen to him while he was here. He was Cooper Lindstrom after all. And she hated to think what might happen to Sentinel Pass if anything bad was to befall the highly public television personality. She could almost picture those horrible TV news vans parked up and down the street. Five-second sound bites that would leave a nasty taste in everyone's mouth.

Beloved television personality Cooper Lindstrom is missing, and presumed dead, she heard an imaginary commentator say.

She swallowed against the sudden lump in her throat. She wrapped up the remainder of her sandwich and carried the cooler to her car. She didn't want to believe her fear meant she'd already come to care about him.

This was a business arrangement. She barely knew the man.

But he kissed you.

He'd turned out to be interesting. Funny. And far more complex than she'd expected.

And you liked it.

She absolutely had to keep their relationship superficial for the sake of her plan.

No fish lips where Cooper Lindstrom was concerned.

She slammed the door of her truck with more force than necessary, then looked around sheepishly to see if anyone had witnessed her uncharacteristic act.

Okay. So she liked him. That didn't mean she was going to do something stupid like fall in love with the man. He already had a return ticket back to La-la land, for heaven's sake. The idea of there ever being anything more between them than what was expressly written in their baby contract was ridiculous.

She wasn't a groupie and didn't plan to become an online member of the Cooper Lindstrom fan club. Not under her own name, anyway.

CHAPTER SEVEN

"So, is this the part of the story where you find a deep hole and push me in to get rid of the body?"

Coop had meant the question as a joke. He hoped. But his guide, who had outfitted him in a protective hard hat with a built-in spotlight and a respirator that was hanging loosely around his neck, didn't appear amused.

"So she told you about Misty, huh?"

"Misty?" The hairs on the back of his neck pricked to attention.

"My late wife. There were some who speculated that I had a hand in her death."

Coop swallowed. The damp chill he'd first embraced suddenly turned unpleasantly cold. "Sh-she died here?"

"No. Car accident. No witnesses. Highway patrol figures something spooked her—a deer maybe. She was going too fast, overcorrected and flipped over the guardrail. We didn't find her for a couple of days."

Mac's flat tone sounded like a recording, but Coop heard the tenor of anguish beneath the man's delivery.

"We'd just had a big fight. Decided to split up. I wouldn't let her take Megan."

"Your daughter?"

Mac blinked as if coming out of a trance. "Uh-huh. Didn't Libby tell you anything?"

Coop pushed back his hard hat. "She mentioned being an aunt, but I'm still trying to figure out the whole cast."

"*Cast*," Mac repeated. It came out like a four-letter word. "You make us sound like a sitcom or something. We're just your typical screwed-up family in a Podunk town in the middle of nowhere. My sister's a beautiful, amazing woman who thinks having a baby will make up for the fact she's never found a guy worthy of her. I'm a truck-driving miner with a little girl who's afraid of the dark. She won't set foot inside this mine, so I spend every spare nickel on babysitters."

Before Coop could ask why he bothered when the return on his time was so poor, Mac said, "Hard-rock mining gets in your blood. Like an addiction. Not like smokin' or drinkin'. Those you can quit. I did both in the past."

"Like gambling?" The question popped out unplanned.

Mac shrugged. "I suppose. Yeah, maybe. You keep thinking the next inch or two is going to produce color. A major vein. The kind that gets investors interested and brings in some serious money that will make up for all the time and money you already wasted."

Coop wondered if his mother had felt the same way. He didn't understand what had driven her to spend every spare minute on a habit that ultimately cost her—and him—everything, but he could see certain parallels between Mac's life and his own. When something controls you, the people around you suffer.

"So you said you'd show me around. How deep does this go?"

"I'm not actively working this part of the mine at the moment. But if I were, I'd reopen a fissure my dad found a few months before he died. There was a cave-in, and until I clean it out and make sure it's braced adequately, I can't tell you much more. I pretty much played out the lode gold I was working before Misty died."

"Can I see it?"

Mac shrugged. "Why not? Wait here. I'll go back to the office and call Libby to see if she'll pick up Megan for me."

Wait here? Alone? Mac didn't give him time to respond. He turned and, three steps later disappeared into the gloom.

Cooper used the heavy metal flashlight he'd attached to his belt loop to look around. The tunnel was wide enough to accommodate a vehicle, which made him wonder why they'd walked. Heavy timbers had been erected in a way that reminded him of a ride he'd once taken at Disneyland. Was this really how modern miners did it? He doubted that, but then, Mac had indicated this was the oldest part of the Little Poke.

He stepped closer to the wall and rested his hand on the surprisingly smooth surface. The rock was cool to the touch and moist, yet he didn't see any water coming from anywhere.

He shone his light upward and his breath caught in his throat. There. A small snakelike trail of something glittery. Gold?

Surely it couldn't be that easy, he thought. No, of course not. The pretty yellow material was probably the fool's gold he'd read about. One historical account had greedy scam artists filling a scatter gun with gold flake and shooting it into the wall of a mine to fleece some unsuspecting investors out of their cold, hard cash.

Well, this gold mine may be played out, he thought, seeing no further hints of color, but he'd come here looking for a different sort of gold mine. And that required him to start thinking with his head. His mother might not have given him much credit for being able to handle numbers, but he knew this much—one plus one, when they were the *right* combination, added up to a whole lot more than two.

Take Bruce Willis and Cybill Shepherd, for example. Pairing them up in *Moonlighting* had been genius. You take a fish out of water and put him in a totally unexpected place, then give him another fish to swim with and—voilà—prime-time romantic comedy. And if you found two fish with the right chemistry, you'd feed the love-starved audience a line they couldn't resist.

"People love dichotomies," Rollie told him once. "How else can you explain all the young chicks who go for me?"

They'd laughed, but Coop had to agree with him to some degree. Although in Rollie's case the girls were drawn to his money and his cozy little five-point-two-million-dollar shack on the Pacific.

Coop spotted a ledge that looked wide enough to sit on and crossed his ankles, leaning back against the rock. To wander aimlessly would be foolish. To get freaked out or pissed off equally futile. His only choice was to wait. And to pass the time, he'd work up a few interesting possible scenes using the dichotomy theory.

Soft, spoiled beach bum meets strong-willed, self-disciplined postmaster. Her brother gets him lost in the mine. A sort of hazing thing. The postmaster comes to find him.

He closed his eyes and imagined their dialogue.

You're a hard man to lose.

I'm not lost, but I am hard.

PM looks shocked. *Did your mother teach you to talk like that around a lady?*

Who says you're a lady?

She tosses her head of shoulder-length shiny auburn hair and puts her hands on her hips. *You think you're pretty clever, don't you? But I've got news for you. I could have had any of the men in this town over the years. My standards are too high. And you're not even up to their level yet.*

She turns to leave, but he blocks her path. *Maybe you'd have more fun if you came down to my level.*

She protests, but a close-up shows she's interested, too.

He moves in to kiss her. She really does have beautiful lips that haven't been kissed in way too long. He can feel her quivering with anticipation. She moistens her bottom lip with the tip of her tongue.

"Hey."

The voice that called out wasn't Libby's. In fact, it wasn't even female. And it was followed by a bright light in his face.

He muttered an oath and jumped to his feet, praying his canvas hiking pants were bulky enough to hide his body's response to his imagination. Good grief. He'd kissed dozens of women on camera and never gotten an erection.

A camera. That's what was missing.

"Did you hope I'd wander off and fall into some bottom-less pit?" he snarled, batting at the beam of light in his eyes. "Was this part of the freak-out-the-city-guy routine? Well, guess what? I'm not freaked."

Mac lowered the light to chest level. "I don't know. You look kinda red in the face."

"That's because I don't like games."

Mac shrugged and started off again, waiting this time for Coop to follow. "I thought that's what you did for a living. Host some kind of game show."

"It's a talent show. And before that I worked on two soaps and had a few bit parts in several prime-time series."

Mac acknowledged Coop's career with a careless shrug. "I don't watch television. My late wife used to have the damn machine on from the time she got up in the morning till she fell asleep at night. I drew the line at having one in our bedroom. I mean, if you're gonna look at a TV instead of each other, you deserve it when your marriage goes south."

"I suppose that means you don't have TiVo either."

The joke appeared lost on him, so Coop tried to explain. "TiVo lets you record things and play them later. So if you and the wife wanted to get it on, she could watch Letterman later. After you were snoring."

Mac ignored the comment. He didn't speak again, which,

unfortunately, left Coop with time to analyze his daydream. In theory, there was nothing wrong with it. He'd always planned for his hero to develop some fiery sexual tension with the heroine. And naturally, as he'd told Shane, he planned to play the lead. But the problem came from the fact that the person he'd been kissing in his mind wasn't his ex or any other actress playing Libby. She was Libby. The real Libby.

And that was a very bad thing.

Use your head, man, he silently chided. Any emotional entanglement would spell disaster for his project—the project he needed to save himself from financial ruin and the jaws of a bloodthirsty bookie. Falling for Libby was the worst thing he could do.

So he'd be cool. He'd keep his distance—both emotionally and physically. After all, his ex-wives were proof that he didn't do love well, so why risk everything for something he was sure to screw up?

LIBBY JUMPED OUT OF her truck and dashed to the door of the rustic-looking, green two-story to pick up her niece from the babysitter. Barb Kellen's big front yard was so littered with plastic playthings it could have been used as a Toys "R" Us ad.

"Knock-knock," she called, opening the door.

A chime sounded somewhere inside the house. A required warning device for home child-care providers, Barb had once mentioned. "Gotta know when kids go out and people come in."

"We're back here," a woman's voice called.

"Libbeee," came a high-pitched squeal.

"Wait. Your other shoe. Megan."

The word came out gruff and impatient. Barb was a nice woman. Early fifties. Retired from a job in Rapid so she could care for her grandchildren. This had led to a new career. But Libby wasn't convinced she had the right personality for handling kids and didn't plan to let Barb babysit her child.

Her yet-to-be-discussed-much-less-conceived child.

She planned to sit down across the table from Cooper this evening and draft their contract. True, she'd said he could take a week to get a feeling for the town and be comfortable with her before making a decision, but after a horrible afternoon at work, she'd changed her mind.

Thankfully Mac had called to tell her that he was showing Cooper the mine, but even knowing that Coop wasn't lost and wandering in the hills hadn't been enough to get him off her mind. Much to the detriment of her job.

She'd filled several dozen boxes with the wrong mail and completely missed a stack of time-sensitive fliers that had to go out. And she may have even snapped at a customer or two when they interrupted her silly schoolgirl daydreams about the handsome movie star.

Nope. He needed to go back home. Sooner rather than later. Hopefully he'd agree to speed up the process if she found a way to put her request diplomatically.

"Libby," Megan cried, throwing herself at her aunt.

Libby put one hand on the wall so she didn't topple over. "Hey, sweets, did you miss me or what?"

"Where's my daddy? He said he was going to pick me up today."

Libby pried her niece's hands apart and went down on one knee. "I know. He told me to tell you he's sorry. He's still at the mine." With Cooper.

"Mac was supposed to pay me today," Barb said, joining them, a pink and brown Keds sneaker in hand. "Is that why he had you come?"

Libby took the shoe from her and helped Megan into it. "He's showing the mine to a friend of mine. Time got away from him. He's had a lot on his mind lately. I'm sure he just forgot what day it is."

"Humph," Barb snorted, crossing her pudgy arms over her

white Child's Play T-shirt. Her business logo was encircled by tiny silk-screened handprints—purple, blue, red and yellow. "He and I have been having this conversation for months now. How come he's always late?"

Libby looked around for Megan's backpack, which she found hanging on a hook above a bench where children could change their shoes and boots in winter. "I don't know, Barb. Maybe he's still getting the hang of being a single father. Misty used to handle the checkbook. I do know that. But he's certainly good for it. You're not questioning that, are you?"

Barb frowned. "No. He always pays. Just never on time. I have my bills, too, you know."

"Don't we all." She made herself smile diplomatically despite her desire to defend her brother. "I'll talk to him. He's juggling a lot right now, but you're perfectly right about deserving to be paid on time."

Barb reached out and ruffled Megan's dark brown hair. "Excellent. I wouldn't want to lose this one. She's a good girl, aren't you, Megan? A little too quiet some of the time but one of the easiest ones I've got right now."

Libby fought to keep from cringing. She hated it when people labeled children—good or bad. Megan was a unique person who had been through an extraordinary time that was bound to have affected her. Mac said she refused to go to sleep without the light on, and Lord help everyone if she lost her "bankie"— a scrap of baby blanket that went everywhere with her.

"I'll remind him to bring a check with him tomorrow when he drops her off. Night."

They were partway out the door—the chime ringing in the background—when Barb asked, "So what's this rumor about some movie star coming to town? Someone saw him at the post office. Why would he be in Sentinel Pass, for heaven's sake?"

Libby had fielded several similar queries today. "He's just passing through. Like most people who come here."

"Isn't that the truth? Flatlanders never last for long in the mountains. Just ask Mac," Barb said cryptically. Everyone in town knew Misty had been from Valentine, Nebraska. She'd made a point of putting heart-shaped bumper stickers on her car.

They also knew that she'd been killed on her way back to the flatlands. Leaving Mac for her former boyfriend. "She loved the mountains at first. Maybe if she'd lived, she would have come back," Libby said.

Barb snorted again. A sound that amplified the pounding in Libby's head. "I doubt it. That type's never happy for long."

That type? Young? Pretty? Blond?

"Gotta go," she said, propelling Megan ahead of her. "Nice talking to you. Bye."

The door closed behind them but not for several seconds. Libby sensed Barb watching. No doubt she was asking herself what a plain-Jane postmaster would know about love.

Not a darn thing, if the asker was referring to personal experience. But she knew quite a bit from observation. From her brother and sister-in-law she'd learned that oil and water didn't stay mixed for long. From Jenna's mother she saw that years of obligation could rob you of the will to be healthy. Her father had proven that a broken heart often never healed. And her grandmother had taught her never to settle for anything less than an honest, mutually respectful relationship.

"Are we going to my house?" Megan asked as Libby helped her into her booster seat. The smaller unit had been a milestone Megan had been proud of, and Libby liked the less cumbersome seat, too.

"No. Mine. Then I'll walk you home. First I need to put on some water for supper."

"You're only eating water?"

Libby laughed. "The water is to cook the spaghetti."

"I like spaghetti."

"I know you do, but I already have a guest."

"The man from the TV?"

"You met him?"

Megan shook her head. "I heard Daddy talking to someone about him. Probably Gene." Eugene Turner. Mac's boss at the gravel pit. A veritable font of negativity.

"Oh," Libby said, poking around with the seat belt until she heard the click. "Well, yes, he's staying in Gran's house and I promised to feed him."

"I could come. Daddy won't have anything fixed."

Poor kid. No hot meal waiting for her. "Well…maybe you and your dad can join us. I'll see."

"See what?"

"See if he lost Cooper."

"On purpose?" Megan asked, her eyes going wide.

Libby kissed her forehead. "Just kidding. I'm sure they'll be there when we get home. Move your foot. Good g—job."

When she arrived home a few minutes later, there was no sign of Mac's truck in either McGannon driveway. Libby helped Megan out and was debating about driving out to the mine when she heard the familiar clatter of Mac's half-ton.

He pulled in behind her Nissan.

She was holding Megan's hand, and neither moved as the two men got out and walked toward them. Both looked somber. She wondered what had transpired between them. Had Mac tried to intimidate Cooper? Or had he simply gone into more detail about the mining industry?

She'd already made up her mind to lay her cards on the table with Cooper. Instead of bothering with mine ownership, she'd offer him a fixed sum for a one-shot sperm-donor thing—no strings attached. If he turned her down, she'd pick someone from the donor list at the fertility clinic and deal with her abandonment issues some other way. Maybe she'd even meet some nice guy and fall in love someday. It wasn't impossible for a single mother to wind up with a happily ever after, right?

Megan's intense pressure on her hand finally broke Libby's reverie. She squeezed back reassuringly, then called out, "Spaghetti at my house. Forty minutes. Megan's going to help."

Stalling, she thought, glancing at Cooper. His handsome face was streaked with the kind of grime that only came from the mines. "You both have time to shower."

Cooper looked at Mac a second, then nodded and turned toward the cabin.

Again she wondered what had transpired. Megan started to pull her toward the house, but she resisted. "Just a second, honey. I want to ask your daddy something."

Mac's step seemed to drag. When he was about a foot away, he pushed back the brim of his Orton Lumber cap and looked her in the eye. "He's here in one piece, isn't he?"

"Did I say anything?"

"I know what you were thinking. That I was going to drop him in some hole and claim he went missing. Even if the thought crossed my mind—which it didn't—I wouldn't have done it. He's not so bad, for one thing. And Meggie and I don't need any more trouble, for another. I still don't like your plan, but I'm going to butt out and let you make your own mistakes."

"Like you did?"

In two steps he closed the distance between them and scooped his daughter up in his arms, surprising both her and Libby. He spun around in a circle, making Megan squeal with delight.

Libby smiled. This was more how he'd been before. Intense, always. Serious. But with a playful side—especially around his daughter.

"I've made plenty in my life, but sometimes something great comes along to shine some light into that deep, dark hole you've dug for yourself."

She knew he didn't mean gold.

"I don't know if you laid out everything about the mine, but I'm going to offer him some of the money in my trust instead of dragging you into this. That's what I should have done from the beginning."

Mac stopped spinning. Megan's ear-to-ear grin faltered. "There's more to the guy than I first thought."

How much more? she wanted to ask but was afraid to hear the answer.

"For one thing, he's smarter than he lets on. He never seemed to run out of questions, and they weren't just about money and the price of gold." He looked at her. "He wanted to know if I ever got claustrophobic."

He set Megan down and said, "I do, you know. Sometimes. When I picture Dad dying under a wall of rock. I think I must be crazy to be doing this." He smoothed down his daughter's thick brown locks and sighed. A second later he said, "I'm gonna clean up. I'll be back with the flashlight so Meggie and I can walk home after dinner."

Then he returned to his truck and backed up with a noisy roar.

Libby shook her head and took her niece's hand again. "One thing you should know about men, Megan. They're a mystery."

"Like the Mystery Spot?" Megan asked.

Libby thought a moment. Jenna's family's tourist trap was a contrivance of optical illusions, but even when you knew you were being fooled, you still couldn't quite figure out how. Pretty much the way she felt about the men she'd dated in the past. "Exactly," she said. "Come on. Let's start cooking. Men like to eat. That's one thing I do know for sure."

CHAPTER EIGHT

"DADDY, WHEN CAN WE get a dog?"

Mac looked up from his plate so fast a long strand of spaghetti dangled from the corner of his mouth.

Cooper blew a raspberry, which made Mac go scarlet.

Libby shook her head. "Boys," she said. "Could we please use our polite table manners?"

"My apologies, Miss Elizabeth," Cooper said with a perfect southern drawl.

Megan's eyes went wide. "You sound funny."

"Ach, m'fair lassie, that's nuthin' compared to me Irish brogue."

Megan giggled. "More, more."

Libby liked the sound of his voice—voices—too much. They'd appeared in her dreams ever since the first time she and Coop had talked on the phone. Live and in person was much worse. Now she was starting to *see* him in her dreams, too. "But then we won't hear about your dog, Meggie."

Megan turned her attention just that quickly to her father. "Daddy, you said in the spring. Remember? Is it spring now, Libby? Miz Barb said it was."

Mac gave Libby a dark look.

She shrugged. "Hey, she's a four-year-old with a steel-trap memory. Don't blame me. You shouldn't make promises you're not prepared to keep."

From the corner of her eye, she saw Cooper's fork pause

midbite. The neatly twirled spaghetti started to slip back to the plate, but he quickly recovered.

"She's too young. And we're both gone all day. I notice you don't have a pet. You haven't even replaced old Thimble."

Libby's late cat—so named because she was so tiny when Gran found her abandoned and starving in the woodpile—had passed away from an untreatable tumor right before Christmas. Libby had been afraid some well-meaning friend might try to give her another kitten as a gift, so she'd spread the word that she needed time to grieve. But in truth, she'd already started researching IVF and had decided to hold off getting a new pet until her child was older. "Don't try to change the subject. I think a dog would be good for Megan. She might sleep better at night if she had a watchdog at her feet."

Mac's mouth dropped open. "Dogs in the house? Are you nuts? You know the rules."

"Dad's rules. He's been gone for how many years? Don't you think you're entitled to start making your own rules?"

"Is that what this is about?" he asked, waving his index finger between Libby and Coop, who was sitting in a place of honor opposite her end of the table. "Some belated stab at rebellion? Gran's the only one left to hold you to some higher standard, and she's not herself anymore. If Dad were here, he'd be appalled. You know that."

Libby pushed away her plate, her appetite gone. "I like to think he'd want me to be happy."

Mac made a puffing sound. "Our dad? He didn't care about stuff like that."

"He used to laugh. I know he did."

"Maybe before Mom died, but when she got sick…well, you remember what he was like. Tell me one time when he smiled."

She couldn't. And she'd blamed herself for that. No matter how hard she'd tried to grow up and fill her mother's shoes, she'd never been able to coax any of the joy she'd once seen in her father's eyes to return.

Cooper cleared his throat. "I don't mean to butt in, but if you decide to get a dog, you should look for a full-grown one, not a puppy. I bought my first ex-wife a pick-of-the-litter standard poodle for her birthday. Unfortunately I thought *standard* meant *ordinary*." He paused, looking thoughtful. "The dog now weighs eighty pounds and has ruined three leather sofas. I know because she sends me the bill every time."

Libby stared in amazement as Mac's initial chuckle spilled over to a laugh. "We're not getting a poodle—big or little," he said, shaking his head. "You're one weird dude. But in case I didn't tell you earlier, you did okay today in the mine. Most first-timers freak out in the dark."

"Thanks. I never went to college, but I played a preppy WASP in one my soaps. We had a story line devoted to hazing during sweeps week. My character *accidentally*—" he emphasized the word "—got locked in a basement room with one of the female leads." He looked to the ceiling and blew out a sigh. "It was supposed to be sexy, but, believe me, I would have preferred to be alone."

"Why?" Libby had to ask.

"Bad chemistry and a broken engagement. She never really forgave me." He shrugged as if such things were the norm in his world.

Maybe they were. Libby had never been engaged, let alone married and divorced. Twice. She took the idea of falling in love and committing her heart and soul to a relationship very seriously.

Cooper and Mac continued to talk. The topic had moved on to sports. Libby wasn't surprised that Cooper could hold his own on that field, too. He was chameleonlike. Charming. Resourceful. Even her brother seemed to have accepted him.

Which made it all the more ironic that Libby was starting

to have second thoughts. Partly because she liked him, too. Partly because she knew she shouldn't believe a word he said.

"Can I get up?" Megan asked.

Libby stood. "Sure, honey. Let me help you. I'm sorry I didn't make any dessert, but there might be an Oreo or two in the pantry."

She pulled back Megan's chair, then held out her arms. The child was almost too big to carry, but Libby loved cuddling the warm little body in her arms. She nuzzled her niece's neck and inhaled the dry, slightly musty scent of her hair. Her heart swelled with a longing so sharp she had to blink back tears as she hurried into the kitchen.

Her goal was in reach. She could almost taste it. But could she trust Cooper to help her get there?

"YOU'RE NOT STERILE, are you?"

Coop almost dropped the china plate he'd been in the process of drying. *Who in this day and age didn't have a dishwasher, for God's sake?* "I'm sorry. What?"

"You're in your late thirties and you haven't fathered any children despite two ex-wives. Is there a chance you can't, um…seal the deal, if we go through with this?"

He carefully set the plate down on the counter with the others then whipped the damp towel over his shoulder with a crisp snap. "*Mid* thirties, if you don't mind. And the reason I don't have any offspring to date is because I'm very careful. Despite what the gossip magazines say, I don't sleep around. Neither of my ex-wives wanted kids, although I lobbied hard when we were first married. Then, as things changed between us, it was a relief that we weren't going to screw up a kid with our divorce."

"Oh," she said, still elbow-deep in sudsy water. "I was just wondering. I mean, you were good with Megan tonight. You seem like you'd be a natural."

"Because I can get down to their level? Are you saying I'm childlike?" He kept his tone light on purpose. He liked spending comfortable time in her presence. He didn't want to ruin their pleasant evening with a serious conversation. He knew one was coming, but the less she asked about his motivation behind answering her Web proposal, the less he had to…fudge. His mother's word for fibbing.

So I fudged about your previous experience, he remembered his mother saying after he was given his first soap opera role as a troubled teen. *They wouldn't even have looked at you if they'd known you'd only worked in commercials. And, hey, you acted. You didn't even like the taste of that cereal they made you eat. It's the biz, son. It's built on lies, but I never lie. Only fudge a little. When it's really necessary.* Toward the end, her lies would have made enough dense chocolate dessert to feed an army.

"…empathic," Libby was saying when he tuned back in to the conversation.

Emphatic? Or empathic? One of them meant sensitive, he thought. He wasn't sure which.

He was saved a reply—which he didn't have in mind, since he had no idea what she was talking about—by the buzzing sound of her doorbell. He'd heard it earlier when her niece pushed it on the way into the home. It had reminded him of an angry hornet.

"Expecting company?"

She shook her head. He handed her the towel so she could dry her hands after pulling the plug on the dishwater.

She wiped her hands, ran the towel around the inside of the sink, then hung it over a knob. After a self-conscious little finger-combing of her wavy locks, she walked into the living room.

The buzzer sounded again, followed by a knock.

"Libby? Are you okay?"

"It's Jenna," she murmured, hurrying to the door. "Hi. Of course I'm okay. What's up?"

Three women crowded through the narrow opening that Libby had obviously meant as a deterrent to keep people out. The first one through was the redhead he'd met earlier. The other two—a blonde with curly hair scraped back in a ponytail, and a petite black-haired woman who seemed to bounce with energy—walked toward the living room without being invited to do so.

Good friends, he surmised. Here to check out the sperm donor. He wished he'd rehearsed his lines. Or even knew what role he was supposed to play.

"Hi. I'm Cooper Lindstrom," he said, addressing the one who had lingered to look him over. "I'm guessing you know why I'm here. A question—is it common knowledge or are you three Libby's best friends?"

"I'm Char," the dark-haired woman said, taking off her black windbreaker to reveal a long-sleeved black turtleneck and black leggings. She was trim and athletic-looking but with plenty of curves. Not his type but someone who would make a great secondary character. Easily recognizable as a girl-Friday type. "Fame is relative."

He cocked his chin. "Einstein?"

"Jones. As in Char Jones."

He liked her. She had spunk.

After dropping her jean jacket on the couch, the blonde walked up to him, hand extended. "My name is Katherine Petroski, but everyone calls me Kat. We're part of the book club."

"Be honest—we *are* the book club," Jenna clarified. "Wine, Women and Words."

"Very alliterative."

"Ooh, sweet play on words," Char said, nodding toward the others as if he'd passed some kind of test.

"What are you guys doing here? It's not book night. Is it?" Libby rushed to the Edward Gorey wall calendar that

Coop had noticed earlier. "No. Not even the right week. What's going on?"

Jenna stepped up as if she'd been elected spokesperson for the group. "We've given you two days. We need to know. Is he the one or not? If he is, he still has to pass our approval."

"Or what?" Libby asked, throwing up her hands.

"Or…" Jenna stuttered. The three looked at each other.

Kat lifted her hand. "Or we won't babysit when you need us."

"Liar," Libby said, her tone more amused than put off.

"We'll only pick dry, boring literary novels when it's our turn," Char threatened.

Libby made a *pff*ing sound. "That from the queen of romance novels," she said in Coop's direction.

"Hey," Char returned defensively. "I like them. They're entertaining. More than I can say for some of those O-books you're fond of."

"Ladies," Kat intervened. "We're not here to talk books, remember? We're here out of concern for our friend. Libby, we didn't want to interfere, but when none of us heard from you, we, um… Well, it's not like we know this man. He could be—"

"A dangerous predator," Coop supplied. "Or a dissipated lush. A deviant. A gambler. A druggie. How would any of you know?"

"Exactly," Kat said, sitting down on the sofa. "Sentinel Pass is a long way from Hollywood. And there's some not very nice stuff written about you. Of course, there are good things, too. I even read that you gave a million dollars to help your neighbor."

He closed his eyes and took a deep breath. He would have strangled his mother if she'd been alive. "Don't believe everything you read in the papers or on the Internet. Rollie is far too proud to accept money. I check on him and make sure he has food, but aside from trying to keep the old fart from falling victim to the kinds of scavengers who prey on the elderly, there isn't much I can do." Especially from here. He'd tried calling Rollie twice and only gotten the answering machine. With no return call.

He looked at his watch and calculated the time difference. Still early by beach standards. He could try again…after the inquisition adjourned.

"See?" Jenna crowed triumphantly. "I told you it was hype. How could we possibly know the truth without being insiders? And could you ever see that happening to any of us?"

All three shook their heads. Libby just watched with a touch of a smile on her lips. Indulgent. As she was with him at times. As if she were some spinster aunt pleasantly amused by the antics of the youngsters around her.

This attitude bothered him. He wasn't sure why. Or if it was something he would include in her TV character. Viewers would probably like her better if she was bubbly and engaging—maybe a combination of all three of her friends rolled into one. But *he* liked the woman he glimpsed through the wall designed to keep everyone at arm's length.

Everyone except her niece. What a touching picture they'd made when Libby had picked up Megan. He'd seen her tears, too, and understood in some small way what she was feeling. Why she'd put that ad on the Internet.

She'd make a wonderful mother, he thought about the same time he realized the four women were talking about him.

"He does that sometimes," Libby was telling them. "Sort of drifts off."

"Maybe he forgot his lines," Char said, eyes narrowed as she scrutinized him.

"What lines?" Kat asked.

"My point exactly. If we knew his agenda, we could decide whether or not Libby's going to get hurt when this is all said and done. Right now he's the only one with a script."

She didn't know how right she was, and he needed to keep things that way until it was safe for him to go home. Once his mother's bookie had cooled off and his exes quit making threats about talking to the scandal sheets, he could go back with a solidly formed nucleus of his idea. On paper. For Shane to take apart and put back together again.

"I apologize for spacing out. It started happening after my mother died. Someone will say something that reminds me of her and I get sucked down memory lane. Sorry."

A lame excuse, but he could tell it won him some sympathy from Jenna…and Libby. Kat was hard to read—she just looked worried. Period. And Char was still on the fence.

He looked at her. "What do you do for a living, Char?"

"I operate a Native American gift shop. It's at the intersection where you turn off the main road to come to Sentinel Pass."

"The one with the big white tepee? Libby pointed it out. I want to see it."

She blinked in surprise. "There are other buildings, too. And a trailer. That's where I live. Year-round."

Year-round. He'd heard Mac use that expression, too. He guessed that winters—without an active tourist trade—changed the makeup of the town. He needed to make a note of that for Shane.

"Well, I know that what Libby and I are discussing is a private matter—friends and family notwithstanding. But I bring a certain element of media attention to anything I do. So far I've been lucky, but there's a chance that might change. If—" he stressed the word for Char's benefit "—word gets out, wouldn't your business benefit from the new blood a few dozen newshounds might bring?"

Kat groaned the loudest. "You just verbalized our worst fear."

"Your worst?"

"Collectively. I, personally, have many others I won't bore

you with. Ever since your name came up, we've been stressing out about what would happen if this was a publicity stunt."

"That's not why I'm here." He hoped he'd managed to put adequate self-righteousness in his tone. "This is a private matter, as I said. The only reason I'm not in disguise is that Libby told me it wasn't necessary. Right, Lib?"

Libby nodded. "So far nobody's mobbed him. Except for a couple of old ladies at the airport."

He managed not to wince. In all honesty, he'd expected a little more fanfare. Not that his ego demanded public attention, but he was used to having people recognize him...and react. Maybe his publicist really did earn the big bucks he paid her.

"What if they blab?" Kat asked.

"I don't think I told them where I live, but Barb asked about him tonight."

"What'd you say?"

"That he was just passing through."

Cooper frowned. The truth of the statement bothered him. He wasn't sure why. He liked the place but not enough to feel badly about leaving it. And he'd be back to film location shots if the series got picked up by a network.

"You could say I'm here researching a new television series," Coop tossed out. Why? He had no idea.

The four friends looked at each other a moment then started laughing. "Set in Sentinel Pass?" Jenna hooted. "Sure. Like they'd believe that."

"What if we say he's looking to buy the mine?" Kat suggested.

"Are you kidding? Nobody's that dumb," Char muttered.

Libby grabbed a very large, knobby stick that had been leaning up against the wall. It looked as if it had been coated with varnish. It also looked dangerous. She held it upright like a wizard's staff and tapped it on the floor.

"Enough. We've had this discussion before, and as I told

you then, the who, what and when of my plan is entirely up to me. The reason I hadn't called to tell you about Cooper is that I haven't made up my mind. This is important, and I want to be sure I'm doing the right thing. For everyone."

Her pals looked slightly abashed.

"But I also know it's only a matter of time before someone stumbles across my online ad and puts two and two together," she added. "If that happens, it's possible the media will find out, too."

She looked at Cooper halfway apologetically. "Hopefully by then you and I will have signed our paperwork and gone our separate ways."

He didn't like the way that made him feel. Sort of used.

Char jumped to her feet. "Okay. Sounds like you have a handle on things. Can we give her the present now? I've been invited to a sweat lodge."

Jenna's mouth gaped. "A real sweat lodge? Pine logs and smoke?"

A slight hint of red brushed across the other woman's cheeks. "Not exactly. This one's more like a sauna except it uses high-tech infrared technology. You still sweat, you just don't get all stinky," she added defensively.

Coop could appreciate that, but her friends laughed as if she'd told a joke. She left in a bit of a huff, but returned a few seconds later with a brown grocery sack. "Here," she said, handing it to Libby.

"What is it? It's not my birthday."

"We know," Kat said. "It's not that kind of a gift. You asked me what Rufus Miller is making and selling on the Internet. He gave me a deal, since it was for you."

Coop remembered the man…and his apparent fondness for Libby. This gesture bothered him, but instead of trying to figure out why, he focused on the item, which Libby produced after digging through several inches of tissue paper.

About the size and shape of an electric can opener, the object resembled a tiny house with aspen bark siding, cedar-chip singles and no windows. The only orifice was a dime-size hole near the apex of the roof.

"Thank you. But…what is it?" Libby asked holding it out for Cooper to see.

"Rufus calls them dream houses. And they're selling like mad. The idea is you write your heart's desire on a piece of paper, then roll it up and pop it through the hole."

Jenna coughed. "We took the liberty of putting yours in it already, Lib, so don't do it again."

"Unless you want twins," Char added.

Libby appeared speechless, which gave Char the opportunity she needed to hug everyone—except Coop—then leave.

He reached for the box. Shaking it gently he heard a scratchy sound from within. The women's gesture—and the friendship behind it—was something to build on. Something he didn't quite understand, though.

He set the gift aside and looked at the two remaining women. "More questions?"

Kat drew in a deep breath before sitting forward, hands clasped between her knees. "What if one of you falls in love? Aren't you worried about how that might complicate things?"

She looked from him to Libby and back. "I mean, that's not so likely to happen to you, Cooper. You're a player. But Libby, on the other hand…"

"Gee, thanks, Kat. Now I feel even more unglamorous than usual."

"Lib, you know what I meant. He's suave and worldly and freakishly handsome. You're not impervious to a man's swoo."

"Swoo?" Coop repeated, unfamiliar with the word.

Libby and Jenna groaned as Kat answered. "It's like a spell certain men cast on women that makes us do things we'd never in a million years do—like marry them. My mama said that's how my daddy got her knocked up, and I seem to be particularly susceptible. I got sideswiped by the swoo twice. And I can tell you have a lot of swoo."

"It's called charisma," Libby clarified for Cooper's benefit.

"No, Lib. It's more than that," Kat insisted. "Charisma wins votes. Swoo gets you laid."

Coop doubled over laughing. He couldn't help himself. This was priceless. A screenwriter's dream dialogue. He couldn't wait to get back to his cabin to text this stuff to Shane.

CHAPTER NINE

THE GIRLS LEFT TWENTY or so minutes later. Long enough for Libby to be fully mortified and bone-deep embarrassed. They'd recounted for Cooper her past amorous adventures so completely that the only conclusion he could possibly draw was that she was a dried-up spinster plodding along the road to Lonely Street. The only thing missing was a dozen cats.

She leaned the talking stick against the wall, where it couldn't fall and hurt someone, then she turned to look at Cooper, who was sitting in her father's favorite chair, watching her.

"I'm sorry about tonight. We didn't get to that serious talk I had planned, and now I have a bit of a headache. I think I'm going to soak in a tub, then go to bed. Okay with you?"

His sandy-blond eyebrows lifted with a slightly rakish nuance that made her feel oxygen-deprived—until she reminded herself that he'd probably stood in front of the mirror for six hours to achieve that look.

"Alone."

"Did you ever watch the show *Moonlighting?* Bruce Willis and Cybill Shepherd. The dialogue was filled with great banter and sexual innuendo. I'm getting a sense that doesn't work around here."

She didn't agree, but she would have felt silly trying to prove that the citizens of Sentinel Pass weren't humorless prudes. Nor did she want to admit that she'd rented season one from Netflix the moment it had become available. "I'm sorry if my friends and I somehow gave you that impression. They're very bright women. Kat is a teacher—well, substitute at the moment, but only because she needs a few more credits to get her degree. And Jenna is a poet. Char is a self-made entrepreneur. They wouldn't normally butt in, but they're worried about me. And how this will all end."

He stood up. "Oh, I know. My best friend isn't a hundred percent behind this either. But he'll come around. Do you think I passed muster with your book club?"

By the time Kat and Jenna had left, the two had been smiling as if they'd just had an audience with the Pope. "They'll call tomorrow with their vote, but I'm guessing you won them over."

He walked toward her. "Good. Being a single parent isn't easy, from what I've heard, and I imagine it would be even harder without their support. What do you think people would say if they found out why I'm here?"

"Honestly? I think there'd be a lot of talk about how pathetic I am. Poor, desperate Libby. No chance at a normal life." She hadn't meant to sound so bitter, but her tongue curled in distaste after the words had passed over it.

"Normal? What's that? I've been married and divorced twice. My mother would say that proves you're smarter than me because you didn't rush into a relationship that anyone could see was bound to end poorly."

Even though his expression remained relaxed, she heard a quality in his tone that conveyed hurt. Had his mother said something that brutal to his face? How awful.

"At least you experienced the rush of falling in love. I can't say that's ever happened to me," she admitted and immediately wished she hadn't. That was the kind of thing you told your girlfriends, not the guy whose sperm you wanted to buy.

"Never?"

She shook her head. "I might have come close once or twice. Then I'd look at them—or myself—and realize I wasn't feeling the kind of light-you-up excitement and joy you're supposed to get from being in love. That's the goal, right? Or am I as bad as my brother? Chasing my own sort of fool's gold?"

She looked at him, wondering how he'd answer. He didn't. Instead he closed the distance between them and said, "Brace yourself. I'm going to kiss you. And there aren't any pillows on the floor to break my fall," he added, his eyes alight with humor.

"I don't—"

He put his finger to her lips. "Don't think. Experience. Isn't that the real reason you went searching beyond the borders of Sentinel Pass to find someone to father your child? You wanted to feel something new, something fresh and exciting?"

"But I never planned to..." To what? Get emotionally involved with her baby's father? Was that even possible? Once someone entered your life, you were involved. But how much that affected you was your decision. Wasn't it?

"You want a child without any of the usual strings that come with love, marriage, extended family and all the commitments those things bring. I get that. But the fact that you reached out into the bigger world tells me you were bored with the choices available here."

She shook her head. "You're wrong. I love Sentinel Pass. This is my home. But I know all the available men and I don't love any of them. I had to look someplace else."

His hands settled lightly on her shoulders. "You have another option. You could do something to open up the town's tourist trade. Draw in new businesses that would add fresh fish to your dating pool."

Libby shuddered from his words, not his touch, which she found warm and inviting. "No, thank you. Sentinel Pass may look dull and boring to you, but I like it the way it is. We've had developers give us the eye in the past, but we've made it clear we're content to grow at our slow, measured pace."

"I didn't say it was dull and boring. In fact, I think your town is quite charming. It's exactly the kind of place my mother used to promise me we'd move to after I got rich and famous. For years I thought she meant it." He looked past her a moment, then suddenly shook his head. "If I were going to live in a small town off the beaten path, this would be my first choice. But tourism can be a good thing. The people leave their money and go. Are you speaking as the town's mayor or as a private citizen?"

Mayor. She'd nearly died when Jenna mentioned earlier that most citizens of Sentinel Pass considered Libby the de facto leader of the town. "The Citizen's Council runs things. And I'm a member, but that doesn't make me the one in charge."

"People respect you and turn to you for guidance."

That was true. And lately she'd felt the burden of that responsibility more than she cared to admit. But she wasn't going to tell him that.

"We're more like a family than a town. Weird as it may sound. So you're right about me looking outside for a sperm donor. It makes the process seem less incestuous."

He smiled at that. *"Less incestuous,"* he repeated more to himself than to her. "That's good."

"Good for what? Are you taking notes or something?"

The question seemed to startle him, and instead of answering, he moved his hands to frame her face and lowered his mouth to just above her lips. "I was about to kiss you and you got me sidetracked. I fantasized about this today in the mine when your brother tried to lose me."

Mac tried to lose him? Not surprising, she guessed, but Coop hadn't stayed lost. Instead, he'd wound up earning Mac's respect by keeping his head and staying put. *Fantasizing about kissing me?* That, Mac wouldn't like.

His breath was warm, and her bones started to melt like ice cream in a bowl. Left on the counter too long. Much too long.

"In my dream, you kissed me back. Can you do that, Libby?" he asked, his lips barely touching hers.

She peered into the bluest eyes she'd ever seen and felt compelled to give him the answer he was waiting for. "Yes." The word came out as a breathless little gasp.

Surely that sound didn't come from my lips, she thought. But only for a second, because Cooper took her answer for an invitation. And maybe it was. She wanted to kiss him. Her curiosity demanded it.

It was only a kiss, right? Not an invitation to fall in love. She put her arms around his shoulders and leaned into him. She knew how to kiss. She'd even been told she was good at it. She was less confident about the parts that came next, but when she put her mind to it…

Coop wasn't expecting her to tilt her head slightly and lean into the kiss. Her tongue made the tiniest foray against his lips, as if testing his willingness to play. And he responded. He was trained to respond. He could kiss on demand—even if his costar had just consumed a Caesar salad with extra anchovies for lunch.

And that wasn't the case with Libby. Her warm breath was sweet and delicious. Her mouth opened a little wider with a sigh that sent all the right messages to the wrong part of his anatomy. He hadn't given sex much thought since his mother's death. Mourning and abstinence seemed to go together. Fitting. And he was still mourning.

But this felt right. Too right. And right was wrong. All wrong.

He lifted his head, ignoring the voice in his mind that cried for more. "It's late. I should go."

She opened her eyes and looked around as if regaining her bearings. "I—I'm sorry. I don't know where that came from."

He did. "Maybe we're both a little needy right now. I haven't thought about anything remotely amorous since my mom passed away, but I had an awful lot of people tell me that life goes on."

She nodded. "I hate that aphorism. We heard it a lot after Misty died. Sadly, it's true."

He moved back to open some space between them. He remembered a question he'd planned to ask her earlier. "What was it like for you when your parents died? You were really young, right? Did you understand what happened?"

"Probably not when my mother passed away, but I was at the mine when they pulled my dad out of the cave-in. I was eleven. It was tough. Scary. But…" She looked at the recliner he'd been sitting in earlier. "Gran and I talked about it. In a way, the accident was a blessing because Dad's heart really stopped beating five years before when my mother passed away. It was like a light had been extinguished in his soul."

"Wow. You lost both your parents just five years apart."

She returned her focus to him. "I was lucky. I had Mac. And we both had Gran. And there was insurance money to make sure we didn't lose the house or the mine. Plus, Dad hadn't touched the settlement he got from Mom's employer—one of the biggest mining operations in the Hills."

"What was it for?"

She hesitated. "Mom was one of four people—young, healthy office workers—who came down with lung cancer within a couple of years of each other. One was a smoker. The rest—Mom included—never smoked. The company settled out of court, but everyone believes their cancer was caused by asbestos in the building where they worked."

"Asbestos? They've known for years that that was carcinogenic. Why didn't the company get rid of it?"

She shrugged. "The owners weren't big on safety—aboveground or below. They're not in business anymore—at least not around here. Or they've morphed into a new conglomerate. I gave up trying to keep track of them."

"Your dad was healthy?"

"Yes. He was built like Mac. A powerhouse. Worked underground from his teens on. Handled dangerous chemicals his whole life. Gran said he was 'hell on wheels' when he was growing up. Smoked and drank until Mom got sick. Honestly I think it was the injustice of Mom's death that upset him most. She wasn't just too young to die, she was a really good person. Lived healthy. Loved by everyone who knew her. He felt it should have been him to go, not her. I can remember him ranting about how unfair life could be."

Coop could sympathize. What was fair about his mother dying and leaving him up to his eyeballs in debt?

Another question popped into his head. One that asked whether or not what he was planning to do with Libby's life story was fair.

An uncomfortable knot formed in his stomach.

"Hey, I'm making headway," he said, starting toward the door. "This time I kissed you without bodily injury. Cool. But I'm going to quit while I'm ahead. I'm going to the cabin now. Night."

She didn't try to stop him. He closed the screen door and started down the steps. Too bad, he thought, because now he was going to be alone with his conscience. Which meant he wasn't going to sleep worth crap.

SOAKING IN HER FREESIA-scented bubble bath twenty minutes later, Libby fretted about what had transpired that evening. Her friends. The inquisition. Sharing a second kiss with Cooper.

"What is wrong with me?" she cried, sinking up to her chin in the hot, silky water. The best part of a claw-foot tub was its depth, but she didn't want to take the time to dry her hair before bed, so she didn't dunk all the way under.

She wiggled her shocking-pink toenails poking out of the water across the bubbly expanse. Silly waste of time and money when she was the only one who ever saw her bare feet. Every day those bright, sexy digits were crammed into shoes one step removed from old-lady orthopedics.

She'd learned the hard way that Gran's advice was spot-on. "Buy shoes designed for the kind of work you do or you'll wind up with sore feet and very-close veins." She'd used the expression Libby had coined as a child to describe the raised purplish-blue strands just under her grandmother's skin on the backs of her legs.

Libby sat forward and pulled her right foot toward her chest, searching for any sign of aging. *So far, so good,* she thought with a sigh. But everyone said age was as much a reflection of attitude as of calendar dates. And she felt older than her years. Except when she was with Cooper.

Why was that? she wondered. Because he seemed so much younger than his years? Blissfully optimistic. Glass half-full. Happy—except when the subject of his mother came up.

That could help explain why she felt so drawn to him. As she'd told Mac, smiles and laughter weren't the first thing that came to mind when she thought of her childhood. Her father had always seemed intense and remote. Only after he was gone and she watched Mac working the Poke did she begin to appreciate the pressure their father must have been under to make a living from the mine.

She wished she could remember her mother better. Gran always spoke highly of her only son's wife, but as Mom's mother-in-law the two hadn't been as close as mother and daughter. Gran had given birth to a baby girl three years after her son was born, but she'd died in infancy. Libby always wondered if that had compromised her ability to love Nieva, Libby's mom.

Nieva Coolidge. *No relation to the president,* she remembered somebody saying. President Calvin Coolidge visited the Black Hills once, and his visit was still mentioned in historic lore.

Nieva had been working for a mining supply company in northern Minnesota when she met Libby's father, Marshall. Even Gran admitted that what happened was love at first sight. The two were married less than a month later.

Libby's maternal grandparents apparently hadn't been thrilled by the speed of the courtship but eventually came around. They were both gone now. They'd been present at their daughter's funeral, and Libby and Mac had visited them a couple of times later on in St. Cloud, but that was a long way from the Black Hills. And once Dad was gone, Gran had had her hands full working full-time and raising two kids at a time in her life when most women were beginning to think about slowing down.

She used her big toe to nudge the stopper out of the drain, then stood and reached for a towel. After drying off, she slipped on her cuddly plush robe, then rinsed the bubble bath residue around the tub. After brushing her teeth, she tossed her robe on a chair and slipped into bed.

The sheets were eight hundred thread count. A luxury she'd grown to love. With sheets this soft, it seemed a crime to wear pajamas. Sexy toes and no nightgown. She wondered what Cooper would say if he knew.

Smiling, she snapped off the light. His kiss had surprised her, but she had a feeling she'd shocked him even more by kissing him back. *What would he have done if I'd invited him to bed?* she wondered.

She pushed the question out of her mind without speculating on an answer. A kiss was one thing, sex something totally different. It wasn't going to happen.

Before rolling to her side, she made a mental note to visit her grandmother in the morning before work. Coop, she'd noticed, wasn't an early riser. She'd peeked in the window that morning to see if he wanted one of the bakery danishes she'd brought home the night before. His bedroom door had been closed. The living room and kitchen looked as though a college rugby team had been living there for a week on spring break. The man was a complete and utter slob.

Strangely, it was his flaws that she liked best about him. His outward perfection unnerved her. His odd mutterings and moments of disconnect concerned her. But his human qualities made her want to curl up with him under a thick quilt for the whole winter.

"I wonder if there's a demographic for women like me on some number cruncher's desk," she murmured. Over thirty. Single. No kids but hungry for one. Pathetic excuse for a dating pool. Financially set but emotionally challenged.

Cooper had been right about why she'd started looking beyond Sentinel Pass for a sperm donor. Distance had implied a certain degree of safety to her. This part of the country wasn't a quick plane flight from any major airport. Tourists to the Black Hills seldom bothered with the sharp turn onto the narrow, frost-pitted road that led into town, and those who did were irked to discover they had to take the same road back once they'd viewed Sentinel Pass's few meager sights.

For most of her life, Libby had considered her town's relative isolation a good thing. But lately—especially since meeting Cooper—she'd begun to wonder if it was possible to suffocate from too much safety.

CHAPTER TEN

LIBBY PETTED THE SQUIRMING little dog on her lap as she studied her grandmother. The early-morning light coming through the east window behind Gran's well-padded glider was soft and flattering, but nothing could disguise the fact that Gran was showing her age. Her heart squeezed with emotion. "How's Onida doing?" she asked, speaking loud enough for Gran to hear. "Calvin said he had to take her to the vet yesterday."

Gran frowned at her pooch, who seemed pretty lively given her age and infirmities—she was practically toothless and given to bouts of incontinence. "She's old. Like me. Parts wear out. The vet says her kidneys aren't so hot. Mine either, come to think of it. Guess we're both running out of time."

Hearing what they all knew was inevitable voiced aloud wasn't what Libby had come for. "Now, Gran, don't exaggerate. You've been saying for years that Onida had one paw on a banana peel. And look at her. She's just fine, aren't you, girl?"

The dog lifted her head and licked Libby's cheek.

"Poor thing. Any praise at all makes her giddy."

The statement caught Libby's attention. Praise had been pretty hard to come by in her home growing up. Her dad had hardly ever expressed any pride in his children or their accomplishments. Lately, Libby had started to wonder if that need for reinforcement had caused her to take a job where everyone looked up to her and came to her for advice.

"Gran, why did you become postmaster?"

"It was post*mistress* back then," Gran corrected. "Sure beat delivering the mail. My dad did that for years. Rain or shine, snow or sleet, seven days a week. You know what the winters are like around here. He got stuck in a drift one time and would have died if he hadn't found a box of Christmas cookies old lady Lytle was sending her son. He ate the whole thing and burned the box to keep warm. Don't tell anybody."

Libby smiled. She'd heard that story before. Many times. "I won't. Gran, do you have regrets about living your whole life in Sentinel Pass?"

"I lived in Colorado with my aunt and uncle after I finished school. Got a job with the phone company. Didn't like it much and was thinking about going home when I met your grandpa. He was mining coal on the western slope. When he found out I was from Sentinel Pass, he said he'd heard there was still some independent mining in the area and had been thinking about checking it out. I thought he was giving me a line, but the week after I moved home he showed up. And never left." Gran looked at her and smiled. "You can endure most anyplace when you're with someone who thinks the sun rises and falls because of you."

Libby sighed. She'd heard that story a couple of hundred times, too. She blamed it for making her hold out for that kind of someone. But coincidence and chance had brought her grandparents together, not an ad on the Internet. And Cooper was not looking for a love match. Actually, she wasn't sure what he wanted, but the idea that he might be her soul mate was ridiculous. The man was flighty, privileged and very, very temporary.

"Gran, do you think a little of that kind of feeling would be better than none at all? Even if the relationship was bound to fail, would the short-term benefits be worth the letdown when it was over?"

"Everything ends at some point. Hearts give out. Kidneys

quit working." Gran patted her lap, and Onida dropped any pretense of liking Libby to try to jump to the old woman's lap. Libby helped her scramble across the distance and managed to get scratched in the process.

She pressed her thumb to stop the bleeding on the gash between her second and third knuckles.

"Even if your marriage lasts, there's no guarantee your husband won't keel over. I know. I've buried two. So I say grab on to whatever happiness you have for as long as you can, then be thankful you had it when it's gone."

Grab on to whatever happiness you have for as long as you can. The phrase echoed in Libby's head throughout the rest of her visit. For a person looking for permission to do something her rational mind was firmly against, Gran's advice seemed pretty clear. And it also affirmed Libby's heart's desire.

Libby left a short while later, after waving to Calvin, who was in the garden. Although no spring chicken, the short, stocky man seemed far younger than her grandmother. He reminded her of Cooper, although she couldn't say why. Cal was small and fastidious. A neat freak. He did all the cooking, shopping and cleaning. Her grandmother once said, "Calvin was my slave in another life."

And this life, too, Libby remembered thinking. But the two truly seemed to care for each other. They had an ongoing game of gin rummy that, at two cents a point had run into the thousands of dollars.

Arriving at the Post Office, Libby brushed past her car, which she'd left parked in its usual spot while she'd walked to her gran's. After checking to make sure there wasn't anything blocking the loading platform, she unlocked the heavy metal door and pulled it open. A wave of familiar smells—paper, ink and toilet bowl cleaner—rushed to meet her as she walked inside.

She'd grown up in this building. Her kindergarten teacher,

Mrs. Nightingale, had walked Libby to the post office every day at noon recess to pick up her mail. From first grade on, Libby came here directly after school. She'd do her homework at the table in the front lobby, where Gran could keep an eye on her. Sometimes she'd take a nap atop the pile of outgoing mail bags, which were made of rough canvas closed at the top with a thick leather belt.

The citizens of Sentinel Pass knew Libby, and she knew them. She'd watched her grandmother interact with patrons and she'd come to understand that Gran was respected, trusted and beloved. Libby never consciously planned to follow in her grandmother's footsteps, but when Gran fell and broke a hip during Libby's freshman year at Spearfish, she'd felt compelled to come home and help. It's what Gran would have done.

And later, when Gran was well enough to return to work, she had decided to use up some of her overdue vacation time to travel. That's how she met Calvin. On a cruise, which he'd taken with his family to celebrate his successful bypass surgery. Cal sold his family home and bought a lot on the edge of town. Gran deeded the house she'd built with her second husband, Gordon, to Mac and Misty, then moved in with Cal—her younger man. And Gran never returned to work, leaving Libby to fill her role permanently—after the tests and interviews, of course.

"Yoo-hoo," a voice called. A familiar voice.

Libby looked toward the back door as Jenna's head popped around the frame. "I've brought a peace offering. Are you still talking to me?"

Libby motioned her in. "Of course. Why wouldn't I be?"

Jenna carried two white paper sacks in outstretched hands. The smell said coffee and doughnuts. Libby's stomach rumbled. Her grandmother's coffee was the color of tea, so she'd only taken a few token sips to be polite. "I was just craving this very thing."

"Ooh, you're experiencing cravings and you're not even P.G. Maybe that's a good sign that you're fertile."

Libby laughed. "Or maybe it means I'm hungry, you goose."

They pulled up two stools at the counter where the rural carriers would be sorting mail in a few minutes. Jenna wasn't working today, if Libby remembered the schedule correctly. Both of the regular carriers would be in.

"How come you're up so early?"

"Mom's got an appointment in Rapid."

Libby pulled a bear claw from the bag and took a big bite, savoring the decadent sweetness and shameless indulgence of calories. She'd pay for this later. "What's wrong with her now?" she managed to get out between bites.

"Oh, who knows? Have you ever heard of MRSA?"

Libby shook her head and opened her coffee container. Pitch-black. Perfect. She took a sip. It burned all the way down. Perfect.

"What is it?"

"Methicillin resistant staphylococcus aureus. Or something like that. According to *Readers Digest*, it's a superbug that can kill in seventy-two hours. Mom's got a scratch on her arm from the cat and she's convinced it's infected with MRSA and she's going to die. I'm thinking about canceling her subscription to the magazine."

Libby tried to look sympathetic. Jenna's mother had been a bit of a hypochondriac even before Jenna's father died, but in the last couple of years her illnesses—real and imagined— had gotten more frequent.

She held up her own hand. "Can you get it from dogs? Call me if I don't have long to live, okay?"

She was teasing, of course, but Jenna looked at her seriously. "Why? So you can make mad, passionate love to your blond hunk before you keel over?"

A spark of excitement traveled down Libby's back and settled much lower. She could almost see that happening. If she took her grandmother's advice and grabbed on— "Can you think of a better way to spend the last hours of your life?" she asked.

Jenna's mouth dropped open, exposing a partially masticated bite of sugar doughnut. Then she burst out laughing. "No, my friend. You're absolutely right. As my dad used to say, 'If not now, when?'" She finished chewing and swallowing before adding, "Would you do it if I called and said you were dying even if you weren't?"

Libby finished her coffee and stood. "The carriers should start arriving any minute. Time to get busy. You know the drill."

Jenna hopped to her feet but didn't leave. "Kat and Char and I took a vote before we got to your house last night. It was two to one in favor of you sleeping with him before he leaves."

Libby stared at her a minute. "You decided this before you even talked to him? Who was the— Let me guess—Kat?"

Jenna shook her head. "Nope. They both think the experience would be good for you—even on the fly. But I told them you're not the kind of woman who settles for easy-come-easy-go. You stick. Anybody you choose to be with has to stick, too."

Libby couldn't process her friend's evaluation right then because two people walked in—Clive Brumley and Sandy Hanson. Jenna gave Libby a long, knowing look, then left, shouldering the razzing from Clive and Sandy for not bringing more doughnuts.

The day began in earnest. Libby did what was required of her, but she couldn't get her friend's words out of her head. *You're not the kind of woman who settles for easy-come-easy-go.* She wasn't the kind who advertised for a sperm donor, but she'd done it.

Could she handle a quick affair? Possibly. But how would that affect their deal? The chance of her getting pregnant from that kind of encounter was nil because there was no way she'd

risk having unprotected sex with a man with Cooper's reputation. But if she and Coop made love, he might decide to
leave without providing the promised sperm. She wondered
if the law would support the claim that any ejaculation would
count toward satisfying their contract.

She didn't think Cooper was that petty, but she'd known
men who would stand on a technicality if they thought there
was money to be made from it. And she'd been adamant from
the start about wanting there to be no emotional strings
between them.

But he was a man. And he had kissed her twice. She was
pretty sure he'd be…up for the task.

"Whatcha smiling about?" Clive asked.

She felt her cheeks heat up. "Nothing. Um…is the first-aid
kit where it's supposed to be?"

She held up her hand to distract him from her obvious em-
barrassment. Plus, there was no sense dying from a simple
wound before she made up her mind whether or not to seduce
the sperm donor.

"WHAT A DUFUS," COOP muttered as he trudged along the path
into town. The shortcut, Libby called it. An opportunity to
break a leg, he preferred to think of it.

His unsteadiness on his feet, he decided, stemmed from his
brand-new hiking boots, which had been delivered a couple
of hours earlier. A big truck had roared into the driveway,
waking Coop from a hot dream. An embarrassingly hot dream
that had slowed his response to the determined knocking on
the cabin door.

"Need a signature here," a voice had called.

Coop had been forced to tug on sweatpants, which hopefully were sloppy enough to cover his still-emphatic woody.
"Coming," he'd called, cringing at the irony.

The deliveryman had been all business, presenting Coop

with a handheld device and a plastic stylus to sign. Coop had blinked to focus and finally managed to scratch his name across the small space. The guy had traded him a box for the device, then asked if he could take Coop's picture. "For my wife. She's a big fan."

Coop knew he looked like hell, even if his hard-on was hidden by the shoe box. He'd tried to close the door, but the guy had snapped a couple of shots using a small digital camera.

Once alone, Coop had splashed cold water on his face and looked in the mirror. "His wife, my butt," he'd groused. But he couldn't blame the man for seeing an opportunity and taking the chance. The Internet had opened up a new market for home-grown paparazzi. And although Coop might have wanted to disappear in theory, he knew his career needed a few "sightings" to keep people's interest. The price of doing business.

He'd quickly dressed and decided to test out his new boots, which he'd ordered for the infamous hike he and Libby were planning. A job he could have left to the location scouts but had decided this kind of overview would prove invaluable when he and Shane really started talking story development.

His only problem: the damn boots hurt.

He found a convenient rock at the spot where the trail intersected the main road and sat. He was still massaging his ankle when a car stopped. Two women. One older but quite beautiful in a Jane Seymour kind of way. The driver he recognized. Libby's friend Jenna.

"Hey, there. You lost?" Jenna asked, leaning across her passenger.

"Nope. Just on my way into town to show Libby my new hiking boots. Although they may take a couple of years to break in."

"I have some great leather treatment that might help. I was a tour guide at Wind Cave one summer, did a bunch of hiking. Hop in."

The trip to Jenna's house only took a few minutes, but it was such a relief to be off his feet he hardly paid any attention to how they got there. "Walking downhill can actually be harder than going uphill because the foot is crammed against the toe of your boot," Jenna told him.

"I had terrible shin splints one time," Jenna's mother, who said her name was Bess, told him. She'd removed her seat belt in order to turn sideways and look at him. Unfortunately that caused the car's alarm to chime incessantly. Jenna ignored it, but from his position he could see her lips flatten together and a nerve in her jaw twitch.

Coop's character sonar went off and he couldn't help investigating the two women's backstory. "Have you lived in Sentinel Pass long?"

"My husband and I started spending our summers here when we were first married. He was a young professor at the University of South Dakota in Vermillion. I was a theater arts major."

He leaned forward. "I thought I picked up an actor vibe. What did you play?"

"Juliet, Lady Macbeth and I had the lead in several musicals. They said I set the bar with my Stella, but I gave up the boards when I got pregnant with my daughter and we moved west."

"Dad was awarded a geologic fellowship with the School of Mines. He was there until he passed away two years ago."

"Oh, I'm sorry for your loss. I don't think Libby mentioned it. I just lost my mother recently, too."

Bess nodded. "I read about that. Jenna printed off a bunch of stuff about you from the Internet."

"Mom," Jenna said sharply. "You're doing it again."

Her mother popped one hand over her mouth. "Sorry. My daughter says I'm guilty of speaking before thinking. I have a bad habit of saying what's on my mind."

"At her daughter's expense," Jenna added.

"True."

"She doesn't recognize social boundaries," Jenna explained.

"I believe it's tied to the stroke my daughter doesn't believe I had."

"Your doctor agrees with me, Mom."

"Which proves I need a new doctor. Look how he bungled your father's case."

A quick twist of the wheel put them squarely in front of a two-story house that was almost identical to Libby's. "Did the same builder construct all the homes around here?"

"Sorta. This was a Sears Roebuck catalog plan."

"No kidding? My mother told me she grew up in a Sears Roebuck house." And she vowed never to sink so low that she had to return to that level of ordinary, he didn't add.

A few minutes later he was sitting on the top step of the wide plank porch, shoeless, while Jenna labored over his boots. He couldn't help but notice that the paint was starting to peel in places, and the gritty runners that had been glued to the steps—for traction in winter, he supposed—were sketchy, at best.

"Can I help?"

Jenna shook her head. "I'm a bit of a perfectionist. Like my dad," she added.

He canted to one side so his shoulder was resting against the solid post. His tailbone was still a little tender from his fall. Through the open window he could hear Jenna's mother involved in a one-sided conversation. "Who's she talking to?"

"I have no idea. Probably one of her actor friends. She failed to list in her credits the twelve years she spent playing the victim. Literally. Her most beloved role was as Poor Penelope Plaingood at the Mellerdrama in Rockerville—until the new highway went in. No one could quail quite like Mom."

"No one could quail quite like Mom," he mutely repeated. Another great line to tell Shane.

"Has anyone ever told you you mumble?" she asked.

The sun made her thick red hair vibrantly alive. She was actually quite pretty, he realized and wondered how he'd missed that. It wasn't like him to overlook beautiful women in his midst. Shane wasn't going to believe that.

"Yes. My best friend. All the time. I don't read well. Probably a learning disability. Mom never had me tested. She compensated by reading my lines aloud to me. Once I hear something and say it back, I remember it."

She held out the yellow flannel cloth for Coop to squeeze another dollop of the pungent treatment from the can she'd handed him. The thick paste came out in a bubble and made a loud farting sound. She looked at him a second, blushed, then went back to rubbing. "I'm just the opposite. I was a voracious note-taker in college," she admitted. "My father had a near photographic memory. Served him well as an engineer."

"I thought you said he was a geologist."

"He had a fellowship in geology, but his Ph.D. was in engineering. He wrote a computer program that geologists use to catalog soil strata and erosion."

"Smart guy."

"Yep. He was passionate about science of any kind. Mom was mad about plays and acting. And I...haven't found my niche, according to Libby." She stopped rubbing to look at him. "Are you going to help her? She'd make a great mom. Have you seen her with Megan? She's all the things I'm not. Patient. Understanding. Forgiving."

He was saved from answering by her mother who returned carrying two three-inch-thick albums. "Come join me inside, Cooper. I'll show you my career in a nutshell."

Jenna groaned. "Mom. Please. He's a nice man. He didn't do anything to deserve this kind of torture."

Her mother ignored her. "I've made coffee."

A bribe he was dying for. He'd been too distracted by the

deliveryman and the arrival of his boots to make his own. "Sounds great."

Bess shot her daughter a smug look and went back inside. "Black or with cream and sugar?"

"Surprise me," he said, leaning over to set the can of leather treatment beside Jenna. "Are you sure you don't need my help?"

"Are you sure you don't want to run—even in your stocking feet—in the other direction while you have the chance?"

He laughed. "I've been around actors my whole life. I can handle one woman's scrapbook."

Jenna dropped the first boot and shrugged. "Don't say I didn't warn you."

He stood, stretched the kinks out of his legs, then went inside. The interior of the house, like the outside, showed signs of wear, not neglect. Dust-free, every little knickknack and framed photograph—of which there were dozens—in place, but the walls could have used a fresh coat of paint and the carpet runners were frayed in spots.

"Come sit by me," Bess said, patting the forest-green sofa. "It'll be easier to point out who's who."

As she walked him through the story of her life, Coop decided Bess reminded him of his mother, for no discernable reason other than she hid her personal disappointments behind a thick layer of bravado. He'd known at some level that his mother was living her life vicariously through him, and that knowledge had driven him to do better. He didn't think there was anything wrong with that. But from a few telling remarks—"Jenna suffered stage fright the first time I talked her into playing a small part and would never go back "—he gathered Jenna didn't buy into his coping mechanism. Apparently she was even more of a disappointment to her father, who had expected her to go to college, graduate with honors and follow in his footsteps.

"Jenna dropped out of college?" he asked, trying to piece together the story.

"Snidely Whiplashes exist beyond the stage, you know. Sometimes they hide behind nice manners and a letter jacket."

"Pardon?"

Bess looked toward the front of the house, where her daughter was hopefully out of earshot. A profound sadness enveloped her. "Something happened to her in college. We don't talk about it." She shook her head and looked at him with false brightness. "More coffee?"

Intriguing. But his insides were sloshing and he wanted to see Libby. He was going to suggest they do a practice hike after she closed up for the day. Maybe he'd buy a picnic from the diner and they could find a nice romantic spot to watch the sunset.

Romantic? No, that wasn't the right word. *Quiet. Intimate.* No. Wrong again. Um... "I should be going. I enjoyed our stroll down memory lane. Have you thought of writing your memoirs?"

"Don't encourage her," Jenna said, opening the screen door. She walked to where Coop and her mother were sitting and deposited his boots on the coffee table, nearly upsetting his half-full china cup. She looked at her mother and shook her head. "Mom's bugging me all the time to do it. I tell her only she can do justice to her story."

"You're writers?"

"Not me," Bess said, shaking her head. "But Jenna's a published poet. Would you like to see one of her books?"

Jenna cheeks turned almost the same color as her hair. "Self-published. Vanity press," she said, giving her mother a dirty look. "Boxes of unsold mouse fodder in the garage. Trust me—you don't want to read it."

"I'd like a book."

"No, you wouldn't."

"I would."

Bess walked to an antique table beneath an ornate oval mirror and triumphantly produced a slim hard-bound volume with a silk-fabric cover. "I pulled this copy out of the garage last week. I was going to donate it to the school. I'll get them another. Give it to him, dear. He's a very nice man. He won't laugh."

Coop nearly winced. That backhanded compliment was something his mother would have said.

"Thanks," he said. "I look forward to reading it." The book fit nicely in the wide pocket on the side of his thigh. He finished tying his laces and stood. "Wow," he said, wiggling his toes. "These feel great."

Jenna seemed pleased with his response. She followed him to the door.

"Which way to Libby?"

She stepped onto the porch and pointed. "Keep going downhill till you get there."

Downhill.

The word held ominous overtones. In the back of his mind was a little voice harping on the fact that he couldn't succeed without his mother's involvement in his career. Life as he knew it was over. But the fear that had been his constant companion for two months had lessened with each e-mail from Libby. He honestly hadn't felt the old gnawing acid in his belly since he'd first arrived in Sentinel Pass. He wanted to believe this was because he'd found a new focus, a positive project that would reward him financially and pull him back from the brink of bankruptcy and publicly humiliating headlines. But deep down he knew it was more than that.

He jumped off the bottom step and headed in the direction Jenna had pointed. He was going downhill to see Libby—and, frankly, he just couldn't wait to get there.

CHAPTER ELEVEN

AFTER THREE DAYS OF CLOUDS, a smattering of showers and a piercing wind that had delayed their hike by a day, Sunday morning had dawned clear and storm-free. The sky almost tasted blue, Coop thought, looking up as they emerged from a narrow corridor lined with skinny, white-bark aspen. The sonata created by the breeze stirring the shiny new leaves had precluded any need to talk, but he didn't want to be accused of lollygagging, so he hurried up to keep up.

"We're going to have our picnic on top of that ridge," she said, pointing to a hill dotted with long-needle pines and an occasional outcropping of shale.

"Great," he said. "I'm getting hungry."

They'd been following the well-marked trail, which Libby had explained was used by hunters, Forest Service vehicles and snowmobile enthusiasts in the winter, for a couple of miles. His left heel was beginning to rub on his boot, but he kept the complaint to himself.

He was breathing hard before they were even a third of the way up the incline.

"This is a lot steeper than it looked from the trail," he said, pressing his hand against the stitch in his side.

She waited for him to catch his breath. "The view will be worth it. I promise."

She was right. A few minutes later, he completely forgot about his aching feet and dry throat as he looked around.

"Wow," he exclaimed, slowly turning in a circle. "You weren't kidding. This is gorgeous. You can practically see California from here."

That made her laugh. "Not quite. But you can see Signal Knob," she said, pointing. "And there's Harney Peak. It's the highest point between the Rockies and Switzerland."

"Did I tell you I visited the Great Wall of China last year? The view had nothing on this place. Of course, China is dealing with air pollution like you wouldn't believe. The air here seems…pure."

"Well, it did rain yesterday. That helps."

She never seemed quite as enthused as he thought she should be about her state. Humility? Or did she take the place for granted?

"Do you know what I like best about the Black Hills?"

"What?"

"When I was in China, there were a couple of hundred tourists beside me. Here, I feel like we're the last two people on the planet, discovering a new world. Do you know what I mean?"

When Libby didn't answer him, he pulled his gaze from the horizon to look at her. "I'm gushing, aren't I? Sorry. This place just… Well, it's surprised me."

He felt stupid and wished he'd kept his mouth shut. His mother would have been shaking her head. *Think before you speak, son. Do you want people to know you only have a G.E.D.?*

"The Lakota considered this area sacred," Libby said, stuffing her hands in the pocket of her black nylon Windbreaker. He'd tied his Dsquared jacket around his waist after following her orders to dress in layers, but even his long-sleeved white polo shirt was getting too warm with the sun bearing down on them. "Hiking these trails is almost a spiritual thing for me. I didn't expect it to affect you the same way."

Her words took the edge off his humiliation.

She motioned for him to follow her to a level spot fairly

well protected from the crisp, steady breeze. "How long were you in China?" she asked, shrugging off her backpack.

"Four days. Two in Shanghai, two in Beijing. That's not enough, believe me."

"Why didn't you stay longer?"

Because his mother had been in charge of his itinerary. A fifteen-hour flight each way, another flight between the two cities, delays at Customs, losing a day in transit… He'd been so jet-lagged on his return he'd nearly been sick.

"I went there to film a commercial and had to get back to the show." He and his mother had had a terrible fight about her pushing him beyond his limits.

You have to make hay, little Sir Sunshine, Lena had snapped. *You're not going to be young and gorgeous forever. This is your moment. You can sleep when you're my age*, she'd argued, utterly unapologetic for subjecting him to the trip from hell.

"I wish I'd had more time there. I want to go back. What little I did see of the country was fascinating, and my guide was really knowledgeable. They attend guide college, you know. It's a legitimate career." He watched her unpack several plastic containers and a bag of potato chips. "Have you been there?"

"Me? Heavens, no. Jenna and I went to New York City with her mom when we graduated from high school. Saw a couple of plays. It was fun, but that's about the extent of my travel aside from a few postal conventions. I haven't even been to California."

He used the wristband of his shirt to wipe a bead of sweat from his brow. "You're kidding. Didn't your family take vacations? Everybody goes to Disneyland, right?"

Now it was her turn to look embarrassed. He squatted beside her and took her hand. "I didn't mean that to sound judgmental. I'm just curious."

She didn't pull her hand free, but he could tell she was uncomfortable with him touching her. Tough. He wanted to know more about her, and she didn't make it easy.

"We went to Yellowstone once. When I was five. I have a picture of my mom pushing me on a swing in front of a log cabin. She looked really thin and she had a scarf around her head, so I think she must have been taking chemotherapy. Someone wrote on the back 'Libby in Yellowstone' and the year."

"I've been there. I think I was nine." He thought a moment. "Yeah. That's right. Mom and I were going to North Dakota to meet some of her family. We took the scenic route, but then she checked with my agent and found out that I was up for a part and he forgot to tell her. A big part. She was furious. We turned right around and drove straight through, but the car broke down in some dusty little town in Utah. By the time the mechanic located the part he needed and got us back on the road, the film was already in production and I missed out on a chance of a lifetime."

She pulled her hand free and unzipped a side compartment of her nylon pack to withdraw a couple of paper napkins. "It was a big one, huh?"

"*E.T.* Lucky break for Henry Thomas, not so good for me. Mom was livid. She fired my agent, sold her car and bought two tickets to the Big Apple. We lived there for a couple of years. I liked it. Went to a regular school most of the time. Made a few commercials. Eventually we came back."

She looked up, eyes wide with surprise. They were close enough for him to see the tiny gold flecks in her irises. He'd never been around women who didn't wear makeup, so seeing her thick, naturally curled eyelashes was strangely provocative.

"Do you ever wear mascara?"

She ducked her chin toward her chest. "Sometimes. If I'm going out. But not at work. Too much dust. And when I'm hiking, the sunscreen can get in my eyes. I'd turn into a smeary mess. Why?"

"Both of my exes would have walked naked down Rodeo Drive with a bag over their head before they'd consider stepping out of the house without being fully made-up. It occurred to me that you're the most real person I've ever met."

She made a dismissive sound. "And you thought I lead a sheltered life," she said drily. "Here. Help spread this out so we can eat. I'm hungry."

She wasn't really, but she needed to put some space between her and Cooper. He'd been crowding her all morning, both physically on the trail and emotionally by intruding on her peace of mind with questions she didn't want to think about.

Makeup? What business was it of his if she didn't know squat about how to doll up her looks? Was he implying she'd look better if she took more time with her appearance? Probably, but there was no way she could compete with the women of Hollywood. She'd been raised by a woman who had spurned her daughter-in-law's attempt to sell Avon products as a waste of time and money. Whatever makeup had been left around after Nieva died, Gran had tossed out or given away. Despite Jenna's attempt to teach Libby the subtle blending of eye shadow and the sculpturing application of blush, Libby always felt like a little girl playing dress-up when she sat down in front of a mirror with a mascara wand in hand.

And as for his question about her limited exposure to travel… Well, she didn't have an answer. Gran had been many places. Florida. A cruise through the Panama Canal. She and Cal even ventured to Alaska a few summers ago. They'd invited Libby to join them, but she'd declined. She couldn't remember why.

She loved to read books that took her to other places, but anytime someone suggested booking a group tour of some kind, she found some excuse to keep her here. Work. Family obligations. Her grandmother's health. Money concerns. Planning for a baby.

She had a job she loved, a terrific retirement plan, benefits most people would kill for—except for the dental, which sucked—and the respect of everyone who knew her. She hated the way Cooper Lindstrom made her question what she had…and want more.

She kneeled on the red-and-white check plastic tablecloth she'd spread on the ground. Coop pitched in to make the corners flat, then he dropped down and crossed his legs.

"The drinks are in your pack, Coop."

He pulled the lightweight daypack she'd borrowed from Mac onto his lap. Mac and Megan had stopped by before dawn yesterday morning to tell her they were making a run to Denver for some diamond bits he needed and wouldn't be back until late Sunday night or Monday morning. Usually Libby went with them when he needed mining supplies.

"I'm not a world traveler, but I do get to Denver about once a month," she said, apropos of nothing.

Coop leaned over to hand her a vacuum-sealed fruit juice. "What do you do there? Shop? See a show? Go to dinner?"

"All of the above. Sometimes." Mostly she helped drive and hung out with Megan at the Holiday Inn. "Megan and I went to the zoo once."

"Oh, well, if she liked that, then she'd love the one in San Diego. It's huge."

"That's in southern California, right? Cities don't really interest me, but I'd love to see the ocean."

"Do you like Denver? We held a tryout there a couple of seasons back. It was more cosmopolitan than I'd expected."

"It's okay. Megan and I had high tea at the Brown Palace right before Christmas. The traffic and the push of shoppers in the downtown area made me feel claustrophobic. I always heave a huge sigh of relief when we get to the South Dakota state line. By the time we reach Edgemont, I'm feeling human again."

He polished off his drink before she even opened hers, then

he stretched out, throwing his forearm across his eyes to block the sun. His Bollé sunglasses were resting by her foot. She picked them up and tried them on. They felt substantial. And expensive. The lens color turned the world an off shade of amber, but the tone somehow sharpened every leaf.

No wonder people spend big bucks on these things, she thought. She caught Cooper looking at her and jerked the glasses off. "Nice color," she mumbled, reaching for a sandwich bag. "You have a choice of tuna salad or egg salad in pitas. They don't get smashed as easy as bread."

He rolled to his side and cocked his elbow to rest his head in his palm. "Egg salad, please. Screw the cholesterol."

She handed him one of the four she'd prepared. "Does high cholesterol run in your family?"

"Apparently. Mom had a heart attack, despite the fact she was taking high-blood-pressure pills. I had a physical last year, though, and the doctor said I was in tip-top shape."

She had to agree with that. When he'd shown up at the post office in his new hiking boots and cuffed shorts with a sweatshirt tossed over one shoulder, she'd had to force herself to quit staring. Even Elana Grace, who ran the Tidbiscuit and was nearly Gran's age, had stopped complaining about the postage rate increase to gawk at him.

"How 'bout you?" he asked.

She figured he had a right to full medical disclosure, since they might have a child together. "Except for Gran—who is a medical marvel, according to Dr. Adrian, and might outlive us all—I can't tell you much about our family health history. I saw a fertility specialist in January to find out if I could carry a child, and everything checked out."

"Was there some reason to question that?"

"Mom had a miscarriage a couple of years after I was born. Gran thinks it had to do with her cancer, but that hadn't been detected at the time, so I don't know. I didn't want to waste my time and effort if my fallopian tubes were kinked or something."

"Logical," he said, before sinking his teeth into the pita. He had perfect teeth. She wondered if they were capped or professionally bleached. Probably, she decided.

"What?" he asked.

"Huh?"

"You have a question to ask me. I can tell."

"You can?"

He nodded. "I read nuances. It's important to an actor to be able to get into a role. I've made a point of studying people's faces."

"Oh." She found that unnerving.

"What do you want to know? You can ask me anything. Isn't that what we're supposed to be doing—finding out about each other?"

"Well, this isn't relative in any way, but I wondered if you bleach your teeth."

He sat up and smiled. His grin was infectious. "Not what I was expecting. Yes." He ran his tongue back and forth under his upper lip. "These are expensively maintained, photo friendly toofies." He flashed her a cheesy smile. "All except for this one. See?" He used his finger to expose his right canine tooth and leaned across the space between them. "Slightly tilted. Mom wouldn't let the orthodontist touch it. She said the minor imperfection gave me character."

Libby agreed. She liked that tooth. She'd noticed it before and wondered how it had managed to avoid being lassoed and corralled into line with the rest of the teeth. Impulsively she reached out and touched it. "She was right."

He removed his hand and his bottom lip touched her finger. Just a tiny touch but one that made her heartbeat jump erratically. She sat back, shocked by the sudden heat that blossomed between them. Was she imagining it or did he feel it, too?

He took in a ragged breath and crossed his legs, putting more distance between them. "Mom usually was. About things that had to do with business. She had a sixth sense where the television and film industry was concerned."

She'd picked up on his carefully worded praise before. Just a hint of anger or some other emotion shadowed his tone when he talked about his mother. Had theirs been a love/hate relationship?

He gave a weighty sigh. "What now?"

Damn. She had to quit telegraphing her silent questions. "Tell me about her."

He made a face that looked as though he'd eaten something sour. "I could, but aren't we supposed to be meeting Jenna at some point today or tomorrow?"

His pithy tone was meant to be a joke, but she decided it hid his true desire not to talk about his mother. "Meaning your relationship is off-limits for conversation."

"No. Meaning she was a complicated woman. We could discuss her quirks and foibles all day and all night and still probably not figure her out completely."

"Well, in that case, you can talk while we walk." She quickly packed up their leftovers and stood. She waited until he replaced his mostly empty water bottle in his pack then held out a hand to help him up.

One quick tug and he was upright. But he didn't let go. In fact, he pulled her closer until their chests were almost touching. "It just occurred to me that we haven't seen another soul for the past hour. Is it possible some cataclysmic tragedy wiped out humanity while our backs were turned and we're the last two people on the planet?"

She gave in to temptation and leaned closer—just for a heartbeat. "You have a wild imagination."

"You could be right. I've imagined doing this ever since our last kiss."

His lips were as smooth and lush as she remembered. She was glad he'd picked egg salad over tuna. She wasn't sure when she'd decided that kissing him was okay, but she was grateful she'd given herself permission to enjoy this small decadence.

What she hadn't agreed to was the…more that seemed to follow as second nature as breathing. The feel of his hand moving slowly down her back to the waistband of her hiking shorts. He drew her closer so she could feel his body responding to the rush of hormones, pheromones or whatever *mones* a man responded to. The thought stopped her. What *was* he responding to? Surely not her sex appeal, which they both knew didn't exist.

He drew back and let out a sigh. "Another question."

"Are you oversexed?"

He let out a harsh laugh. "Just the opposite, if my recent history is being judged. The question you should be asking is, why can't I quit kissing you?"

"Okay. Answer that one."

"I like kissing you. In fact, I think I want to make love with you."

"No. That's not part of our agreement."

"I know, but you made the rules. You can change them if you want. They're not written in blood, are they?"

Her heart was beating painfully fast. She couldn't remember why that rule had seemed so important when she wrote it, but she was sure the rationale was sound. To protect her unborn child. Or was it to protect her heart?

She started to walk away, but he stopped her. "Libby, I'm serious. I came here planning to play by the rules, but something's going on between us that seems worth exploring. What would it hurt?"

Who would it hurt, he should have asked.

She knew the answer to that question. *Me.* "Coop, every

woman under the age of eighty finds you attractive. Me included. You came here for one reason and one reason only. It's better if we stick to the plan."

"Another word for *script*," he corrected. The word sounded austere and bitter. "'Follow the script, Cooper,' my mother always said. 'Don't think. Don't extemporize.'"

He stormed off. Into the forest. In the wrong direction.

"DAMN," Libby SWORE. Coming to an abrupt stop, she pulled out her map.

They'd been walking for hours, it seemed, and still hadn't reached the trail Libby thought would lead back to where they were supposed to meet Jenna.

Coop drew on a reserve he usually didn't have to rely on to walk the extra ten feet to reach her. His Cole Haan boots felt three sizes too small, and he was certain he had a blister the size of Connecticut on his left heel. "What now?"

"See that stream? It must be Crooked Creek. That definitely means we're on the wrong trail. Probably the Deerfield."

He regretted that their earlier camaraderie had been lost when he stormed off. He thought he'd been headed back to the trail they'd been on, but his sense of direction had probably been thrown off by the low, purplish clouds that had swept in while he'd been lusting after Libby.

His actions had been that of a spoiled child—or an ego-centric TV personality—but at the time his only thought had been to put some distance between them. He did want to kiss her and make love to her, but if that had happened, he would have felt obligated to tell her about his plan to turn her life story into a television series.

He wasn't ready to do that. He didn't have a clear vision of the story's take-away. Was this going to be about a woman who was prepared to do anything to get pregnant? Or did the focus need to be on the self-involved hero who was willing to use her for his purposes? He just didn't know yet.

"Can I soak my feet in the water before we go any farther?"

She glanced at her watch. "Jenna's probably starting to worry."

Her friend had dropped them off that morning with the promise to pick them up at the trailhead at three. They were definitely behind schedule.

"What's her number?" He pulled his phone out of his pocket. Holding it to the light, he stared, dumbfounded. No bars. "Why the hell don't I have cell reception? We're several thousand feet closer to the damn satellites here than on the flats."

She refolded the map. "Look around. Do you see any towers?"

He hated her complacent tone. "If I lived here, I'd lobby the cellular companies until they built one."

He didn't check to see if she was rolling her eyes. Instead he sat on a giant boulder that looked as though it had been placed in that spot for that exact purpose and started to pick at the reddish dirt that had filtered into his laces.

"Don't do it," she cautioned. "You'll never get that boot back on if you take it off."

"My feet are killing me. I've got blisters on my blisters."

"And your extra shoes are where?"

She'd put that on his prehike checklist, but he hadn't wanted to carry the extra weight. "If I had the energy, I'd push you into the creek."

He could tell by the bright shimmer in her eyes that she was trying hard not to laugh at him. "I've been thinking about what your Lakota name should be. Pouts With Shoes On sounded good, but now I think I like Dances No More."

Her lips quivered from the effort it took to remain serious. God, he wanted to make love with her. Right here. Right now. On the hard ground. Boots on or off, he didn't care. He'd followed her shapely ass for too many miles to quell the lust he'd felt building.

She stepped back as if reading his mind—and almost fell into the marshy edge of the bubbling stream. He lunged to grab her hand and pull her to safety.

"If I hadn't caught you, would that make you Dances-In-Water?"

She yanked her hand free. "Better than Freezes in Snowmelt. Come on. If we keep heading downstream, we'll get to the road eventually. There's a trailhead where you can wait while I backtrack to find Jenna."

Even taking another step sounded brutal. "How 'bout you leave me here and send a rescue helicopter?"

"How 'bout you suck it up and follow me?"

She turned and started away, paralleling the sparkling water that tumbled musically over fat boulders. She didn't look back to see if he was capable of following, which meant he had no choice but to overcome his pain and go after her.

For what felt like hours.

His right foot was on fire by the time they stumbled into the graveled lot of the trailhead. A smart little shelter had been erected with a bench that Cooper sank onto with a loud, gusty sigh.

There was no cars parked in the lot, which told Coop Libby's map-reading had been correct. He'd gotten them off course and they now had to walk farther to find Jenna. Luckily they'd reached a wide, well-maintained gravel road.

"Maybe we could hail a passing car," he suggested after Libby returned from using the rest room.

"The Daugherty Gulch trail is only half a mile or so in that direction. You can wait here. I'll go find Jenna. She's probably worried sick."

He felt badly about that. And Libby was probably smart to leave him behind since she could cover the ground faster alone. But the second she turned to leave, he heaved himself up to follow. She started to say something but didn't. They walked the whole way in silence.

And not a single car passed going in either direction. Maybe they were the last people on the planet.

They found their driver asleep behind the wheel.

"Jenna," Libby called, tapping lightly on the windshield.

Jenna jerked awake, eyes wide with terror, hands lifted defensively. She took a frantic glance around, then appeared to come to her senses. Whatever her dream, it hadn't been pleasant.

"Hi," she said, rolling down her window. Her voice was shaky. "You're late. What happened?"

"We…um…turned left when we should have turned right. Sorry."

Jenna used a master switch to unlock the rest of the doors of her Subaru Outback, then got out. Libby opened the rear hatch and motioned for Coop to come over. He limped to the car. "Thank God. I couldn't have gone another step."

"You never know what you're capable of until you're tested," Libby said cryptically. "Give me your foot."

He sat down and barely managed to lift his left boot about three inches off the ground before his thigh muscles started quivering. It plopped back to the gravel. Libby didn't laugh. Instead she bent over and picked up his heel, settling it on her bent knee.

"I can do that," he protested when she started unlacing the boot. Jenna's scrutiny made him feel like a wimp.

"I can do it faster." She was right. Flick, pull, flick and it was done. "Brace yourself," she told him. "This might hurt."

"Why would it hurt? I can't wait to get the damn things off…off, off, ouch. Oh, God, my toes are on fire. Put it back on."

"Can't. Sorry." She tossed the boot into the car beside him, then quickly pulled off his sweaty sock. "Jen, do you have any ointment or lanolin?"

"Um…maybe. Let me look in the first-aid kit. You know Mom."

Coop heard her poking through a box of some kind that she'd pulled from under the seat. Curious about what Jenna meant, Coop looked at Libby with his unasked question.

"Bess is a bit of a hypochondriac," she said softly, leaning toward him.

Hmm, he thought. One more character trait to file away. He'd been considering making someone like Bess the heroine's mother. Lots of good conflict to work into the stor—

"Yow," he cried out, lifting his butt off the tailgate using his arm strength alone. He tried to wrench his foot free of Libby's hold, but she had a firm grip on his ankle and was determined to spread some stinky, stinging alcohol-based goop on his open sores.

"Stop. That hurts worse than the blisters. Ouch. You're killing me." He squeezed his eyes tight against the pain. A few seconds later he started to relax. He sank back down and opened his eyes. "Oh. Better."

The two women exchanged a look. Jenna's expression seemed to say *For heaven's sake, what a baby.* But Libby's knitted worry lines on her brow remained constant. She fixed things. She'd led them out of danger when he got them lost. She'd nursed his poor feet without saying "I told you so." His mother would have rubbed in the fact that he lacked an internal compass, pointing out yet again how dependent he was on her.

Without knowing it, Libby had passed a test it hadn't even occurred to him to require. She was going to be a terrific mother.

CHAPTER TWELVE

"HE'S ASLEEP," JENNA hissed, glancing over her shoulder, then back to the road.

They'd only traveled about five miles before a muffled snoring sound had started to emanate from the backseat. Libby used the makeup mirror in her visor to check on Cooper. Twilight had descended swiftly, as it usually did in the mountains, so she couldn't clearly see his face. "He could be faking it. He's an actor, you know."

The orange dash lights cast a mellow glow that made Libby wish she could nod off, too. She was drained. Although she'd tried not to let Cooper see her distress, there had been a couple of times when she'd felt completely lost and out of her element. They could have been hiking on Mars, for all the good her natural sense of direction was doing her. Reaching the stream had helped her get her bearings, but that had reinforced just how lost they'd become, and she'd known they were going to be way late getting to the car. She hated to make anyone wait for her, which was probably why she was neurotically punctual when it came to opening the lobby window every morning.

"You know, Lib, I like him. How come you act so uptight around him?"

Libby didn't answer right away. She shifted in the seat, adjusting her lap belt so it didn't cut off her breathing, then she leaned across the middle console and said softly, "Because I like him, too. Probably too much."

"Oh. *Oh.*" The second one told her Jenna understood.

"Are you going to do what Kat and Char suggested?"

"No. I don't dare. It might screw up everything. No pun intended."

"But, Lib, the actual screwing could be worth it."

Libby glanced in the back. Cooper looked out cold, and she didn't blame him. They'd pushed far beyond his flatlander limitations today. She actually felt sorry for him. "Don't be crude."

"I'm just saying—"

"Don't. Don't say it. I'm this close to making the mistake of a lifetime," she admitted, using her thumb and index finger to show the tiniest of spaces. "Knowing you approve might push me over the edge. It would be more helpful if you'd strongly disapprove. Or, better yet, remind me of my role in the community and how people look up to me and that I still want to be able to look them in the eye after he leaves. I don't want anyone to feel sorry for me. I had enough of that growing up."

The car swerved sharply to avoid a pothole. "What are you talking about?"

"Pity." She sat back and slumped down in the seat so her knees touched the dashboard. "It's inescapable when you're an orphan in a small town. You know that."

"Lib, nobody feels sorry for you. Maybe when you were a kid, but you're an adult now. Responsible. Stable. No one could fault you for wanting a baby."

Libby wished that were true. "Not if I were doing this the normal way. But I'm not, Jen. My plan isn't the least bit normal—not by Sentinel Pass standards, anyway. But by keeping the donor aspect a business transaction, I can at least maintain a certain degree of dignity. I'm not going to blow that on a quick thrill."

"Who said it would be quick?" her friend returned with a roguish chuckle. "Given his party-boy reputation, he should be pretty experienced. You might be passing up a chance of a lifetime."

Libby laughed. "Stop it. You're not helping."

"I'm just saying you have to do what's right for you and not worry about what the town thinks. Nobody is going to judge— Wait, that's not true. Everybody is going to judge you, but they're going to do that whether you have sex with Coop or just get pregnant by him. Either way, they'll talk, so why not grab a little gusto in the process?"

"Because…how do I put this?" *I'm a lousy lay.* "The few guys I've been to bed with haven't been impressed. John said I was too uptight. Tobin suggested I see a sex therapist." After she refused to give him a blow job in the kitchen while Megan was in the adjoining room watching a video. John, her first serious boyfriend, had taken her virginity after an evening of too much drinking and had been put off when she complained that it hurt.

"If—" she stressed the word in a low whisper "—I gave in to this weird attraction between us, the experience might be so bad he'd leave without honoring our agreement."

Jenna shook her head slowly from side to side. They were approaching the outskirts of town, so she eased her foot off the gas and let the car coast down the long hill. "We both know I'm no expert on men, but I think most of them would take bad sex over no sex in a heartbeat. And if the scandal sheets are to be believed, Cooper's a bit of a hound dog. As long as you have a good supply of condoms handy, I think you should go for it."

The funny buzzing sensation in her abdomen returned. "He has a bad foot."

Jenna reached out and touched Libby's arm. "Honey, that's not the part of his body you need to worry about being impaired."

Libby slugged her on the shoulder. The car swerved but only in jest. Jenna was a safe driver, even if she was an X-rated sounding board.

Coop decided he deserved an Oscar. The women bought

his sleeping act one hundred percent, which meant they'd been utterly candid the whole drive home. He'd missed a couple of things when they'd talked in whispers, but he'd managed to get the important stuff. Libby didn't dare make love with him because she was afraid the town would find out and she'd be embarrassed when he left.

He wasn't sure how to use that for his heroine or how to get around it where Libby was concerned, but he understood her better now. Not only was Sentinel Pass a security blanket of sorts, she felt she owed the town something for helping to raise her. The proverbial *village* everyone was always talking about. His mother had been the only citizen in his village. She'd made sure of that.

And Libby gives back by assuming the role her grandmother once filled, he thought. *Damn, this is good. Heroic, even.*

Which, he realized, made him look like an opportunistic scoundrel by comparison. He let out a soft groan and shifted on the seat.

"Coop?" Libby called tentatively. "Are you awake?"

He knew he'd blown his cover, so he stretched and tried to sit up. A crick in his neck made him choke on a stabbing jolt of pain. Muscles he hadn't known existed suddenly cried out in protest.

"I'm going to fire Evan," he snapped through clenched teeth. "My personal trainer. My God, I'm falling apart."

When he rolled his shoulders, every tendon and synapse shrieked. Even if he'd wanted to show Libby he was more than a *hound dog* as Jenna had put it, there was no way he could perform. Thank God they weren't on a set; the director would have called for a body double and Coop would have missed all the fun.

And he honestly didn't see why he couldn't have his cake and eat it, too, as they say. There was legitimate sizzle between him and Libby. She'd admitted she was interested in him. And Lord knew he was hot for her. So a couple of guys didn't get her. Big deal. Reviews meant nothing to him unless they pertained to his performance. Maybe he could offer to sign an addendum to the paternity agreement promising to honor his side of the bargain even if they did have sex.

LIBBY FILLED THE quilted tote bag she'd bought at the last Founder's Day festival with everything she thought she'd need: Gran's electric foot bath, a jar of Epsom salts, her manicure kit, the organic pedicure cream Megan had given her for Christmas and a three-pack of condoms.

Her cheeks heated up as she hid the strip—which she'd purchased six months earlier when she'd been dating Tobin—under the plastic foot bath. Tobin Arness was a postal clerk from Hot Springs she'd met at a union meeting. They'd only gone out half a dozen times. Five times too many. His scathing assessment of her ability to please a man in bed had been one of the motivations behind her decision to try IVF. The doctor doing the in vitro fertilization wasn't going to give a damn how well she spread her legs as long as her insurance covered the cost of the procedure.

"These are just a precaution," she murmured under her breath as she left the house.

Yeah, right, her practical voice returned.

Libby hated that she couldn't fool herself. Sometimes a little self-delusion was allowed, wasn't it? A foot bath and pedicure wasn't a blatant invitation to fool around. And despite Jenna's assurance that a blister or two wouldn't impede the average man's ability to have sex, Cooper might not be feeling all that amorous.

"Uh-huh. Right," she muttered, closing the door behind her. "He's in pain. I can help. This is what I do. I take care of people. My family. My town. My hired sperm donor."

She stopped midway between her house and the cabin and took a deep breath. It was only a little after eight, but without

a moon, the night sky was a cloak of black velvet with thousands of tiny pinpricks of light showing through. The stillness
was alleviated only by the chorus of frogs coming out of hi-
bernation in the nearby creek. She glanced toward her
brother's house. Completely dark. Mac had left a message on
her machine saying he hadn't been able to get the part he
needed so they were staying over another night.

No help there if she wanted someone to talk her out of
doing this.

The roof of the cabin was visible against the sky, even
given the darkness. A single light shone through the gingham
curtains in the rear window. The bedside lamp.

She treasured honesty, and the God's honest truth was she
wanted to make love with Cooper Lindstrom. Not the celebrity that most of the world knew but the man she'd spent the
past five days getting to know. As bizarre as their pairing
might sound—postmaster and TV star—she desperately
wanted to taste a little bit of the vibrant light he gave off.

Even though being with him was sure to end badly and
would probably mean exposing herself to criticism and
possible ridicule—she could almost hear the women of
Sentinel Pass shaking their heads and saying, "Poor Libby.
She actually thought he cared for her"—she made up her
mind to do it. If the worst happened and he left without ful-
filling his part of the bargain…well, she'd deal with that, too.

If you think about it, she told herself, *I'm not any worse off
now than I was before he came. I'm still me. Alone. Back to
square one.*

She resumed walking toward the cabin. And the truth was,
she was ready to take the risk and stroll a few steps on the wild
side. Just once in her safe little life.

HEROINE DECIDES TO make love with hero.

Coop looked at what he'd just typed on his laptop.

Wrong, wrong, wrong. It was too soon for them to hook up. Consummation would ruin the sexual tension that had to build for a couple of seasons. Only after the viewing public was fed up with the will-she-or-won't-he repartee did the main couple get to fall into bed together.

He sighed and closed the laptop. Plot was Shane's strong point. Coop was the idea man, and at the moment the only idea that zipped around his head was how to get laid. His libido had been on hold for too long—even before his mother's death. He didn't know why. Dissatisfaction? Lord, he hoped not. He was going back to that life in a few short days, and Libby was staying here. So, if by some wild stretch of the imagination he could talk her into his bed and they actually hit it off… Well, crap, the whole thing sucked.

A light tap sounded on the outer door. He sat up, swinging his bare legs to the floor. He started to stand up, but a shooting pain in his foot made him drop back. He adjusted the sheet and blanket across his lap. "Come in. It's not locked."

He'd left the bedroom door ajar, so he had a clear view of Libby as she walked in carrying a big bag. "Whatcha got? Food? I am kinda hungry."

She popped her head around the door. "How do you manage to stay so slim the way you eat?"

"Mom said I had a quick metabolism."

"Lucky dog."

"She said that, too."

He heard the sound of water running at the sink. A moment later she appeared in the doorway with a large molded-plastic tub in her hands. As she drew closer, he recognized what she was carrying. A foot massager. He'd seen one in a catalog on the airplane. He'd had several professional pedicures in his life, although those had involved a fancy chair that massaged his back while his feet soaked.

"Oh, cool," he said. "You didn't have to, but…thanks."

She set the contraption on the throw rug beside the bed and reached under the bedside table to plug it in. A soft roar sent a cascade of bubbles over the rim. He leaned down to catch the spill, but she beat him to it. Their skulls bumped.

"Oops. Sorry. I filled it a little too full. I haven't used it since Gran moved. Let it run a few minutes to warm up, then put your feet in. I'll get another towel."

She disappeared into the small bathroom. After returning home from their hike he'd stood in the shower until the hot water had run out. He felt much better, except for his feet.

"This is pretty generous of you, considering I got us lost today," he called.

She returned with the damp towel he'd used and another that had been hanging on the bar. "It was partly my fault. I thought the trail you wound up on looped back. If I'd stopped you sooner, we could have turned around."

"Well, I appreciate you not leaving me behind. I can be a bit of an ass from time to time. Probably comes from having people pander to your every whim and desire. Thank God I wasn't born to be king. Or president."

She smiled. They'd talked a little politics during the early stage of their hike and had agreed they had not a smidgen in common. She listened to NPR every day, while he caught the occasional sound bite on CNN.

"Okay," she said, setting up a small plastic stool she'd brought with her. The clever contraption folded shut until she pushed out the sides. Noticing his interest in it, she told him, "I bought a couple of these for Megan so she can reach the sink. They're cheap and strong."

Once she was seated, she nodded toward the water. "Go ahead and put your feet in. Oh, wait, I forgot the Epsom salts."

She dashed into the kitchen, then quickly returned. "There," she said after dumping half the bottle into the water. "Will it sting?"

"I don't know," she said soberly. "I called Gran to ask what was good for sore feet and she said Epsom salts. I don't even know what they are."

"Your honesty isn't as reassuring as a good lie would have been," he told her.

"Is there such a thing as a good lie?" she asked.

He was sorry he'd brought up the subject. Instead of answering, he made a production of slowly lowering his feet into the water—big toe first. "It's hot."

"It's supposed to be."

He closed his eyes and plunged his right foot all the way in. The initial shock immediately gave way to soothing comfort. "Not bad." He put the left in. "Nice, in fact."

She rocked back with a satisfied smile. Glancing at the clock near the lamp, she said, "You should soak at least ten minutes, then, if you want, I could give you a pedicure before I dress your blisters."

A pedicure? The idea sounded sort of intimate given where they were—and the fact that he was naked beneath the covers that were pulled across his lap. He swallowed. "Sure. That would be great. Do you do this for all your hiking partners?"

She grinned. "Actually, last fall, our bookclub read a book by John Muir, then we did a fourteen-mile hike on the Mickelson. When we got back, we all took turns soaking our feet and giving each other pedicures."

"Sounds like a Sentinel Pass version of an orgy."

She threw back her chin and laughed. She'd never looked more beautiful, relaxed and happy. And the feeling that grabbed him midchest—right around his heart—was one he'd felt twice before. Shortly before he'd proposed to his wives.

Oh, crap, he thought. *Not good. Not good at all. Bad timing for my hero and really bad timing for me.*

Ignore it, he told himself. *You can have sex without falling in love. You heard her when she was talking to Jenna. Other*

*men have made love to her and didn't wind up walking down
the aisle. Get a grip, man. You're about to exploit her life. Even
if you tell her the truth and she agrees it's a great idea—which
it is—she's bound to have second thoughts somewhere down
the line. You'll make your mother's prediction come true and
be a three-time loser.*

Sex? Yes.

Love? No. Hell, no.

CHAPTER THIRTEEN

LIBBY DECIDED IF SHE lived to be Gran's age, she'd never be more embarrassed. What was she thinking? She didn't know how to seduce a man. She needed to put all thoughts of sex out of her mind and concentrate on what she did know how to do—give pedicures.

"I'll do your right foot first," she said, picking up the fluffy white towel she'd rushed to Bed, Bath & Beyond to buy as soon as she'd found out he was coming. As if fancy towels might somehow bridge the gap between his world and hers.

She draped it across her knees and modestly averted her eyes while he situated himself on the bed. It hadn't escaped her notice that he was probably naked beneath that layer of sheets and blanket bunched around his lap. She could see his tan line. Low, low on his hips. Her mouth went dry.

A heavy weight settled on her knee. She looked down. Dripping wet foot. Long and a bit bony, but a beautiful shade of honey. Of course, he'd have to be that gorgeous, surreal color you saw in magazines. He lived on the beach, she reminded herself. If anyone was going to be that color, it was Coop.

She used the towel to wipe the foot, rubbing the coarse dark-blond hair that was wet to just above the ankle. His calves were substantial and beautifully sculpted. His knee… "Is that a scar?" she asked, touching her finger to the thin white happy-face smile someone had etched just below his kneecap.

"Yeah. Skiing accident."

She resisted the urge to lean over and kiss it. "Must have hurt."

He heaved a great sigh. "Actually, I've never been skiing in my life. My mother thought it was too dangerous. My various trips to Vail were spent drinking and making excuses for not skiing. This happened on the set when I tripped over a power cable and landed on some kind of equipment. Bled like it hit an artery. The director talked Mom into keeping things quiet because of some OSHA infraction, so I didn't go to the emergency room. She made up the story about the ski injury years later when some reporter asked about the scar."

"It could have gotten infected."

"It did. Mom knew somebody who had some left over antibiotics. I know, I know, that's a crazy way to screw up your body. Jenna's mom got on a rant the other day about the medical profession's abuse of antibiotics and how it grew a superbug. Don't tell her I was one of the guinea pigs, okay?"

She chuckled and returned her attention to his foot. "It'll be our little secret," she said. One among many.

She made sure each toe was dry, then she picked up her clipper and carefully trimmed each nail. "You have nice feet," she said idly. "Strong, masculine toes."

His laugh made her look up.

"What?"

There was a poignant edge to his smile that made her heart skip a beat. God, he was handsome. Too handsome. Especially when his hair was standing up in places. His lashes looked too heavy for him to keep his eyes open.

"Nothing. Inside joke. What is it about you that makes me remember all these weird things? Like the fake ski accident. I repeated the first version so often I think I started believing it happened—but as soon as I said it, the truth hit me."

"So what memory did my praise of your toes dig up?"

He eased back on his elbows and looked at the ceiling.

"When I was twelve or so, I did a bunch of print ads. Catalogs. JCPenney. Macy's. That sort of thing. Not very glamorous but fairly good money. The lady who booked me made some lewd comment about the size of my feet. I guess they seemed disproportionately big for my age or something. Mom put her up against the wall and told her never to call us again. That was…memorable."

"Do you remember what she said?"

"Something like, 'Big feet mean a big you know what. He ought to have a great career in porn. Some of the best are fags.'"

Libby felt her mouth drop open. "The witch. I'd have smacked her around, too. I bet your mother was livid."

"Actually, I think she was afraid the woman might have been right about me being gay. I never had a serious girlfriend until my mid teens. Then I landed a role on a soap opera. Believe me, what happens on-screen can't hold a candle to what was going on when the camera was turned off."

She worked the soothing cucumber lotion into his skin, massaging the sole of his foot. "Isn't that where you met your first wife?"

He made a soft moan of appreciation. "That feels great. Huh? Oh, yes. Tiffany joined the cast a few years later. She was twenty, but she was playing sixteen-year-old Shannon Montworthy, my adopted stepsister who, it turned out, may or may not have been my father's illegitimate daughter. Gasp. Did we commit incest? And since my character was twenty-two, had I committed statutory rape—even though she was a prick tease from the word go and begged me to do it?"

She laughed. "Was she acting or playing herself?" she asked, setting his foot on the floor. She patted her knee for the other one.

Cooper sat up and bent over to unplug the foot bath, then gave her his left foot. The skin around his toes was withered from soaking so long. She was careful to avoid the huge raw circles on his heel and under his big toe.

"T-fancy—my pet name for her—was and still is a serious actor devoted to her craft. She's gone on to do some very good stuff. The problem is most people still think of her as a soap ingenue. Tough label to shake, although Meg Ryan did it, and I think Tiffany will too—eventually."

She was curious about his past but didn't want to pry. Clippers in hand, she tackled his big toe and asked, "How long were you married?"

"A lifetime, by Hollywood standards."

She glanced up.

"Eighteen months."

"Oh."

"Morgana and I only lasted four. So T-fancy claims I loved her more. Morgi hates that."

"Is she right?"

He didn't answer right away. His beautiful lips puckered as if in deep thought. "I loved them both…at the time. Still do…in a way, even though they drive me crazy and are bleeding me dry. We were mutually beneficial to each other at the time."

Mutually beneficial. The expression made her uncomfortable. His rationale sounded a lot like the one she'd used when she put her ad together for the Internet.

She quickly finished his toes, then put some antibiotic ointment on the sores before picking up the bottle of lotion. He wiggled his toes when she applied some to the arch of his foot.

"That tickles."

"Sorry."

"Don't be. It feels good. Better than I deserve."

"You were actually a very good sport today. Certainly better than I expected you to be."

"Because I'm a self-absorbed celebrity?"

She shrugged. "You have a different kind of lifestyle."

"Not necessarily better or worse. Just different, right? Mom used to say that when I asked why our family was different from 'normal' people."

Her hands stilled. "Gran used to tell me the same thing."

She looked into his eyes and felt a pull so strong and so deep in her gut she had no choice but to follow it. He must have felt the same thing, because he opened his arms and motioned "come" with his fingers, the way she did to guide a delivery truck to the loading dock. The towel across her knees dropped to the floor and she was in his arms.

They tumbled backward when her weight knocked him off balance. She felt foolish at first—fully dressed up against his bare torso—but his arms were strong and they held her close, as if he was really happy she was there.

"We're going to make love, aren't we?" she asked.

"I think so. I want to. Do you?"

She couldn't speak, her throat was too tight. She couldn't believe she'd found the nerve to ask. But she nodded.

He turned them so they were lying side by side, facing each other. He very tenderly touched her hair, brushing her bangs back so he could see her eyes. "I like you, Libby. I didn't expect this to happen and I don't want to do something that might jeopardize our agreement, but…"

She was amazed he could think clearly when her brain had turned to absolute mush. All she wanted at the moment was to experience more of what she'd felt when he'd kissed her. She might not be able to give pleasure—aside from a foot massage—but she could receive it. And no matter what this experience cost her, she was ready. "I won't hold you to our bargain if this doesn't turn out well. I promise."

His low chuckle reverberated through the mattress and into the base of her spine. She shivered from the simple joy it gave her.

"I'm not worried about tonight. We're going to be great together. I meant outside influences… There are things—"

She stopped listening after *going to be great together.* Nobody had ever said that to her before, and for the first time in her life she could almost believe it was possible. She felt different with him. Relaxed. Joyful. Complete. Womanly.

"Can we not talk anymore and kiss?" she asked, bringing his head to hers.

His smile was his answer. She memorized it before closing her eyes and diving into the warmth of his skin, his smell and his touch.

I tried to tell her, he rationalized in one small part of his mind, even as her sweet, inquisitive tongue rubbed across his crooked eyetooth. *In the morning. Won't be too late.* He hoped. Because he might have arrived in Sentinel Pass with an ulterior motive, but he was in bed with her with nothing else in mind other than making love with her.

She was so very different from his exes that she made this experience wholly new. He honestly felt tingles of excitement run from fingertips to toes. Soft, pleasured toes. Hands that could pleasure toes could pleasure other parts of his body, as well, he decided. From what he'd overheard earlier, she didn't think of herself as a sexual creature. Some idiots had traumatized her. His job, he decided, was going to be bringing her inner sex goddess back to life.

He was the man to do it. He didn't know how he knew that, but he did—once he got her out of her clothes.

"You're still dressed. Serious oversight on my part." He kept his tone light to make sure she didn't take the observation as a criticism. "Fortunately, I'm quite practiced at removing women's clothing. I won a Daytime Emmy for it. 'Best new actor-slash-boy-toy in a featured role.'"

He raised up, dragging the sheet with him to keep from exposing himself. She had some catching up to do on several levels, and his hard-on was going to have to wait.

He gently pushed her onto her back, then paused a few

heartbeats for dramatic effect. "The top of the blouse is the best place to begin because it's strategically placed. A slight brush of the heel of the hand across the breast. *Intentional or accident?* the audience wonders."

She looked around. "What audience?"

"Good point. The seducee wonders," he amended.

"Are you sure you're the seducer? What if I told you there's a strip of condoms in my tote bag?"

The mischievous glint in her eyes made him laugh out loud, then swoop in for a kiss. "I'd say I lo—I think you're wonderful," he smoothly amended. "Now, back to the play-by-play."

She sighed. "Could we speed things up just a bit? You're naked and I want to be."

He shook his head. "Everybody's a director. I'm coming to the naked part. Shirt first…" He finished off the buttons. "Then bra." He delicately nudged the soft flannel panels apart to reveal bare skin and perfect breasts. "What? No bra?"

He made light of the fact, but inside his head he couldn't quite get around the idea. His body knew how to react without conscious thought. Her skin was a luminous shade of peach. Her breasts full and perky, with rosy nipples all puckered up as if saying, *Kiss me, you fool.*

He touched them first. Just to make sure they were real. So real. She inhaled deeply, bringing them closer to his face, his mouth. He outlined one nipple with his tongue. It danced under his playful manipulation while Libby squirmed in response.

"Can I change my Native name to Dances With Nipples?" he murmured, his mouth watering from the barest taste of her.

"That…feels…go-good," she said on a staccato release of breath.

He leaned closer, slightly pinning her legs and pelvis with his weight, then took the nipple in his mouth and suckled. Her chin arched and she groaned. One of her hands moved in his hair, urging him closer. The other trailed up his bare arm to his shoulder. Her leg looped over his hip.

She might not think she knew how to play this game, but her body had all the right moves down pat, he thought, levering her thigh a little higher. He reached down with his free hand and applied pressure to the juncture between her legs.

"Oh," she moaned. "Why are my jeans still on?"

She sat up and looked at him, her languid half-closed eyes giving him a sexy, pouting appraisal. "Boy-toy-of-the-year needs my help, I think." She quickly shrugged out of her shirt, tossing it carelessly toward where she'd been sitting, and then wiggled free of her jeans and underpants. He caught a glimpse of white against the blue as both pieces of clothing went sailing past his head.

"Much better," she said. "Where were we?"

He laughed. "You aren't as shy and demure as I thought."

"Apparently you bring out some latent wanton wench in me."

"Wanton works for me. Come here, me pretty." He closed one eye in a Johnny Depp impression and gave a piratelike leer.

Her feminine giggle sealed his fate. He was hers. Heart and soul. And now he got to prove it—even if he didn't dare tell her how he felt.

"I…I BOUGHT A BOOK. O-ordered it online," Libby said, her voice coming in little bursts. The feel of his tongue on her breasts made her pant most tellingly. "A h-how-to on s-sex."

She couldn't believe she was admitting something so private and silly, but Libby had decided if she ever got the chance to make love again, she was going to do it right. The book had been frank and unapologetic about a person's right to not only have sex but enjoy it.

"Did you read it?" Cooper asked. He was lying partly on top of her. Enough that she could feel the length of his erection against her thigh, but he hadn't made any attempt to straddle her, as her previous partners would have.

She nodded.

"What did it say about foreplay?"

He moved his chin with its hint of five-o'clock shadow back and forth on her breast bone in the valley of her bosom. The friction went straight to her core.

"The author was in favor of it," she said, striving for normalcy.

"Me, too," he said, smiling that famous grin that made her heart stop momentarily.

She knew what the book said, but she was curious about how he perceived that part of the sex act. "Why?"

He rubbed his nose along the underside of her breast, ever so softly tasting her skin. "Discovery. How else are you going to know what the person you're making love with likes? How else can you tell her what you like?"

He caressed her ribs.

"I like that. D-do you?"

She splayed her fingers against his warm skin and pressed firmly to feel each bone of his rib cage. He shivered slightly. "Oh, yeah."

His hand traveled over her bare hip and she sucked in a breath involuntarily. His smile encouraged her try the same thing on him. In the past, she might have hurried right down to his you-know-what, since she'd been told that men liked to "get the show on the road," as one of her lovers had put it. But Cooper moved languidly—as though he was memorizing every inch of her.

So she took her sweet time, too. And, oh, there was so much to feel. His body was perfection—but not perfect. Her fingers paused when they found a tiny divot near the small of his back.

"I had a suspicious mole removed," he said. "Too much sun. Makes living on the beach a bit challenging."

She put his hand on her thigh, rubbing his finger across an

inch-long ribbon of scar tissue. "The bottom fell out of a canning jar. I was wearing shorts. Blood and peaches all over the kitchen. It was a mess."

"Poor baby," he murmured, inching down to kiss the spot. Then he kept going, turning her slightly so he could tenderly caress the backs of her knees.

Shivers raced upward and outward. She closed her eyes, reveling in this new and amazing sensation. She could feel herself opening, moist and eager.

Patience builds anticipation, the book had said. She'd had no idea what that meant until now.

He cleverly worked his way along the inside of her thigh, drawing closer to the mound of curly hair at the junction of her thighs. Was this the point where he'd suddenly bury his face in her crotch and expect her to rejoice in orgasm?

He must have sensed her sudden tensing, because he lifted his head and looked at her a moment. "Your turn to find my erogenous zone. *Zones,*" he corrected. "There are at least two major ones."

He flopped on his back, arranging the pillow under his head, then dropping his arms flat, palms up. His naked body lay exposed to her complete appraisal. So…she looked.

"If I looked that good naked, I'd never get dressed," she said, not meaning for the words to come out. But they did.

He smiled, but there was a serious look in his eyes now. He'd put himself out there, and it was her turn to take the plunge. So she explored. With her eyes, then her hands. She started at his ankles and worked her way up, detouring around the most obvious erogenous zone.

She let her hair trail over his penis and she heard him suck in a sharp breath. She liked the sudden sense of power his response gave her. She'd never felt in control of her lovemaking experiences in the past, but now she had him where she wanted him, and they both knew it.

Boldly she ran her tongue along the inside of his pelvis and upward to his belly button. His abs rippled in response. She glanced at his face and saw him grimace with pleasure. "Found one," she chortled triumphantly.

He licked his lips and let out the breath he'd been holding. "Definitely."

She tried his nipples next, but even teasing them with her teeth, as the book had suggested, didn't earn her that coveted response. She moved on to his neck. She buried her nose against his skin and inhaled. She loved his scent—masculine and delicious. She worked her way up to his right earlobe.

His whole body clenched.

"Bingo," she whispered, running the tip of her tongue around the outer rim.

"Common. I know. But...oh..." The word was lost in a shiver as she worked the delicate lobe between her teeth. His moan triggered something inside her she'd never felt before. A need that for once seemed to match her partner's.

She kissed him and reached for the part of him she'd only touched with her hair. He explored, too, gauging her body's readiness with first one finger, then two. With a low, hungry moan, he asked, "Condoms?"

"Bottom of the bag."

He worked fast, his languid pace behind them. He sheathed himself as she watched. His hands liquid and sure. The sight of him took her breath away—but in heady anticipation, not fear.

And once he entered her, the answer she'd always sought was there. In his breadth and instinctual response to her rhythm. The one she hadn't even known she possessed. And moments later, to her breathless joy and only slight amazement, she experienced exactly what the book had spent two chapters explaining.

CHAPTER FOURTEEN

LIBBY CAREFULLY stretched and opened her eyes. Her internal alarm clock served her well, she realized, confirming the time with Cooper's watch on the bedside table. He was sleeping on his side, facing the wall. And hour or so earlier, they'd been spooning. A position that had naturally led to a joining unlike anything she'd experienced before in her life. Her heart raced just thinking about it. So natural, so easy.

Sex with Cooper had been fun, exhilarating, second nature. She never once froze or felt foolish, awkward or embarrassed. She didn't know why that was except to put the credit on him. He'd been easygoing, gentle and self-deprecating. If something didn't work, he made her laugh, turning the joke on himself.

She'd never had more fun in bed. Her only regret was they were in the cabin. She wished they'd spent the night in her bed so she could relive the memory each night when she closed her eyes. This truly had been the experience of a lifetime. She didn't regret a moment of it, but now it was time to get up.

She slipped out from under the covers, gasping at the morning chill. She picked up her discarded jeans, undies and shirt. She'd never forget the look on his face when he realized she wasn't wearing a bra. A bold move on her part but one that had paid off. He'd lavished praise on her breasts all night long. The poor man probably never got to see a nonsurgically embellished pair, she thought with a naughty grin.

As she prepared to leave, she noticed the foot bath sitting

to one side, still filled with disgusting-looking grayish water. She'd have to leave it for Cooper to clean up. She did grab the towels to add to the laundry at her house, though. As she started to stuff them into the bag, she paused. An unopened condom package sat staring up at her.

How was that possible? she wondered. *I'm pretty sure we did it three times.* The first, which she would forever call their foreplay game. The second, when she was on top. A revelation unto itself. And then the third, when they were both still partly asleep.

"Oh, no," she murmured.

Cooper made a quiet snuffling sound and rolled over. His hair was sticking up in every direction, like a little boy's. Her heart swelled to fill the inside of her chest. God, she loved him. And when he left in two days, she'd carry this precious memory close to her heart, letting it shade the perceptions her child would form of his or her father.

He'd promised not to go back on their deal for any reason. He'd even hinted that he had more to tell her about his plans for the future, but they'd been too busy making love to talk.

She stuffed the towels into the bag and shoved her feet into her loafers. They'd managed to discuss the health factor, and she felt reasonably safe, even though she would have preferred that they'd used protection every time. The chance she'd get pregnant from that one time seemed remote, if not ridiculous. But since she was going to use the IVF with his sperm once he left, why even think about it? The fertility doctor would tell her if he'd been less than honest with her diseasewise.

Half an hour later, she hurried out the door of her house and started her car. She was going to be late for the first time since she'd become postmaster. Probably thanks to the lack of sleep, she just didn't seem able to stay focused on what she needed to do: shower, dress, eat…. She felt jittery inside. As though small earthquakes were going on all around her and she was the only one who seemed to notice.

Had the stars realigned themselves in the night? Quite possibly.

She parked in her usual spot, grabbed her purse and got out. Then remembered her keys, which were on the seat. She quickly retrieved them, grateful she hadn't locked the door with them still in the Xterra, and walked to the rear door.

Both rural carriers were waiting.

"You sick?" Clive asked through the steam of the mug he held to his lips.

She could smell the butterscotch-flavored java from four feet away. "No. I'm fine. Just overslept."

"Not like you."

She unlocked the door and went inside. Everything was the same…yet different. She couldn't put her finger on it.

She started a pot of coffee and kept out of the way of the carriers as they did the initial sorting that she usually had done by the time they arrived. She didn't hear a word of their chatter until Clive said, "Hey, lookee there. Your fancy boy's got his picture on the cover of the *National Perspirer*." His name for the periodical several of the patrons on his route received.

"He's not my fancy b—" she started to say, but her words got caught in her throat when she read the headline over the blurry photo that was indeed an image of Cooper standing in the doorway of Gran's cabin.

Coop's New Love Nest?

She tried to laugh, but the sound came out strangled. Talk about art imitating life. Whoever took this shot couldn't have known that she and Cooper were going to be fooling around last night—*she* hadn't even known it.

"Pure trash. They make up everything. You know that."

"I told you word would get out about him being here,"

Clive said. "You can't keep a lid on that forever. Although you still haven't told us why he's here."

And she wasn't about to. Not yet. She didn't trust people to understand—especially since she wasn't quite sure how she felt at the moment, either. Last night had changed things. She knew that much, but she couldn't say what would happen next.

Clive kept reading. "Says here he's making a pilot for a TV show about a postmistress who goes on the Internet to hire a guy to be a sperm donor. Don't they know you're a post*master*, not a postmistress?"

All the blood ran out of Libby's head and pooled in her feet. She swayed and had to grab the edge of the sorting desk to keep from falling over. She grabbed the paper out of his hands, nearly shredding it in the process.

"Hey," Clive groused. "That's Milly's paper. She'll have my head if you tear it."

Libby didn't give a damn. She needed to read the article and dashed into her tiny office, closing the door behind her. "No, no, no," she muttered, willing it not to be word for word what Clive had just read. "A mistake. A lucky guess. Please don't let it be the truth."

The leak was attributed to Cooper's ex-wife. His first ex-wife, Libby thought bitterly. Infancy. The name suited. A bitch who sold out Cooper to get her name—and a small color photo—on the front page of this rag.

He told her. She could picture the two of them reading her online ad out loud. Laughing.

Her face felt fiery-hot. Humiliation surged through her veins, as powerful and intense as what she'd felt in his arms the night before. "The bastard came here planning to use my story as the basis for a television show," she whispered. "A comedy."

She continued reading, her mind besieged by a monsoon of emotions. Fury. Hurt. Dismay. And finally…panic. When she read the closing quote: "I'll probably be joining Coop on-site in·Sentinel Pass soon. He's been there scouting locations for our upcoming shoots. Think Mayberry meets Bedrock."

Her brain flashed to the image of his amused murmuring when she'd pulled into the parking lot of the Flintstones theme park in Custer. Her stomach turned over as the undeniable truth hit her.

"Not the town, Coop. Me? I deserve whatever ridicule comes from what I did. But not Sentinel Pass." If she'd had more than a few sips of coffee that morning, she would have vomited all over the standard bulk mail.

She read the entire article again. Only two direct mentions of the town's name. Maybe the Pass's remote location would keep the newshounds at bay, she thought. For a little while. Until she could figure out what to tell the people she had inadvertently betrayed.

But that small consolation didn't ease the horror of Cooper's subterfuge. She'd trusted him with her most intimate secrets. She'd opened herself up to him in every possible way. Would her character on his show be as naive? Would he use what happened between them last night?

A small sob burst from her lips. The pressure of unshed tears made her squint in pain, but she refused to cry. There'd be time for that later—after she called her PMR to take over so Libby could go home and kick Cooper Lindstrom the hell out of her grandmother's cabin. The lying dog could damn well keep his sperm and go directly to hell.

COOP AWOKE FEELING as if the weight of two full-grown elephants had been removed from his shoulders. He could take a deep breath and feel the air go all the way to the bottom of his lungs, instead of getting stuck halfway there because of a tightening in his chest.

Worry. Grief. Fear. Constant companions since his

mother's death seemed to have left the building. He didn't understand how one night in the arms of a woman he barely knew could produce such a radical shift in his perspective, but he knew this change was due to more than sex alone.

He sat up and looked around. The sun—had it ever shone so brightly?—filled the room with a pure yellow-gold he'd never noticed before. He grabbed his watch from the bedside table and put it on as he swung his legs over the side of the bed. He paused to run his hand across the slight impression still visible in the pillow Libby had used.

What a surprise she'd been. From not wearing a bra beneath her prudish flannel shirt to the breathless joy they'd shared when she realized she could not only control but prologue their pleasure by taking the top position.

He smiled a moment longer, then stood.

The rag rug had become lost under the bed, so the painted wood floor was darn chilly. His toes—bandage-free and feeling no residual effects of the hike—curled tight. He showered and dressed before cleaning up the mess from the foot massages. He was just dumping the brackish water on a rosebush near the front porch when the roar of a truck engine caught his ear.

"Libby?" he murmured, his smile growing.

No. Alas, the four-wheel-drive diesel belonged to her brother. Mac pulled to a stop and got out, then opened the back passenger door to help Megan out of her booster seat. The little girl jumped down excitedly and ran to greet him. "Hi, Mr. Coop. We're back. We went to Denver. I played with Fayth and Mariya. They both have y's in their names. Daddy says that's because their mommy and daddy have to be different."

Coop set the plastic foot bath on the porch and gave his full attention to Libby's niece. He'd never been around children outside the set, but this girl fascinated him. She seemed so articulate and bright—like a miniature adult. Would his and

Libby's child be so gifted? The question startled him. Would he have any way of knowing if he or she were? The answer seemed pretty obvious, and he didn't like the bad taste it left in his mouth.

He talked to her a minute longer, learning that Fayth was "sebben" and Mariya "three and a half." She made it clear that those months between her birthday and the younger child's were a gulf that only Megan's superior patience and age were able to bridge.

"Did you get the part you were looking for?" he asked Mac once Megan's attention had turned to picking flowers from the nearby bushes. "How'd you get back so early? Fly?"

Mac shook his head. "Naw, we drove. I bought the new bits I needed on Saturday, but the fittings for the drill are out of date. You can't buy them from a regular manufacturer. Luckily, I have a miner friend who is also a machinist. He can tool just about anything. Unfortunately, he didn't have it done until late last night."

"You must have left awfully early this morning."

Mac shrugged. "Megan was asleep. Made for a fast trip. Not so many stops."

Coop could understand that. Sort of.

"Lib at work?" Mac asked.

"I assume so. I just got up."

Mac's dark eyebrow arched, but he didn't say what Coop could clearly read in his expression: *Lazy bastard.*

The words echoed hauntingly in his mind. He didn't know why. Some leftover stigma from childhood? He doubted it. His mother had been candid about the circumstances surrounding his birth. "Your father didn't want to be a father, but I wanted to be a mother. Your mother. His loss was all the better for me because I didn't have to share you with him or his family."

People didn't use those kinds of labels anymore. Did they? He didn't have an answer. He wondered if Libby had thought about that question and had something planned to answer when their child asked why he or she didn't have a father. Or had she assumed that his inclusion via the Internet would make that stigma a nonissue? He mentally added the question to the list of things they needed to discuss before he left on Wednesday.

"I have to drop Megan off at the sitter, then I'm headed to the mine to put the new drill bits in. Wanna come?"

The offer sounded friendly. "You won't let me vegetate in the dark for a couple of hours, will you?"

Mac's grin looked rueful but not apologetic in the least. "No reason to go into the mine. We'll be working in the toolshed. But you might get dirty."

"Cool. I've got a couple of calls to make to the West Coast, but I'll be here whenever you're ready."

Mac whistled for Megan and pointed to the car. "We have to stop at home so you can brush your teeth."

"I already did, Daddy. Yesterday."

Mac looked skyward and shook his head. "Now. Pronto."

Megan skipped past, flashing Coop a smile that reminded him a lot of her aunt. He waited where he was until the truck had backed up, then he returned Megan's exuberant wave.

"Neat kid," he murmured, walking inside for his phone. He knew it was too early to call Shane, but he wouldn't have cell reception at the mine, so it was now or never.

The phone rang half a dozen times before a grouchy voice answered, "Go to hell and call back at a decent hour."

"Wuss. It's seven. Some people have been up for hours."

"None that went to bed at four."

"What were you doing up so late? Partying? You dog, you."

Shane made a growling sound that reverberated over the line. "Damage control, you ass. Your bigmouthed ex-wife decided to share what little she knows about this project with the world."

The world? "What could she say? I didn't tell her anything."

"Then she got it from your teenage assistant. The two have been seen all over town partying till the wee hours. They're tight. Probably working on a tell-all book about what it's like to sleep with and work for Cooper Lindstrom."

Coop's stomach started to churn—and he hadn't even had coffee yet. "Any mention of Mom's gambling problem or my finances?"

"No. The focus seems to be trained on your new love interest—the postmaster. Somebody snapped a shot of you poking your head out of some log cabin surrounded by evergreen trees. Secret love nest. Picture the bold print?"

He could. All too well. He wondered if there was any way he could keep Libby from seeing it. He muttered a few choice epithets about the opportunistic delivery guy who'd probably sold the photo for more money than he made in a week.

"What are you going to do?" Shane asked. His voice was starting to sound less grouchy.

"I have no idea. Should I wait to see if Libby gets wind of this? Believe it or not, I'd planned to tell her about the show today. I figured if she really hated the idea, we could still back out. It's not too late. We don't have to pitch it until August."

There was a stilted pause, then Shane said, "Um…well, actually, I took a meeting with the network yesterday. One of the shows they had in production fell apart. The female lead just got busted on drug trafficking. The good news is they loved the concept, the name, everything."

"The name? What name? We didn't decide on a name."

"I had to give them something, so I went with *Sentinel Pass Time*."

"What? That sucks, man. I hate it. Who came up with that?"

"I did. What's wrong with it?"

Libby was going to kill him. That was what was wrong with it. Bad enough he was using *her* story, but now her town was about to become a common household play on words, a potential tourist destination and at the very least a punch line in some late-night television host's monologue. He was dead meat.

CHAPTER FIFTEEN

"CALM DOWN, LIB. THIS steely-eyed Valkyrie isn't like you. You're scaring me."

Jenna's voice barely penetrated the haze of fury that had been building inside Libby's head all morning. She'd managed to get through four hours of torture by faking a sore throat. Whenever anyone came to her window asking about her "houseguest," she coughed and pointed to her voice box. "Laryngitis," she'd croak.

Luckily, no one had dropped in specifically to ask about the article. There'd been one call from the *Rapid City Journal,* the largest newspaper in the greater Hills area, but she'd played dumb. Not a stretch, considering how dumb, gullible and foolish she felt. Screwed, both literally and figuratively. And the worst part was she could almost see Coop's side of things.

Almost.

He'd seen an opportunity and gone for it. She'd invited him here. She was to blame for what happened next. But that didn't mean she could ever trust him again. He'd destroyed any chance of that happening by not being up front with her from the start. He'd toyed with her dreams and her heart, and now he had to leave. And he could take his sperm with him. As much as she wanted a child, she couldn't—wouldn't—use his sperm, because staying connected to him in any way would only prolong the pain of remembering what they'd shared.

"You don't get it, do you?" Libby said, pacing from the

picnic table to her Xterra and back. "He stole my story, used me to scope out the town and will be laughing all the way to the bank while we're left picking up the pieces after his stupid film crew and lookie loos leave. Sentinel Pass will never be the same, Jenna."

"Is that what you're upset about, Lib? Or are you afraid *you're* never going to be the same?"

She stopped pacing and faced her friend. "That's a given. We were together last night, Jenna. Lust and heavy breathing. The whole nine yards. It was g-good." *Perfect.* "For the first time in my life I experienced what all the women's magazines are always raving about. Finally I get why sex is such a big deal. But one of the reasons last night worked was because I trusted him. Just like he trusted me to get us out of the forest. But after this, I could never trust him again. Ever."

Jenna didn't try to argue with her. Some truths were self-evident. "So you want me to take over for you this afternoon. You're sure you don't need more time to cool down? I don't want you to make a mistake you're going to regret later."

Libby picked up her purse and started toward her car. "Believe me, I have a million regrets. The biggest is ever putting that ad online in the first place. Kicking Cooper Lindstrom out of Gran's house is going to feel great. I might not be able to stop what's coming, but I can get rid of some of the evidence."

Jenna frowned. "You're not talking about dumping his body down a mine shaft, are you?"

Libby could picture the image with some degree of pleasure, but she shook her head. "I'm going to make Mac drop him off at a motel in town. If he can't change his flight, he can rent a car and do whatever…as long as he never comes back here."

"What about his sperm?"

Libby hopped in her SUV, then rolled down the window. "He and his sperm can go to hell. I'm stopping by the bank and withdrawing as much of Mom's settlement money as I dare, then I'll run by the lawyer's office and get them to type up some kind of paper negating our earlier agreement. Maybe if I pay him, he'll call off this television project and leave us alone. Our original deal was based on a share of the mine over eighteen years. What I intend to offer will more than make up for that."

Jenna rushed to the truck. "Oh, Lib, no. Not the trust. That money was going to be the baby's college fund."

"There isn't going to be a baby, Jen. If I'm this stupid where men are concerned, what business do I have raising a kid? Maybe after I'm not so damn pissed off, I'll even thank Coop for keeping me from making the biggest mistake of some poor kid's life."

Jenna started to say something, but Libby cut her off. "I've got to go. Thanks for coming into work. When the calls start coming—and we both know they will, given the way gossip travels in this town—tell them I'll explain everything at the next town council meeting."

Then she backed up and headed toward the highway. Her bank was in Hill City. The money, which her father had always considered tainted, was a small price to pay for extricating herself from this mess. She hoped it would be enough to save her beloved town from certain disaster.

Coop perched on a fairly clean surface—a stool that had been the repository of a towering stack of dust-coated mining magazines. After being given permission to set the outdated periodicals on the floor of the shop, he'd pulled the wobbly wooden hunk of furniture closer to where Mac was working.

Everything in the cramped workshop appeared both old and greasy. The smell was something totally foreign to Coop's experience, but he liked it. There was a certain element of manliness to it. One got a sense that real men had sweated and toiled in this place and, in the process, talked about the issues of the day and the problems confronting them. Maybe. Or they might have been like Mac—silent to the point of consternation.

"What are you doing?"

"First, I'm rebuilding the starter."

"For your truck?"

"For the motor that runs the pump that takes water out of the mine."

"How does the water get into the mine?"

Mac took a deep breath as if drawing on his reserve of patience. "Seeps through the strata of rock. The Black Hills were formed by an uplifting of igneous and metamorphic rock covered by a thick marine layer that has been eroded away over some sixty-five million years or so."

"You know a lot about geology."

"Helps to avoid wasting time and money looking in the wrong spot for gold. If you know where to expect it, you have a better chance of finding it."

"Do you really think the Little Poke has gold left?"

"Hell, yes. I wouldn't be doing this if I didn't. All I need is a promising-looking vein to interest one of the big outfits. I've held off selling partly out of respect for my dad—this was his dream—and partly because of Lib. She doesn't want to do anything that will result in drastic changes to Sentinel Pass."

Coop swallowed hard. Maybe if he revealed the true reason he was here, Mac could help him figure out a way to tell Libby.

"Um, Mac, what would you say if I told you I had an ulterior reason for coming here?"

Mac stood up straight, a very large wrench in hand. "What kind of reason? Publicity?"

"No," Coop answered honestly. "I was hoping nobody would find out about this trip until…much later. After I had time to develop a television program loosely based on Libby's online ad. You know, selling a share of a mine in return for sperm."

Mac's eyes narrowed. "Did you tell her this?"

Coop felt his cheeks heat up. "I plan to. Today. I hope to make her see that the story has universal appeal. A lot of viewers will be able to identify with her situation."

"But you'd set it somewhere totally different. Like Beverly Hills or something. Right?" The look in Mac's eyes seemed to suggest that Coop should slither off the stool and disappear under any nearby rock.

"I can see how that might have been a good idea, but from what she told me about Sentinel Pass in our e-mails…well, the place emotes setting. This could be good for the town. Lots of new money coming in. I don't have any figures in front of me, but I'm sure *Northern Exposure* threw a hell of a lot of business Alaska's way when it was running. What town doesn't want money?"

Mac put a gloved hand to his face and rubbed his brow, leaving a black streak behind. "Oh, God," he groaned. "You really blew it, man. Lib's gonna take you to the most remote tunnel she can find and bury you to your eyeballs. What were you thinking?"

A chill passed down his back. "It was just an idea when I left L.A., but my friend talked to a few people who are interested. I didn't break any laws. By publishing her story online she sort of made it public domain."

Mac shook his head. "All that means is you've covered your ass enough to ease the pain when she kicks it back to Hollywood."

Coop slumped over, put his elbow on his knee, then plopped his chin in the palm of his hand. "You're right. I know you are. I blew it. Especially after last night."

Mac dropped the wrench and slowly turned to look at Coop. "What happened last night?"

Coop slid off the stool. The hairs on the back of his neck stood up and his breathing quickened. He'd never been in a fight—a real fight—in his life. "Uh…nothing. I mean, whatever happened is between your sister and me. I better go."

"Good idea. There's a plane leaving for Denver at four. That should give Mac plenty of time to get you to the airport."

Mac looked past Coop's shoulder. Coop didn't need to look to know who had just spoken. He recognized her voice. A softer, loving version of it had whispered sweet nothings in his ear all night. He spun around. "Libby. I'm glad you're here. We need to talk."

She looked different. Cold. Distant. A female version of her brother. "I read about your plan to make a sitcom out of my story—my life. I don't know why I'm surprised. Someone like you would probably find my situation amusing, and I'm sure our town presented ample opportunities for caricature. Naive buffoons that we are."

She lifted one arm and pointed. "How did you plan to portray Mac? Lonely, rough-hewn widower with a dark cloud hanging over his head? Did he murder his wife or somehow arrange for her to drive off a cliff just hours after deciding to file for divorce?"

Coop looked at Mac, whose ruddy complex had turned a deep burgundy. "I never even heard that rumor."

"But he fits a stereotype. Single dad. Workaholic. Going nowhere fast."

Coop held up his hand. "She said that, not me." To Libby, he said, "I like Mac. He'd make an interesting three-dimensional character. And your niece is charming, delightful."

She advanced on him without warning, her index finger landing squarely on his chest. "Leave Megan out of this. She's been through enough, you conniving dog."

He tried to reach for her hand, but she jerked it back. "I'm not here to beg you to cease and desist. My lawyer says the constitution allows you to do whatever you want with an idea you picked up on the Internet. I can't stop you from doing this. But I can try to buy my way out of this mess."

He looked from her to Mac and back. "What are you talking about?"

"I looked back over our e-mails while I was waiting for my lawyer to call me. I did the homework I should have done before you came here. Your mother won big at a couple of casinos, but don't gamblers routinely lose more than they win? I'm guessing you need money to pay off her bills."

He was too shocked to answer.

"Here's a cashier's check for a hundred grand. All you have to do is sign this paper agreeing that our earlier deal is null and void. This means you forswear any claim on the Little Poke."

"I don't want your money, Libby. If the network buys this story, I stand to make ten times this amount in the first year alone. This money could put our child through college."

"There isn't going to be a child, Cooper. I've changed my mind about the in vitro, but even if I were still going through with my plan, you are the last person on the planet I'd ask for DNA."

Her biting tone hit hard. It never occurred to him that she might decide not to have the baby. He was shocked by how disappointed he suddenly felt. "Libby, I screwed up. I'm an ass. I admit it. Can't we at least talk?"

She shook her head. Her chin fell just a bit, and he caught a glimpse of her pain. "Just sign the paper and take the check, Cooper."

Mac walked to Libby and put both arms around her in a bear hug. "I knew this was a bad idea, Lib, I just had no idea how bad. I'm sorry."

She murmured something Cooper couldn't hear, but he saw Mac nod. Then he stripped off his gloves and walked to the small cluttered sink to clean up.

Coop reached out imploringly, but Libby had her back to him. She took an envelope from the pocket of her lightweight jacket. Mac produced a pen, still slightly damp from his wet hands.

Two against one. Proud and wronged. He had very little defense against that. He'd go home and regroup. She was right about one thing: he had unfinished business to take care of. He'd take the check and return it to her as soon as possible.

He signed his name without reading a single sentence or clause. Why bother? She wasn't out to screw him. He did that well enough on his own.

CHAPTER SIXTEEN

IN THE MONTH SINCE leaving Sentinel Pass—and Libby—Coop had learned two irrefutable truths: less than one percent of the population, male or female, should wear thong bikinis; and it really, truly *was* five o'clock somewhere.

"How's your drink?" he asked Rollie, who seemed to intuit the exact moment when Coop was reaching for the bottle of Grey Goose.

The two had assumed their usual positions on padded chaises beneath the teal-and-orange canvas awning artfully looped between the dozen or so cast-metal poles surrounding his redwood deck. He vaguely remembered approving the unique design that in hindsight was completely wrong for an oceanfront application. Metal of any sort when mixed with salt air corroded. Libby would have known that.

"Still full. You might think about slowing down there, buddy boy," Rollie said. "Last night you wound up sleeping in your chair, didn't you?"

"Was that last night?"

Rollie—who only shaved once a week, right before the visiting nurse his children had hired to check on him was due to drop by—looked like a scruffy homeless person. Faded green beachcomber-length shorts that appeared to be held up only by his bony pelvic saddle. A stain-splattered T-shirt sporting the menu from his favorite hamburger joint up the road—"Saves looking up the delivery number," Rollie liked to say—and rubber flip-flops that probably cost him under a dollar. The man was worth millions but dressed like a bum.

Coop looked down at his own apparel and sighed. Same cheesy Hawaiian-print shirt he'd had on yesterday, he was pretty sure. Lately the days seemed to run together.

"I'm thinking about selling the house," he said, stirring the sunset-colored mixture of orange and cranberry juices in his acrylic highball glass. He'd switched from martinis to the fruitier drink for Rollie's sake. The man needed more nutritional value than what three or four olives afforded.

"Why? Not enough good-looking women walking past in bikinis?" Rollie asked with a low chuckle. "I'd buy it from you if I was ten years younger. Best thing you can invest in is dirt—or in this case, sand. My advice? Rent it."

"That's what my friend said, too." Shane had come unglued when Coop told him his plan to sell out and move back east. Maybe give Broadway a try. Preferably in a dark, morose tragedy.

"Where ya going?"

Crazy.

"I haven't decided. Just too many memories here. Mom loved this place."

Rollie was quiet a moment. "You know your mom and I had a thing once. She ever tell you about us?"

A wave of chilled pink vodka sloshed over the hand holding his glass. "I don't think so." He licked a few drops from his wrist while pretending to ponder the question. "Nope. Definitely not. I'm pretty sure I'd have remembered if she'd mentioned fooling around with my neighbor."

Rollie made an offhand motion. "Wasn't anything serious. I thought it could have been, but she said the only man in her life was her son. I told her I didn't think that was fair to either of you, and she told me to get screwed." He laughed. "She was the most outspoken woman I ever met. Refreshing. Reminds me of your secretary."

"Assistant. Ex-assistant. She and my first wife have decided to become lesbians. They're collaborating on an off-Broadway play about women who don't know they're lesbians." He grinned. "God, Mom would have laughed her butt off over that, wouldn't she?"

Rollie nodded. "She never thought any of the women you dated were good enough for you. She called them Popsicles—sweet on the outside but cold on the inside."

Cooper knew a woman who was just the opposite—a little cool at first meeting but warm and delicious on the inside. God, he missed her. If the past month was a precursor of what he had to look forward to for the next forty or so years, he was in big trouble.

"So how's the investigation coming? Did they nail your mom's bookie yet?"

Coop had confided in Rollie as soon as he got back in town. On the flight home Coop had decided that he wasn't going to pay the man a dime. What was the worst that could happen? The bookie could have him killed. Big deal. And if the guy threatened to expose his mother's gambling habit…well, if Coop was dead, what did it matter? But he'd decided it was important to warn Rollie because the old man might become collateral damage if the bookie sent some goons to the beach house and got the wrong address by mistake.

Instead of being surprised by the news, Rollie had come unglued.

"I warned her this would happen," he'd shouted, shaking his fist in the air. "Goddamn, low-life scum-suckers preying on people's weaknesses. I had a good friend who lost everything—his house, his business, family, self-respect. He committed suicide rather than get help. You can't let this happen again, Coop. Your mother wasn't strong enough to fight this jerk on her own, but she can with your help."

"I'm a little late, aren't I?"

"Why? All you gotta do is call the police, give them access to your mom's computer and help them find this asshole."

"What if someone leaks it to the tabloids? Mom's reputation—"

"What reputation? My God, man, your mother was a bull terrier with a nasty bite. She never let anybody close, and most people were scared to death of her. Letting people know she was human might be the kindest thing you could do for her memory."

Coop wasn't entirely convinced that was true, but the detective who'd come to the house to check out the threatening e-mails told him this particular online syndicate had stepped over the line many times and Coop's documentation might prove instrumental in closing them down.

As soon as he was given permission to do so by the police, he'd called a journalist he halfway trusted to get the facts right and went public with his mother's story. The reporter asked questions that really made Coop think. What did he know of the woman who was his mother? When he emptied her condo, he'd stumbled across half a dozen boxes filled with clippings and memorabilia she'd saved over the years. At first he'd thought everything pertained to his life, but gradually, as he'd sorted through the layers, he'd found bits and pieces of a young woman who hadn't fit in the world to which she'd been born. A small-town beauty queen with acting aspirations. Not quite pretty enough to compete with the leading ladies of the day but smart enough and resourceful enough to make a life for herself on the fringes—until Cooper came along. Then he became her ticket in.

He found his original birth certificate. On the blank for father was the word *Unknown*. But there was an address. He looked it up online and found it belonged to a studio that had been gobbled up years ago by another company.

When the article came out, Coop was deluged by requests for interviews. But, much to his publicist's despair, he'd turned them all down. Maybe in the back of his mind he hoped Libby might read the piece and feel a tiny bit of understanding of why he did what he did. But he knew that wasn't likely. She didn't have time for the triviality of celebrity. No interview was going to change that.

Still, he'd felt a certain measure of satisfaction when his publicist told him his Web site was getting thousands of hits per day and his fan mail was running ninety-nine percent supportive and positive. Big deal. None was from Libby, so what did it matter?

The sound of a door slamming inside the house made him look over his shoulder. Shane, of course. The only one with a key.

He'd had to change the locks after he fired Daria, his ex-assistant. Despite his best effort to bow out of the project that had been his idea, the juggernaut called *Sentinel Pass Time* was becoming a reality faster than global warming.

"Hey, Shane," he called. "Make yourself useful. Rollie and I need another drink."

"Speak for yourself," Rollie said, slowly getting to his feet. "I have a date tonight. My nurse. The blonde. Turns out, she has a thing for older men."

"Especially one with a house on the beach."

Rollie waggled a gnarled finger at him. "Anybody ever tell you you're a cynic when it comes to love?"

"Wrong. I'm a born-again hard-core believer. Love exists. But for most of us it just never works out."

"That's what your mother said, too, but I told her she was a coward. Once burned doesn't mean you give up entirely. You grow another layer of skin and try again." He started toward the steps that led to a stretch of sand between the two houses. "I've got so many layers of scar tissue the doctors who perform my autopsy are going to need dynamite to get into my chest."

Coop was still smiling when Shane joined him a minute later. "Where'd Rollie go?"

"To get ready for his date. I hope that includes showering. The man's getting a bit ripe."

"You should talk. If the paparazzi found you like this, they could use Photoshop to put you on the street with a shopping cart, and everyone in America would think you were a bum."

"Thanks."

"You're welcome. Why don't you jump in the shower and we'll go to Spago?"

"I'm drinking my dinner. Besides, this is Friday. Morgana and her friends are probably there."

Shane turned to face Coop. "Her agent said she wants the role of postmaster. So bad, in fact, she's willing to sign off on the spousal support clause of your divorce if you agree."

Coop blinked. "What do *I* have to do with it?"

Shane's poker face gave way to a smirk.

"Oh, crap. What did you do to me now?"

"Made you executive producer. You have final say in casting. And story line."

Coop gulped down a swig of his drink. A part of him saw an opportunity to make amends to Libby. He could make the show less of a comedy and more real. But would that be enough for her to forgive him? Probably not. The name was in place. Shane's scouts were headed to the Black Hills to take stills and background footage. Negotiations were underway to build the sets they'd need on-site and rent existing facilities. "It won't be enough to fix things, Shane."

Shane stood up and held out his hand. "How do you know if you don't try?"

Coop looked at the shimmering glow of the sun setting

across the waves. "She hates me, man. I screwed up her life. I don't blame her. I hate me, too."

Shane took the glass from Coop's fingers. "Yeah, well, join the club. Both of your exes said the same thing, but now they're singing your praises. Did you see the public apology Tiffany's publicist issued after the story about your mother's gambling addiction came out? Maybe, given time, Libby will forgive you, too."

Coop shook his head. "What are you talking about? Morgi's only playing nice because she wants something from me. And Tiffany…" He didn't know what was going on with her. They hadn't spoken since she broke the news about her love affair with his assistant.

"T-fancy needs your permission to disclose certain facts about your marriage that she agreed never to talk about in the divorce settlement. Standard wording that you probably don't even remember your lawyer putting in but significant enough that her publisher won't go to contract until you're on board."

"Publisher? Oh, right, her tell-all book." Coop shook his head. "What kind of things?"

Shane nodded toward the house. "The excerpts in question are on your counter. I read them. Ballsy, I know, but I figured, given your present depression, you wouldn't care. And the deal benefits you more than her. The only bad part is she claims you never satisfied her as a lover, but she's quick to point out that this isn't your fault since she was a lesbian and didn't know it."

Coop put his head in his hands and groaned. "God, my life sucks. I want to go back home."

"Home? Where's that?"

Sentinel Pass. The only place that he'd ever felt truly comfortable. At peace. And he'd screwed up any chance he ever had of staying there. With Libby. And their child, which she'd decided not to have.

Shane cuffed him on the shoulder. "I've been patient—and we both know I'm not a patient man—but this is getting stupid now. If you want a life with this woman in this off-the-map town in the middle of nowhere, then get off your butt and do something to fix the problem. Are you your mother's son or not?"

"What do you mean?"

"Lena Lindstrom, for all her faults, thought the sun rose and set on her fair-haired boy. What would Lena do if she were here?"

Coop sighed. "She'd make me go back to work. 'These bills won't pay themselves,' she'd say."

"Agreed. And you were adamant about not cashing the check Libby gave you, so even though you don't have to pay your mom's bookie, you still need to start bringing in some dough. Call your agent. Tell him I've got a part for you. Sweet money up front."

"Doing what?"

"Playing yourself. In the pilot."

"No."

Shane shook his head. "Think, Coop. Do you want to make this character a real person who goes to this town with one idea, then falls in love? Or do you want Woody Harrelson to give it his take? He was suggesting a washed-up show biz type with a drinking problem who goes there—"

Cooper knew he was being played, but the image that came to mind stuck. And burned. "You've changed the story line?"

Shane shrugged. "Not yet. But…"

"If my character falls in love right off the bat, what about the sustained sexual tension and conflict?"

"Do you see any resolution in sight?"

Coop shook his head.

"Then there's a story. We're still using the town. We're adding our own people, like in *Cheers*. You're the hero and you're fighting to win the heart of the postmaster and the townsfolk, both of whom you unintentionally wronged. They want their way of life back—or they think they do—and most would be happy to see your head on display right beside Felix the dinosaur."

"Seymour. As in, come to Sentinel Pass and *see more*."

"Whatever."

Coop took a deep breath to clear the vodka haze, then stood. "Okay. Let me shower, then we'll work on the script. Order a pizza or something from the burger place down the road. Rollie's got the number if you need it. It's tattooed on his chest."

Shane's low grumble was carried away by the onshore breeze, but Cooper wasn't listening anyway. This plan might not work, but at least it would provide a way to publicly tell Libby he was sorry. And that he loved her. Something he hadn't been brave enough to say out loud when he had the chance.

LIBBY KNEW A GOOD week before she bought the home pregnancy tests what the results would be. She hadn't even missed her like-clockwork period yet, but every day began a roller-coaster ride of emotions that started in the pit of despair, chugged through "Oh, my God. Oh, my God," peaked at "I'm going to be sick," then bounced through varying degrees of panic.

She was pregnant. She knew it. But it took three different brands of prediction sticks before the reality sank in.

"One lucky shot in the dark," she muttered for the hundredth time. "That kind of thing only happens on soap operas."

Which was exactly what her life was turning into. First, people were full of questions. "How could you, Libby?" seemed to be the most prevalent. Then, gradually, the tone changed to fear. And finger-pointing. Customers who normally stopped to chat would stalk straight to their boxes, retrieve their mail, then exit without a word. Others would mumble and grouse, never really making eye contact with Libby.

Everywhere the citizens of Sentinel Pass gathered, the division between the pro-isolationists and those who saw a prospective economic boom became more pronounced.

Her town was in an uproar, and it was all her fault.

Mac had stood by her, telling people, "Libby never saw any of this happening. Who could have? The guy was stringing us all along."

That's how she'd felt then—and still did—like a puppet whose strings had been suddenly cut. She went through the motions of the act she'd perfected over the years, but she didn't feel anything. Most days were a blur, punctuated by concerned phone calls from her book club friends, visits with Gran, who didn't seem to grasp the problem facing the town or her granddaughter, and tender moments of escape with Megan.

The possibility that she might actually become a mother seemed to give her a different perspective on simple acts like reading Megan to sleep at night or making finger-paint masterpieces on the back deck. Probably just hormones, she guessed, but she always felt on the verge of tears.

And now she was facing another dilemma. Did she tell her friends, her brother, her town, about the baby? Or did she wait until she was sure she could carry it to full term? First-trimester miscarriages were common, she'd read. Especially among women her age.

And what of Cooper? Should she tell him?

A part of her said no. The sneaky bastard didn't deserve the truth—couldn't handle the truth, as Jack Nicholson had barked on film.

In the weeks since he'd left she'd become a Netflix fanatic, catching up on back seasons of television shows she'd heard about but never watched, as well as watching a new title every night. She didn't know why. Maybe because that industry was *his* life and she craved the connection—regardless of how remote.

She closed the lid of the washing machine and pushed the start button. The quiet chugging sound made her long to curl up on top of the machine and take a nap. *Nap?* That was so not her. This was Sunday. Her day to catch up. But she'd arranged to take the next day off, as well, so she could go to Rapid City to the doctor.

The sound of the phone ringing made her hurry into the kitchen. She checked the caller ID before picking it up. Although the new service had added an extra five bucks a month to her phone bill, she'd found it saved her a good dozen "No comment" responses a day to calls from the media.

"Hi, Kat. Are you and the boys back from church?"

"Didn't go. Jordie has a cold, and Tag is at his dad's for Father's Day. I actually spent a decadent morning reading the *Denver Post*. They're doing some kind of promo and one was delivered to my doorstep. Free."

Nobody was thriftier than Kat. Not even Libby. "That's nice. What's my horoscope say?"

There was a long pause. "I didn't think you believed in those kinds of things."

"I don't, but…never mind."

She heard a rustling of newsprint. "Hold on. Here it is. You're a…got it. Okay, listen… *Fate opens a door that was previously marked Do Not Enter. Now is your chance to find a part of you that was missing. Do not be afraid. Do not pass Go. Do collect all that you are entitled to.*"

Libby's knees went wobbly and she sat on the closest chair. "You made that up."

"Wh-what? No. I—I…okay, I did. But that's what it should have read. The real one says something about your finances being on the upswing. Who gives a fig about that?"

I do. If I'm going to be a mother, I need to work extra hard to rebuild my baby's college fund. But at least, she told herself, *I still have my entire share of the mine.*

She shook her head to refocus on their conversation. "I've never known you to fabricate horoscopes, Kat. What's going on? Why'd you call?"

Kat sighed. "There's an article in the lifestyle section about Cooper. I think you should see it."

"I don't—"

"It's more about his mother and her gambling addiction than him. She really screwed up her life and his finances, Lib. You might not hate him so much if you read it. I mean, I feel sort of sorry for him. He really loved her, you know."

"Love? The only kind of emotion that man is capable of is self-adoration. You shouldn't believe everything you read, Kat. We've had this discussion before in book club. You're the resident softy, remember?"

Kat made a frustrated sound. "I knew you were going to say that, but I still think you should read the article. Aren't you the person who values fairness and impartiality when Jenna gets on a rant or Char goes all mystic on us? You always say opinions are only as good as the information behind them."

"I say that?"

"Yes, you do."

Libby didn't want to admit it, but a part of her craved an explanation for his actions. "Okay. I'll try to find a paper. There might still be one—"

"Jenna's on her way over with a copy as we speak. I would have come, but I don't want to expose you to Jordie's germs."

"Is he really sick?"

"No. Just a cold, but you…you're fragile right now."

Libby's heart skipped a beat. Kat was intuitive, but surely she hadn't guessed about the baby.

"I know you're not sleeping well. And you blame yourself for the uproar around town. Guilt is a heavy burden. It can run down your body's natural defenses."

Libby let out a sigh of relief. "You're right about not

sleeping." Her nights were filled with memories and what-ifs. And ridiculous dreams of scenarios that couldn't possibly come true. Images of her and Cooper making up, sorting things out, starting fresh.

"And the initial trimester of any pregnancy is problematic—especially when it's your first."

The phone slipped from Libby's grasp, but she managed to catch it before it hit the table. "What did you say?"

"Don't worry. No one else knows. I just have a sense about these things."

"Kat…I… Oh, God, this can't be happening. What am I going to do? When people find out, they'll probably run me out of town on a rail. It's his baby, of course."

Her friend made an exasperated sound. "Like there was any question of that. Nobody is going to hold this against you— or your baby. Believe me, Lib, I know. I got pregnant out of wedlock not once but twice. The only people who like to remind me every chance they get about my tendency to shoot myself in the foot are members of my family."

"Mac is going to be furious."

"He'll get over it."

The words were comforting because deep down Libby knew they were true. Despite being completely justified in telling her "I told you so," Mac had been in her corner ever since word of Cooper's plan came out.

"Thanks, Kat. I appreciate your support. Do you think I should hold off telling the others?"

"Only if you're prepared to put up with several months of pouting."

Another truth.

"Gotcha. Hey, I hear a car. It's probably Jenna. I'll talk to you later, okay?"

"Sure will. Book club's Tuesday night, remember? *Botany of Desire*. I'm bringing everything. Since we try to shape our menu around some aspect of the book, I had to get creative. The chapter about marijuana was challenging, since I don't want my kids to even guess that I know what it is. But I found some beer made out of hemp. You can take a sip. I promise it won't hurt the baby. Gotta run. See you tomorrow."

Libby hung up, then walked to the door just as Jenna started to knock. She didn't give the other woman a chance to speak. "Come in. Kat told me you were coming. Let me read the article first, then we'll talk."

Jenna presented her with the folded paper. Cooper's photo was visible and half the headline: —*ing a Gambler*.

Loving a gambler? Supporting? What?

She spread the page wide. *Her Famous Son's Secret: Hiding a Gambler.*

"Got any coffee left?" Jenna asked, shouldering past Libby, who felt rooted to the spot. She couldn't wait to dive in to the story.

"I had tea. The water's probably still hot."

"Tea?" Jenna exclaimed, picking up a box of Celestial Seasonings Lemon Zinger. "You never drink tea unless you don't feel well. Oh, God, no." The box went flying. "Don't tell me. You have AIDS."

"Huh?" Libby picked up the box and handed it to her.

"Did he give you some kind of STD, and you're on a powerful antibiotic and can't drink caffeine?"

Libby shook her head. "You've been spending too much time with your hypochondriac mother. I'm not sick, you big dufus. I'm pregnant."

The box tumbled from her friend's fingers a second time, and she clapped a hand over her mouth to lessen the shrill squeal that followed. "Libby! How? I thought he didn't…you said you used protection."

Libby shrugged. "We did. Except one time."

Jenna threw her arms around Libby and squeezed. Hard. "I'm so happy for you, Lib. I really am. Despite what a rat fink Coop turned out to be. I'll be your baby's acting aunt until…Mac gets his act together."

Libby knew Jenna had had a terrible crush on Mac before his marriage to Misty. She wondered… No, Jenna wasn't still in love with her brother. She hoped. As much as Libby adored him, she knew Jenna could do better. Mac was a lost cause.

"You go read about the big creep and I'll make us both a fresh cup of tea. Do you have any muffins or anything? We're eating for two now, you know."

Libby laughed. Two friends down, one to go. Then she had to break the news to her brother. And Gran. And the rest of Sentinel Pass.

She sat in her father's chair—the one Cooper had favored when he'd been here—and opened the newspaper. She still hadn't decided whether or not to tell Coop. Word might get back to him if a film crew showed up. Maybe she could stay behind the chest-high window at the post office and nobody would know the difference.

Yeah, right. But if he did hear about her condition and he called, she could always lie. After all, she'd learned from the best—a man who lied for a living.

CHAPTER SEVENTEEN

"SIT STILL, WILL YOU? My God, do they make Ritalin for grown-ups?"

Coop ignored Shane's grousing. The SUV they'd rented at the Rapid City airport was only ten miles from Sentinel Pass. The tall ponderosa pines and Black Hills spruce had already started filling the air with their distinctive welcoming scent. He was home. His olfactory sense knew it even if his mind was still reluctant to admit the truth.

Or, rather, was afraid the truth was going to disappoint him. *He* might have come to the conclusion that he needed to make a large part of his life in the Black Hills—he wondered if Kevin Costner had felt the same way after filming *Dances with Wolves*—but that didn't mean Sentinel Pass or its postmaster were going welcome him back.

"Do we get a motel before or after you prostrate yourself at the feet of your postmaster?" Shane asked, subtly emphasizing the second half of Libby's title.

"After."

"You're sure? Coop, I'm worried that you're underestimating just how much groveling is going to be required to woo this woman away from the point of wanting to gut you in public."

Coop smiled. "That isn't Libby's style. She's more likely to suffer in silence."

"Then stick it to you later. Behind closed doors," Shane mumbled.

Despite the fact they were best friends, Coop knew practically nothing about Shane's private life—except that he liked to keep it private. Mostly Shane was a workaholic who shied away from the glitz and glamour that Coop had courted at his mother's insistence.

"Are you speaking from experience?"

"My family has mastered the art and science of passive-aggressive behavior. On the surface, we epitomize the standard American norm, but when the doors close, look out."

The personal revelation was so out of character Coop turned to look at him. "You've never mentioned your parents before."

Shane's scowl told him the man wished he'd kept his mouth shut. "They're both dead now, but they were married nearly thirty years when my mother passed away. My father remarried four months later to a woman twenty years his junior. After his stroke, she started sleeping with my brother...while running his campaign for the Minnesota congress."

"Wait a second. Isn't that a story line from *The Young and the Restless?* If not, it should be. Where's your brother and your stepmother now?"

"Still one state over in Minnesota, as far as I know. We're not exactly close."

"But isn't he your twin?"

"We're the yin and yang of fraternal evolution."

Coop wanted to know more, but the turnoff for Sentinel Pass loomed. He spotted the large white tepee that housed Char's Native Arts gift shop. There were only three vehicles in the parking lot. Impulsively he pointed and said, "Pull in. Libby's friend owns this place. She might tell me what to expect when we get to town."

Shane slowed down and put on the blinker. Looking around, he frowned. "Are you sure? This looks like the kind of place that has bows and arrows for sale. Is she a friendly native?"

"Char's as white as you or me, but she likes to promote Native American crafts and artisans."

"Is this Char person one of the secondary characters you mentioned? The book club ladies?" He parked and turned off the engine.

"Uh-huh. The one I labeled 'Quirky. Weird-colored hair.'"

Shane got out. "Ah. I can't wait."

"Then you go first. I—I'll slip in behind you and make sure there aren't any Wanted posters with *Dead or Alive* above my name."

Shane rolled his eyes, but he opened the door and walked directly to the main counter. To Coop's surprise, the person working the cash register wasn't Char. It was Jenna.

"Hi," she called out, sitting up straight on her stool behind the counter. The round layout of the tepee was somewhat restrictive in size, but the sunlight filtering through the canvas and the shafts of light angling through the conical opening of the ceiling gave the place a bright, open feel. "We have a great sale on jewelry at the moment, if you're interested."

He looked over his shoulder in Coop's direction, but Cooper wasn't ready to reveal himself.

"Is this the right road to Sentinel Pass?" he asked.

Coop almost snorted. Lame question.

But the dreamy expression on Jenna's face told him she was too intrigued by Shane's dark good looks to notice. "You're one of the TV people Libby warned me about, aren't you?"

Shane looked down as if questioning what aspect of his black jeans and long-sleeve black shirt gave him away.

"It's the tan," she said as if sensing his unasked question. "The only people around here with tans just got back from a cruise. And you don't strike me as the cruise type."

"You're right," Shane said. "I'm not. I, um, I'm here with a friend."

"Girlfriend?" she asked. Even from a distance, Coop could

see her face turn red as she stammered, "L-like I said, we have some nice jewelry on sale."

Good save, Jenna, he silently applauded.

Shane shook his head. "No. My friend and business associate. I think you know him. Cooper Lindstrom."

She jumped off her stool so abruptly it fell backward, crashing into a desk of some kind behind the counter.

"Coop's here? In Sentinel Pass?"

"I sure am. Is it safe to come out?"

She crossed her arms in front of her. "You've got a lot of nerve showing up here."

Shane let out a laugh. "God, Coop, you were right. This place is wonderful. That line was straight out of an old Western. Miss Kitty to a gunslinger at the—what was the name of her bar?"

"The Longbranch," Jenna supplied, her gaze never leaving Cooper. "Didn't you cause enough grief the first time around?"

He shrugged. "Who's to say what's enough? I'm back because…well, to paraphrase Ricky Ricardo, 'I've got a lot of 'splaining to do.' To Libby and to the town."

Jenna looked from Coop to Shane and back. "What if I told you you're too late? We had a town meeting last night and we voted *not* to cooperate with your film operation."

Coop didn't believe her. She kept glancing at Shane, which was probably a tell. "Then I'd say you need to convince Libby to call another meeting. This show is going to happen. This is Shane Reynard, the producer," he said, motioning Shane to come closer. "He's here to get a feel for the town, its people and how much the show can borrow from the *real* Sentinel Pass without stomping on too many toes."

She leaned over the counter to look at his feet. "I can't believe I helped you break in those boots." She shook her head and sighed. "You hurt us, Coop. You lied. Do you have any idea how much stock Libby puts in the truth? You should.

Remember how mortified she was when she thought you'd misinterpreted her ad?"

Coop didn't need to be reminded. He'd thought of little else over the past month. "Libby's a better person than me, Jenna. There's no disputing that. I don't deserve her and I don't for a minute think that winning back even some small part of her affection is going to be easy. But I'm here to try.

"And because I know how much she loves Sentinel Pass, Shane and I want to do this right."

Shane moved to Coop's side. "We plan to get a motel room somewhere close by and write the script for the pilot and the first couple of shows. Coop told me there's a popular diner right downtown. We'd try to make ourselves available to take input from anyone who wants to contribute."

She seemed to be studying his friend's face more intently than seemed fitting for one as shy as Jenna. "You're a writer? I thought he said you were a producer?"

A memory clicked in Coop's brain. "Jenna writes, too. Poetry. Deep, poignant poetry. I read your book, but I didn't get a chance to tell you so before I left. It was…intense and insightful—a little troubling because I felt like I owed you an apology and I didn't know why."

"Well, you know why now."

Shane smirked at the quick comeback.

"I do. I know and I apologize. So are we even? Do you want to work for us? Maybe do some copy editing or something?"

Coop looked at Shane. The man's eyebrows were practically touching. Not a good sign. Coop didn't know why the idea had upset his friend. What could be wrong about hiring a pretty girl who knew the town to help them?

She didn't reply right away. She looked at Shane again, then quickly dropped her gaze. There was something maidenly about the gesture that Coop stored away in his memory bank. "I'll have to think about it," she said. "The

Mystery Spot is opening soon. It takes most of my time during the summer."

Coop explained to Shane about Sentinel Pass's lone tourist trap.

"There's your answer. She's busy."

"During the day. But she could help us in the evenings after the Mystery Spot closes."

Shane didn't say anything.

Coop didn't know what was wrong with his friend, who was known for his diplomatic prowess. He seemed to have a problem with Jenna, but Coop couldn't imagine why. If any of Libby's friends were going to give him a hard time about trying to worm his way back into her life, he would have put his money on her.

"Well, in that case," Jenna said, "I might be available for a few hours each day, provided my mother's health remains stable." She looked at Coop. "And I might know a place you could rent short-term."

She quickly explained about a house that had recently come on the market. "*If* it's still available."

"We'll take it," Coop said just as Shane's elbow drove into his side.

Jenna didn't seem to notice, as she'd already picked up the phone and was dialing.

Coop motioned for Shane to follow him a few feet away to give her some privacy. Beside a shelf of Sioux pottery he whispered, "What?"

Shane took a deep breath and let it out before answering. "I know her."

"Jenna? How?"

"I went to college with her. I don't mean we hung out or dated or anything, but I knew who she was. Something happened—"

"He said okay," Jenna hollered out, stopping Shane midsentence.

"Great," Coop called, waving to her. "We'll take it." To Shane he said, "How come she doesn't seem to recognize you?"

"I don't know. Maybe she made more of an impression on me than I did on her. Plus, my hair was a lot longer. And I wore glasses."

"Oh, yeah. You had LASIK surgery about the time we met. But surely she'd recognize your name...."

"Reynard is my mother's maiden name. I legally changed it when I started making movies."

Coop had no idea what was going on or if this was going to play a factor on the show, but he could tell his usually unflappable friend was flapped. He still had his sunglasses on—a social gaff he found pretentious and silly.

"So how do you want to play this? Are you going to say something or not?"

"No. Definitely not," Shane said. "In fact, I'll wait for you in the car. That was a dark period for both of us. She isn't going to want to relive it any more than I do."

Coop watched him leave. But as intrigued as he was by the glimmer of revelation into Shane's history and the bizarre happenstance that made two lives intersect for a second time, Coop's first priority was to get to Sentinel Pass. There would be time later, when he and Shane were discussing plots and story lines, to delve into the misty past.

"The key, my good woman," he said, returning to the counter. "My kingdom for the key." He bowed with a flourish.

She rolled her eyes, but her smile was softer and more indulgent than it had been earlier, lending hope that he'd win her—and Libby—over eventually. If he could dredge up just the right amount of *swoo*.

"It's the yellow house two blocks off Main. Oh, and by the way," Jenna said before laying the key, which was attached to a cast-metal key fob in the shape of a moose, in his open palm, "I lied about the town meeting. It wasn't last night. It's tonight. At seven. Libby said she was parking the truck facing outward in case she caught a whiff of hot tar and feathers."

Coop closed his fingers around the key and doffed an imaginary hat. "Thanks, Jenna. I owe you one." He turned to leave but stopped. A scenario started to unfold in his imagination. He looked over his shoulder. "I'm not going to ask you to lie, but if you could avoid mentioning the fact that Shane and I are here… Well, did you ever see *Mr. Smith Goes to Washington?*"

Her smile seemed genuine. "It's one of my mother's favorites. She's a huge Jimmy Stewart fan. I can picture what you have in mind. A grand entrance. But you know why women loved Jimmy, right? He wasn't the most handsome of the male stars of his time. He was the most sincere."

He took his time walking to the car. Basically she was suggesting he strip naked emotionally and let everyone—especially Libby—see the *real* Cooper Lindstrom. The boy who knew at a tender age that he wasn't very bright. *Beauty without depth*, he overheard his mother say on his fifth or sixth birthday.

If he laid himself bare, Libby might feel sorry for him, but she certainly wouldn't love him. And would she want to expose her children to his flawed, learning-challenged genes? His mother had taught him how to make people like the man he pretended to be, but who in the world could love the man he was?

CHAPTER EIGHTEEN

LIBBY RUSHED DIRECTLY from work to her grandmother's house. She only had about an hour to prepare for the town meeting that was scheduled to take place at the history center. There wasn't a great deal she could say except "mea culpa" and offer to resign from the community board.

She opened the back door of the small house, calling out, "Hello? Anybody home?"

Onida answered with a series of sharp, high-pitched barks. Her grandmother's usual reprimand failed to follow.

Libby bent to pick up the excited, wiggling poodle. "Hey, girl, where is everybody? Did they leave town to avoid seeing me? Now I really *am* feeling like an outcast."

Onida's long pink tongue licked her chin—a shade too close to Libby's lips for comfort. She put the dog down with a pat on the head, then looked around. "Gran? Calvin?"

"We're on the back porch," Cal called.

Libby hurried through the kitchen, surprised to see pots and dirty dishes sitting around. Calvin was meticulous as a rule. She pushed open the screen door. The temperature had climbed into the mid eighties that day, but it was cooling down nicely.

"Hi. Keeping cool outside, I see," she said.

Her smile faded. Cal and Gran were sitting on the glider, gently rocking back and forth. But with one arm around her grandmother's shoulders and the other diagonal across her body, he seemed to be restraining the older woman, not relaxing with her.

"What's wrong?"

"Your grandmother had a rough day, didn't you, dear?" he said, looking at Mary. His tone and expression were compassionate and loving, and Libby relaxed some. She rushed to where they were sitting and drew up a faded wicker foot rest.

"I'm sorry to hear that, Gran. You're not feeling good?"

"I feel fine as fish feathers," the woman answered forcefully. "But I need to go home. Why won't anybody take me there? Marshall will be there. I'm supposed to make dinner for him. I think it's burning."

She struggled to stand, but Cal was prepared. He started them rocking again and whispered something low and soothing that Libby couldn't hear into her grandmother's ear. Libby reached out and stroked Gran's bare forearm. "Marshall was your son, Gran. He's been gone a long time. You moved into the big house and took care of me and Mac after he died, remember? And now we're here to take care of you. Us and Cal. We love you. We're not going to let anything burn. I promise."

Gran relaxed and a moment later closed her eyes. Her head dropped to one side to rest on Cal's shoulder. He relaxed his hold and let out a long sigh. "I have a call in to her doctor. She woke from a nap agitated and paranoid. Didn't seem to recognize me. I'd just started making vegetable lasagna and suddenly I had this stranger trying to get out the door without her walker. I was afraid she'd fall and break her hip."

Libby leaned over to give him an awkward hug. "I'm so sorry. What does the doctor think happened? Could it be the new meds he started her on last week?"

"Possibly. Or just an aspect of dementia. She's had a few episodes. Nothing this scary."

"What can I do to help? Shall I sit with her? Or go clean your kitchen?"

He chuckled. "No offense, but you young people don't know how to clean. How 'bout you help me get her to bed? If she wakes up, I'll give her an Ensure and one of her sleeping pills. That way I don't have to worry about her getting up in the middle of the night."

Libby groaned. Had she been so self-absorbed that she'd completely missed her grandmother's decline? And what was she going to do without her grandmother's advice? She wanted to cry, but she had to be strong—for Gran's sake.

"Heard about the big meeting t'night," Cal said, securing the brake on the wheelchair that Libby had brought close. "Someone tried to get me to sign a petition to force you off the committee. As if I'd sign such a thing. What's wrong with people?"

"I like that petition better than the one suggesting I ride sidesaddle on a rail on my way out of town. There was one of those tacked to the door of the post office this morning."

His low chuckle seemed so normal and familiar she was finally able to calm—just a bit. "Mary and I were talking about the situation earlier. She seemed pretty clear at the time. Said you were too levelheaded to do anything to put the town in jeopardy."

"But my online ad is going to turn Sentinel Pass into some late-night comedian's punch line."

"So what? Haven't you heard the saying there's no such thing as bad publicity?"

"Yes, but—"

He put his gnarled hand on her arm. "Is there a chance your grandmother and I might be cast as characters? We both thought that sounded like fun. They can make us as old and quirky as they want so long as they include the part about us being in our eighties and living in sin."

Gran woke up as they helped her into the wheelchair. She lifted her chin and looked at Libby. "Hello, dear. Where'd you come from? I haven't seen you in ages."

Libby's heart broke a little, but she managed to smile. "I know, Gran. I'm sorry. Been busy with work and…stuff."

Gran touched her cheek. "You need more stuff in your life. Work is what you do, not who you are."

"Thanks, Gran. I came here for advice and, like usual, you knew what to say."

"Come back tomorrow, Nieva," Gran said with a sigh. "I'm so tired I can hardly keep my eyes open."

Nieva. Daughter-in-law, not granddaughter. "I will. I promise." She kissed her grandmother's peachy-soft cheek, then held the door open so Cal could wheel her inside.

"I can handle everything from here," he said. "Don't want you to be late for the meeting. Sorry your grandmother and I can't be there to stand in your corner."

"Me, too. But Mac is coming. Besides, I got myself into this mess, I'll just have to get myself out."

His low chuckle was oddly comforting. "That sounds just like your grandmother. Go get 'em, girl."

She made sure the dog was safely inside, then she walked around the side of the house to her truck. She would handle this. She might be pregnant, unpopular and missing a crucial member of her support team, but she would handle this.

She put the key in the ignition and turned on the motor. She had time to run by Jenna's but wasn't sure her friend was home. Jenna had failed to return Libby's call earlier in the day. Hopefully that didn't mean she'd had to take her mother to the doctor. Libby already knew that Kat wasn't going to be at the meeting. Her eldest son had some school function, and his flaky father had bailed, so Kat was stuck in Deadwood. Char had spent the day in Pine Ridge, where she met quarterly with a group of artisans whose work she sold in her shop. She'd promised to try to get back in time, but when Char was on "reservation time," as she put it, anything could happen.

Libby had never felt more alone in her life.

She put the Xterra in gear and backed up. She drove straight into town and parked in her usual spot at the post office. Since she was early, she took her time, pausing to read a poster that someone had stuck to a telephone pole using hot-pink thumbtacks.

Oust Libby McGannon the headline read.

Her stomach heaved, but pride helped her keep from throwing up.

Her town had turned on her. She'd felt the dirty looks, heard the pointed remarks in the lobby. Where was the unconditional love she'd always heard about and had hoped to find? She'd always tried to do the right thing, and the one time she made a mistake—granted, a very public mistake—the support she'd hoped to find wasn't there.

She felt lost, rootless. And, to her profound surprise, liberated.

She had a career, vested time in a government job. She could move anywhere. Start over. Maybe Mac and Megan could go with her. *Not Gran.* No, her grandmother needed to stay where she was for as long as was possible. But she would have been the first to encourage Libby to spread her wings and fly if she were still herself.

Maybe I could transfer to Cheyenne or Sheridan, she thought, looking with longing at the road that would take her out of town. Both cities were within reasonable driving distance so she could visit her grandmother.

She kept walking toward the small square where schoolchildren loved to visit. There were already a good number of cars in the parking lot. Her palms were damp and she had a bad taste in her mouth, but pride kept her from crumpling.

She put a hand on her still-flat tummy. She needed to look ahead—and not just for her own sake anymore. She wouldn't look back with any more regrets than she already had. She'd blown it with Coop, but she wasn't going to let anybody say anything bad about him. She planned to stand up for her child's father, and if her town didn't like it…

"THE MEETING IS called to order. I make a motion that we skip the old news and minutes from the last meeting to get down to business," Art Gadoya said. He'd been elected secretary of the group about ten years back and, since nobody else wanted the job, was still in office. "Second?"

Libby could have raised some objection to the abuse of protocol, but instead she stood. "I'll second that."

A collective gasp told her the audience of around a hundred people, including those smokers hanging just beyond the open door at the back of the building, hadn't expected her to be so bold.

The board murmured its yeas. There were no nays.

Since she had the floor, she decided to lay out her side of the story. "The business we're here to talk about is whether or not I should step down from the city council. I will. I do. Art has my formal letter of resignation in front of him." She looked over her shoulder. "Sorry, Art. I should have made copies, but we had three full-coverage circulars today." Art had been a mail carrier when Libby's grandmother was postmaster. He understood.

"No problem," he murmured.

"I'll let you get on with the business of electing someone to fill my spot as soon as I tell you what I assume you're here to hear. How did this happen? How could Sentinel Pass go— almost overnight—from a sleepy little mountain town to the subject of a proposed television sitcom?"

"Yeah," somebody in the back shouted. "How could you sell us out, Lib? Did that Cooper fellow promise you a leading part?"

"Naw," another voice said. "He promised her a kid. Women her age start hearing the tick-tock of their biological clock and—"

Libby grabbed her chair and moved it back away from the desk so she could stand on it. She searched through the many faces until she spotted Robert Greise. "I thought that was your voice, Bobby. And the reason you know so much about women is why? Because you watch *Dr. Phil?* It can't be because you've ever been married or had a serious girlfriend."

The man's blush went all the way into his receding hairline. "I know you had to put an ad on the Internet to find a man," he charged.

"You're right. And I found one. The wrong one, perhaps, but that's the trouble with Internet dating. A guy who's short, balding, thirty pounds overweight and still lives with his mother can portray himself as tall, well-built, gorgeous and successful. By the time you realize you've been sold a bill of goods, it's too late. He knows where you live."

Since she'd basically described Bobby to a T, a low murmur of snickers filtered through the audience. She looked around and let out a sigh. "I made a mistake. I'm sorry. There's no putting this genie back in the bottle. So unless you want my head on a stick, I suggest you elect a new board member, then create some kind of plan to deal with the onslaught of media attention once the film crew arrives."

She turned to step down and realized too late that she hadn't eaten since breakfast. The table appeared to wobble, and she blinked to regain her equilibrium. She heard someone cry "Uh-oh," then suddenly she was falling.

The sensation didn't last long. Miraculously, someone caught her. Strong male arms pulled her into a tight hug that felt comforting and protective. Mac, she thought, smiling. She hadn't seen her brother in the audience, but obviously he had her back.

Then, to her horror, he kissed her.

"Oh, God, what are you do—?" Blue eyes, not brown, smiled back at her.

"Coop," she cried, unable to fully grasp that he was here. Holding her as if she were the most precious thing in the world.

"I couldn't have written a better opening than that, my love," he said, kissing her again. "Thank you. Now I need to set a few people straight about what's happening. Are you okay? Can you sit down?" Someone moved the chair she'd been standing on so he could lower her to it. "You still look pale. You haven't been eating, have you?" He made a tsking sound. "My bad. But things will be better soon. I promise."

If she'd been able to think straight, she'd have told him his promises were as worthless as a T-Rex's arms. But her heart was pounding too hard. She could barely make out what he was saying.

He stepped to the table. "Citizens of Sentinel Pass. Hello. My name is Cooper Lindstrom. Some of you know me from television. Others I met the last time I was here, about a month ago. I'm absolutely sure each and every one of you has an opinion of me." He paused for effect. "All good, no doubt."

His mocking look garnered a few snickers and even more catcalls.

"No? Well, then, I hope to change your opinion tonight. Not for my sake but for Libby's."

With a glance back at Libby, he planted one hip on the table, then swung his legs around so they were hanging over the edge. His back was to her, but the pose made him seem friendly and accessible, one of them. He shrugged out of his black wool sports coat and laid it to one side. His pale blue oxford shirt was just the right degree of casual.

At least he hadn't opted for flannel or plaid, Libby thought. That would have been too condescending.

"First, let me say that before I came to Sentinel Pass, I had absolutely no understanding of the concept of a hometown. You see, I was born in Hollywood." A murmur of chatter broke out, but he talked over it. "So when I read Libby's online ad, offering to trade a share in her family's mine for a chance to become a mother, the last thing I was thinking about was how her friends and family might be impacted. It didn't occur to me because I don't have that kind of history."

He threw up his hands. "If you've read anything about me, you know that I'm a single child born out of wedlock to a classic stage mom. I started working while still in diapers. I went to school on the lot. It was a great adventure for a kid. I'm not complaining. I just want you to understand that coming to Sentinel Pass was like landing on a different planet."

"Yeah, real people are from Earth. Movie stars are from Uranus," someone muttered, making certain the word came out "your anus."

Coop roared with laughter. "Good one. Write that down, Shane." He pointed to a man dressed all in black who was standing near the rear door.

Libby remembered hearing Coop talk about his best friend, who was also a producer of some sort.

"Everyone, this is my friend and colleague, Shane Reynard. He's the guy who took my idea—which I stole from Libby—and turned it into a viable proposal that the network snapped up."

The body of attention turned Shane's way. Libby gave the man credit for not slipping out the door and running for his life. Instead he took a step forward and casually waved, as if accepting credit for something good.

"Shane and I are here to set the record straight and get your input on how this show is going to morph into something we can all be proud of. But more of that later. First, I want you all to apologize to Libby."

Libby's mouth dropped open. "What?"

"Why should we?" Bobby boldly challenged.

"Because if not for her, Sentinel Pass would be stuck in a time warp, never realizing its true potential."

Art pounded the gavel to quiet down the crowd. It was obvious very few shared Coop's assessment that their beloved town was somehow lacking.

"We happen to like our town just the way it is, Mr. Hollywood big shot," Bobby said. "Who are you—"

"Damn it, Bobby. Shut up and let the man talk," a new voice cried.

Libby glanced to her left and saw Jenna push her way through the crowd. She squeezed between Libby's chair and Elana Grace, who was sitting to Libby's right. The Tidbiscuit owner groused but shifted sideways to make room.

"You were saying, Mr. Lindstrom," Jenna prompted.

"Thank you, Ms. Murphy. I didn't mean that to sound disparaging. Sentinel Pass is one of the coolest places I've ever visited—and I've pretty much been around the world. It's a unique treasure, but unless you take steps to preserve it, Sentinel Pass will become a has-been. Or, worse, a could-have-been. Believe me, I know what that's like."

Libby looked at Jenna, who winked.

"You have the opportunity to decide Sentinel Pass's future," Coop told them.

"Didn't you take that out of our hands when you decided to name a television sitcom after us?" Libby asked.

He shifted on one hip and scooted sideways so he could look her in the eye. "I was the catalyst for change, yes. I admit that. And it was wrong of me to do that without being upfront with you from the beginning. But what happens next is completely in your hands."

Her heart stuttered. The subtext of his words came through loud and clear. He wanted another chance with her. Oh, God, she didn't dare hope... No. He'd lied to her. He'd used her. Made a fool of her. She couldn't forget that.

CHAPTER NINETEEN

COOP SAW A FLICKER of possibility brighten Libby's eyes, then disappear like a flame on a candle extinguished by someone pinching it between their fingers. He understood. He hadn't expected his path back to be easy.

He faced the crowd again. The citizens were turning out to be an easier sell than Libby.

"Let's be clear about something. Sentinel Pass is not hip or cool or happenin'. Am I right?"

"No, and we like it that way," the older woman sitting to the right of Libby said.

"But your taxes go up every year. Your property values are rising modestly. Everything costs more—the gas to drive to the city for the groceries the outside world produces. But the only money coming into town is what you, its residents, earn outside. You've become a sort of bedroom community. And maybe that's all you want to be. But why can't you be both—a destination and a bedroom community? Why can't the coffee shop start selling lattes to people who expect to pay premium? Do you know what the markup is on anything chocolate?" He addressed his question to the woman he remembered seeing behind the counter of the corner café.

She shook her head.

"Why can't the Murphys' Mystery Spot do enough business to actually pay for itself? Jenna will tell you how expensive it is to advertise in travel magazines and on billboards. Free advertisement is like a gift from the gods."

"I'll second that," Jenna murmured loud enough to be heard.

"Char's gift shop has the best chance of making money because it's on the highway, but the people traveling that highway are always on their way somewhere else—Mount Rushmore, Hill City, Deadwood. There's nothing compelling them to stop. But there could be. If they were curious about the place that had a TV show named after it, you could charge admission to the sets after we're done filming. On weeks that our crews are in town, you can advertise real-life celebrity sightings. We all know how exciting that can be," he said facetiously.

A few chuckles became a few more. Questions came at him, but they were no longer bitter and antagonistic. He had a sense that the tide had turned, until the sound of a chair scratching along the floor made everyone go silent. He turned to see Libby standing.

She gave him a weak but valiant smile and a nod that seemed fairly encouraging. "I'm glad Cooper came back to make his case in person. I think that speaks highly of his sense of integrity. Since I'm no longer on the board and you don't need my vote, I'm going home now."

Nobody tried to stop her. He wasn't sure if that was out of respect because she looked so tired or because they really didn't care that she was in pain and felt betrayed and rejected by the people who were supposed to love her.

"However," he said, projecting his voice as he'd been taught, "it's not too late to call this project *Hill City Blues*. Or *As Rapid City Turns*. Or…" He pointed at Shane. "Help me out, Reynard."

"Um…*The Not-So-Scarlet Letter Carrier*."

Coop's mouth dropped open.

Shane tossed up his hands. "What? You asked."

"How 'bout *Off Your Rockerville?*" Jenna called out. "I

heard someone who lives there complaining because Libby wasn't *their* postmaster."

"You could offer this opportunity to Lead," Jenna's mother, who was sitting in the front row, suggested. "Maybe call the program *Get the Lead Out*." To Coop she explained, "People always pronounce it wrong. They call it Led, not Lead."

"Not bad," Shane said, stepping forward. "I like it. That's the town with the big gold mine, right?"

"Hey, wait a minute. This is our show," the big-mouth idiot who had attacked Libby complained. "You can't just give it away. Libby is our postmaster, and it was her idea that started this whole thing."

"Correct," Coop said. "And I think you all owe her an apology."

He turned to see her reaction, but she was gone.

He caught up with her in the parking lot. She seemed to be walking in a daze, which wasn't like her at all.

"Libby? Lib. Wait up."

She stopped but didn't turn to face him.

He dashed between cars, dodging prominent side mirrors and oversize all-terrain tires.

"Lib," he said breathing hard, "are you okay? Something's wrong, isn't it? They want you back inside. All's forgiven. You're their new hero."

She lifted her chin and looked at him. Her lips pulled sideways in a rueful smile. "Anybody ever tell you you should be in show business? You could sell ice to Eskimos, as my grandmother used to say."

"You're still mad at me, aren't you?"

She started away. "Don't, Coop. I'm tired. I'm going home. It's been a long day. A long month. I... Just don't."

"Can we meet for breakfast? Jenna said you have a sub filling in for you tomorrow. We need to talk, Lib."

She muttered something about her so-called friend selling her down the river, but he was pretty sure she also said to drop by around eight. "Eight. I'll be there. Sleep well, my love."

Her steps faltered at his casual endearment, but she didn't stop.

That didn't bode well, he feared, but he refused to admit defeat. She was the love of his life—even if she could do much, much better.

WHEN LIBBY OPENED her eyes the next morning, her first thought was she couldn't believe how well she'd slept. She'd crawled into bed after a brief phone conversation with her brother, expecting to toss and turn all night. Mac had reiterated everything Coop had told her. All was forgiven. The town loved her and wanted her back on the board.

"Tough," she muttered, throwing back the covers.

She got up and looked out the window. Overcast. Perfect. It matched her mood exactly.

She got dressed, washed her face, applied her usual sunscreen and flavored lip gloss, ignoring the makeup and mascara on the counter. She was done trying to be someone she wasn't. She was tired of trying to live up to the town's expectations of who she should be.

"I make one mistake and they're ready to rake me over the coals," she told her reflection. Despite Mac's reassurances, Libby knew that people would be talking about this for years. The respect she thought she'd earned by sacrifice and duty weren't worth the ink it took to write the words. "Screw Sentinel Pass. I hope Coop does change his mind and takes the show somewhere else. It would serve them right."

She walked downstairs and straight into the kitchen. The smell of coffee brewing served as a warning, but she still jumped backward in surprise when she spotted Coop sitting at her table, newspaper spread open.

She grabbed the door frame to steady herself and lend support to her wobbly legs. "What are you doing here? How'd you get in?"

He picked up the set of keys she'd given him when he was staying in the cottage. "You never took them back. I made coffee." He pointed to a pink box partly open to display an assortment of doughnuts. "And brought breakfast."

She craved caffeine, but even the smell was giving her a bad taste in her mouth. She walked to the counter and flipped the switch on her electric teakettle. "Green tea is better for you," she said, grabbing a box from the cupboard.

She knew her tone was surly, but she wasn't in the mood to be friendly. Her life was a mess, and this man was almost as much to blame as she was.

"Doughnut?" he offered.

"No. Yes." Her mouth started watering again. She couldn't tell if this was in expectation of a maple bar—her favorite—or because she was going to throw up.

She stepped close enough to grab one, then scuttled back out of reach. His sandy eyebrow arched questioningly, no doubt interpreting her avoidance all too correctly. She decided to be blunt. "I don't want you to touch me. There's no point. But we do need to talk, so you stay there and I'll sit across from you once my tea is ready."

"There's no point? What does that mean?"

"Don't be obtuse."

"Is that a fancy way of saying don't be dumb? Because I am, you know. Dumb. You have to spell things out for me."

An undercurrent of anger in his tone made her swallow her overly sweet bite of maple-flavored calories without chewing completely. She choked slightly.

He was on his feet in a blink. He quickly filled a glass of water from the tap and handed it to her. "Are you okay?"

Her eyes were blurry with tears and her nose was starting

to run, but she could breathe again. She nodded, handing him back the glass. "Chew first. Then swallow. Talk about dumb."

He set the glass on the counter at the same moment the bell chimed on her kettle telling her the water had reached boiling point. He filled the mug she'd prepared and carried it to the table. "Come sit down. Are you sure your throat is okay?"

She followed him. "I'm fine."

He gave her plenty of room to settle in her chair, then he returned to his place. "I'm sorry if I surprised you by being here early. Usually you're up at dawn. When you weren't, I thought you might appreciate having the coffee made when you came downstairs."

She would have if…things were different. Which they weren't. "You should give me the key back."

He wiggled it off the ring and nudged it across the table.

Libby dunked her tea bag a few times, stalling. When she looked up, he was watching her, a bemused expression on his handsome face. "What?"

"You do that as if you're trying to drown the tea bag—or someone you *wish* was a tea bag."

She gave him a stern look. "I'm not happy. My life is a mess. Everything is wrong and mixed up and there's nothing to smile about, so quit trying to make me smile."

"Sorry."

"No, you're not."

He leaned forward, resting his elbows on the table. "You have no idea how much I regret screwing up what could have been the best thing that ever happened to me."

His words sounded heartfelt and real, but she reminded herself that he was an actor. "How long did you practice that line?"

He frowned and started to deny it but then stopped. "I can see why you'd think that. And the fact is, I've said those words a dozen times or more in my head. Not to memorize them so they'd sound truthful and sincere but because that's all I think about anymore. You. Me. What could have been."

"We never had a could-have-been, Coop. We come from different worlds, with different values. There's no common middle ground. I put my heart on the line and you turned my story into a sitcom. What does that tell you?"

"It's my story, too, Libby. I'm the jerk who answered your ad and saw a way to profit from it. There's no way to make me look heroic. I was a greedy opportunist with only my own needs in mind when I typed in a reply to your e-mail. I suck."

His bluntness robbed her of any reply.

He jumped to his feet and started pacing. "But something happened when I got here. Shane tried to explain this to me in the airplane. Something about the hero's journey. Your ad was my call to adventure, and I thought I was answering it for one reason—the gold mine, but it turns out I really came here for another."

"What?"

"Redemption. You saved me, Libby. I was drowning in a sea of debt and denial, loss and fear. For the first time in my life I was calling the shots. I didn't have anyone else to blame when something went wrong. And something was bound to go wrong."

"Why?"

"Because I'm…not the brightest bulb in the pack."

Her expression went from confusion to dismay. "Why do you believe that?"

He shrugged. "Mom never used those words, of course, but there was no denying I had certain learning challenges. She had to help me with my lines when I was younger because I'm a slow reader. And I've never had a head for figures—although I did balance my checkbook for the first time last week." He'd been surprised to find that it wasn't as difficult as his mother had led him to believe. "I can't tell you the number of times I'd suggest something and Mom would point out all the reasons why my idea sucked. A smart person would have known better than to think that in the first place, right?"

She didn't answer, but he could tell by her frown that she was troubled.

"Mom liked to say she was the brains of our outfit. She was smart, clever, resourceful. Like you."

She made a face. "You're comparing me to your mother?"

"You're all of those things, along with kind, generous, patient, humble, fair and nurturing. Mom was none of those. I loved her, but in the months since her death I've come to see that she was also petty, self-involved, greedy, deceitful and, above all else…afraid."

"Afraid of what?"

"Of being poor, I think. I heard from two of my aunts after the article about me and Mom's gambling addiction came out. I'd never met them."

"That's too bad."

"That was Mom. She used her beauty as currency. It wasn't enough to buy her a husband, but I'm sure whoever my father was, he had wealth and power. The money he gave her to get lost—or get an abortion…she always dodged that question— gave us a start. Once I was born, she became the CEO of Cooper Lindstrom."

"But you don't hate her, do you?"

"Dumb, huh? I supposed I should. Shane does on my behalf. But despite her mistakes and lack of parenting skills, deep down she loved me. I know that."

She sat back in her chair and folded her hands across her belly. "Wow. It just hit me that the decisions I make now are going to have lasting repercussions in my child's life. Someday he or she might be having this same discussion."

"The hypothetical child you and I were going to make together before you told me take my sperm and leave?"

She swallowed. "No. The child we created the night we were together."

His blood suddenly rushed everywhere but to his head, where he needed it. Her words didn't quite make sense. He looked at her waist. "You…you're…pregnant?"

She nodded.

"We took precautions."

"Not every time, apparently."

His knees turned wobbly and he pulled out his chair to sit down. He knew some kind of response was expected, but emotions he'd never expected to feel overwhelmed him. Tears rushed to his eyes. His throat constricted. Something powerful and scary exploded in his chest. Not panic, as he would have thought, but joy. A laugh that probably sounded more like a cry burst from his lips. "We're going to have a baby," he shouted, jumping to his feet. "Oh, my God, I'm going to be a father."

Panic followed on the heels of that word, and he sat back down clumsily. "I don't know how to be a father. I've never even played one. Playboy Lothario? Yes. Talent show host? No problem. Daddy? No way." He shook his head and looked at Libby. "You weren't going to tell me, were you?"

"I hadn't made up my mind." Honest, as usual. "Until last night. When I saw you at the meeting, I knew I didn't have any choice.

"In my mind I'd made you out to be the bad guy, Coop. That way I didn't have to shoulder all the blame. I don't like to make mistakes. That doesn't fit with who I am—a people-pleasing good girl who never rocks the boat or asks herself what she really wants out of life."

He started to say she was being too hard on herself, but she stopped him. "I wrote that ad. It was an impulsive act probably brought on by sleep deprivation and worry—not some imaginary clock sound ticking in my brain. My sister-in-law's death shook us all. My grandmother's health problems served as another reminder that we don't have forever. I think I knew at some gut level that this was my last chance to live a life of my own choosing."

"I know exactly what you mean. Up till the day she died Mom was still e-mailing me my daily schedule."

She nodded. "If you keep busy enough, you don't have time to worry about whether or not what you're doing is making you happy."

"What will make you happy, Lib?"

She didn't answer right away. "I've given that a lot of thought over the past month. At first I thought feeding your body parts to a shark might be nice." She grinned, then quickly added, "But then my breasts started to hurt and the smell of coffee made me queasy. I took a couple of home pregnancy tests and decided it was time to develop a plan B."

"Which is?"

"Still under debate. But…I'm open to suggestions. Yesterday, moving to Wyoming figured high on the list of possibilities."

He stood up and walked to her. "What's in Wyoming?"

"Devil's Tower. Yellowstone. Cody. Cheyenne."

He took her hand and pulled her to her feet. "Brat. I meant why'd you pick Wyoming?"

"It's close enough to visit Gran and Mac and Megan regularly, but it's not Sentinel Pass."

He wrapped his arms around her, knitting his fingers to rest on top of her butt. "Ah…another rat jumping ship before the marauders from Hollywood arrive. What if I told you I just bought a quarter interest in a gold mine and plan to live in Sentinel Pass six months out of the year?"

"The Little Poke?"

"Your brother and I worked out a deal while you were sleeping. I had this cashier's check burning a hole in my pocket. I could have saved it for a college fund for our kid, but I didn't know about our kid. Mac, either, huh?"

"Only Kat and Jenna. Kat's some sort of baby psychic, and Jenna's nosy. I planned to tell Char tonight at book club."

He nuzzled her neck and jaw. "That means we just have to work together to make sure *Sentinel Pass Time* is a big hit so we can tuck away a nice chunk of change—in case we want to give our daughter a brother or sister later."

She looked up. "We're having a girl?"

"God, I hope so. She can have my hair and your eyes."

"What's wrong with my hair?"

He threw back his head and laughed. "I love you, Libby McGannon. You rescued me from myself. And now you have to do the right thing and marry me."

Her long, deep sigh wasn't exactly the answer he was hoping for. "I've done the right thing my entire life, Coop. I was kinda looking forward to being a rebel for a while. It was refreshing. For a few minutes I felt like I was you. Thumbing my nose at society."

"If that's important to you, we can take turns being outrageous—until the baby comes. Then I'm going to do my best to set a good example. I don't know how to be a dad, but I promise to try my hardest not to screw up."

His honesty was unmistakable, but he was wrong. "You know as much about parenting as I do, Coop. We'll learn together. The hard way, I'm sure."

"Does that mean you've forgiven me?"

"You told me you don't hate your mother for gambling away your money. Despite everything, you still love her. But last night, at the meeting, the town that supposedly loved me—helped raise me—had to be bribed into overlooking my mistake."

"They still love you, Lib. They just freaked out for a minute."

"Well, we're not going to do that with our children, Cooper. Promise me. We're going to love them no matter what they do…or don't do."

He squeezed her so tight she let out a little yip. Then he let go and took her face in his hands. "I promise."

Then he kissed her, and Libby knew she was right where she was always meant to be—home. In Cooper Lindstrom's arms.

* * * * *

Don't miss HIS BROTHER'S SECRET,
Debra Salonen's next installment in the
SPOTLIGHT ON SENTINEL PASS *series!*
Coming in September 2008
from Harlequin Superromance.

THOROUGHBRED LEGACY
*The stakes are high when it comes to love,
horse racing, family secrets
and broken promises.*

*A new exciting Harlequin
continuity series coming soon!
Led by* New York Times *bestselling author
Elizabeth Bevarly—
FLIRTING WITH TROUBLE*

Here's a preview!

THE DOOR CLOSED behind them, throwing them into darkness and leaving them utterly alone. And the next thing Daniel knew, he heard himself saying, "Marnie, I'm sorry about the way things turned out in Del Mar."

She said nothing at first, only strode across the room and stared out the window beside him. Although he couldn't see her well in the darkness—he still hadn't switched on a light…but then, neither had she—he imagined her expression was a little preoccupied, a little anxious, a little confused.

Finally, very softly, she said, "Are you?"

He nodded, then, worried she wouldn't be able to see the gesture, added, "Yeah. I am. I should have said goodbye to you."

"Yes, you should have."

Actually, he thought, there were a lot of things he should have done in Del Mar. He'd had *a lot* riding on the Pacific Classic, and even more on his entry, Little Joe, but after meeting Marnie, the Pacific Classic had been the last thing on Daniel's mind. His loss at Del Mar had pretty much ended his career before it had even begun, and he'd had to start all over again, rebuilding from nothing.

He simply had not then and did not now have room in his life for a woman as potent as Marnie Roberts. He was a horseman first and foremost. From the time he was a schoolboy, he'd known what he wanted to do with his life—be the best possible trainer he could be.

He had to make sure Marnie understood—and he understood, too—why things had ended the way they had eight years ago. He just wished he could find the words to do that. Hell, he wished he could find the *thoughts* to do that.

"You made me forget things, Marnie, things that I really needed to remember. And that scared the hell out of me. Little Joe should have won the Classic. He was by far the best horse entered in that race. But I didn't give him the attention he needed and deserved that week, because all I could think about was you. Hell, when I woke up that morning all I wanted to do was lie there and look at you, and then wake you up and make love to you again. If I hadn't left when I did— the way I did—I might still be lying there in that bed with you, thinking about nothing else."

"And would that be so terrible?" she asked.

"Of course not," he told her. "But that wasn't why I was in Del Mar," he repeated. "I was in Del Mar to win a race. That was my job. And my work was the most important thing to me."

She said nothing for a moment, only studied his face in the darkness as if looking for the answer to a very important question. Finally she asked, "And what's the most important thing to you now, Daniel?"

Wasn't the answer to that obvious? "My work," he answered automatically.

She nodded slowly. "Of course," she said softly. "That is, after all, what you do best."

Her comment, too, puzzled him. She made it sound as if being good at what he did was a bad thing.

She bit her lip thoughtfully, her eyes fixed on his, glimmering in the scant moonlight that was filtering through the window. And damned if Daniel didn't find himself wanting to pull her into his arms and kiss her. But as much as it might have felt as if no time had passed since Del Mar, there were eight years between now and then. And eight years was a long time in the best of circumstances. For Daniel and Marnie, it was virtually a lifetime.

So Daniel turned and started for the door, then halted. He couldn't just walk away and leave things as they were, unsettled. He'd done that eight years ago and regretted it.

"It *was* good to see you again, Marnie," he said softly. And since he was being honest, he added, "I hope we see each other again."

She didn't say anything in response, only stood silhouetted against the window with her arms wrapped around her in a way that made him wonder whether she was doing it because she was cold, or if she just needed something—someone— to hold on to. In either case, Daniel understood. There was an emptiness clinging to him that he suspected would be there for a long time.

* * * * *

THOROUGHBRED LEGACY
coming soon wherever books are sold!

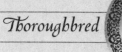

Thoroughbred *Legacy*

Launching in June 2008

A dramatic new 12-book continuity that embodies the American Dream.

Meet the Prestons, owners of Quest Stables, a successful horse-racing and breeding empire. But the lives, loves and reputations of this hardworking family are put at risk when a breeding scandal unfolds.

Flirting with Trouble

by *New York Times* bestselling author

ELIZABETH BEVARLY

Eight years ago, publicist Marnie Roberts spent seven days of bliss with Australian horse trainer Daniel Whittleson. But just as quickly, he disappeared. Now Marnie is heading to Australia to finally confront the man she's never been able to forget.

The stakes are high when it comes to love, horse racing, family secrets and broken promises.

A new exciting Harlequin continuity series coming soon!

www.eHarlequin.com   HT38984R

Cole's Red-Hot Pursuit

Cole Westmoreland is a man who gets what he wants. And he wants independent and sultry Patrina Forman! She resists him—until a Montana blizzard traps them together. For three delicious nights, Cole indulges Patrina with his brand of seduction. When the sun comes out, Cole and Patrina are left to wonder—will this be the end of the passion that storms between them?

Look for

COLE'S RED-HOT PURSUIT

by USA TODAY bestselling author

BRENDA JACKSON

Available in June 2008 wherever you buy books.

Always Powerful, Passionate and Provocative.

REQUEST YOUR FREE BOOKS!
2 FREE NOVELS PLUS 2 FREE GIFTS!

HARLEQUIN®

Super Romance®

Exciting, emotional, unexpected!

YES! Please send me 2 FREE Harlequin Superromance® novels and my 2 FREE gifts (gifts are worth about $10). After receiving them, if I don't wish to receive any more books, I can return the shipping statement marked "cancel." If I don't cancel, I will receive 6 brand-new novels every month and be billed just $4.69 per book in the U.S. or $5.24 per book in Canada, plus 25¢ shipping and handling per book and applicable taxes, if any*. That's a savings of close to 15% off the cover price! I understand that accepting the 2 free books and gifts places me under no obligation to buy anything. I can always return a shipment and cancel at any time. Even if I never buy another book from Harlequin, the two free books and gifts are mine to keep forever.

135 HDN EEX7 336 HDN EEYK

Name _____ (PLEASE PRINT) _____

Address _____ Apt. # _____

City _____ State/Prov. _____ Zip/Postal Code _____

Signature (if under 18, a parent or guardian must sign) _____

Mail to the Harlequin Reader Service:
IN U.S.A.: P.O. Box 1867, Buffalo, NY 14240-1867
IN CANADA: P.O. Box 609, Fort Erie, Ontario L2A 5X3

Not valid to current subscribers of Harlequin Superromance books.

Want to try two free books from another line?
Call 1-800-873-8635 or visit www.morefreebooks.com.

* Terms and prices subject to change without notice. N.Y. residents add applicable sales tax. Canadian residents will be charged applicable provincial taxes and GST. This offer is limited to one order per household. All orders subject to approval. Credit or debit balances in a customer's account(s) may be offset by any other outstanding balance owed by or to the customer. Please allow 4 to 6 weeks for delivery. Offer available while quantities last.

Your Privacy: Harlequin is committed to protecting your privacy. Our Privacy Policy is available online at www.eHarlequin.com or upon request from the Reader Service. From time to time we make our lists of customers available to reputable third parties who may have a product or service of interest to you. If you would prefer we not share your name and address, please check here. ☐

HSR08